things to be lost

Also by Lionel Newton
getting right with god

lionel newton

things to be lost

A DUTTON BOOK

DUTTON
Published by the Penguin Group
Penguin Books USA Inc., 375 Hudson Street,
New York, New York 10014, U.S.A.
Penguin Books Ltd, 27 Wrights Lane, London W8 5TZ, England
Penguin Books Australia Ltd, Ringwood, Victoria, Australia
Penguin Books Canada Ltd, 10 Alcorn Avenue,
Toronto, Ontario, Canada M4V 3B2
Penguin Books (N.Z.) Ltd, 182–190 Wairau Road,
Auckland 10, New Zealand

Penguin Books Ltd, Registered Offices:
Harmondsworth, Middlesex, England

First published by Dutton, an imprint of Dutton Signet,
a division of Penguin Books USA Inc.
Distributed in Canada by McClelland & Stewart Inc.

First Printing, February, 1995
10 9 8 7 6 5 4 3 2 1

 REGISTERED TRADEMARK—MARCA REGISTRADA

LIBRARY OF CONGRESS CATALOGING-IN-PUBLICATION DATA:
Newton, Lionel.
    Things to be lost / Lionel Newton.
        p.   cm.
    ISBN 0-525-93755-2
    1. Fathers and sons—United States—Fiction. 2. Parricide—United
States—Fiction. 3. Family—United States—Fiction. 4. Boys—United
States—Fiction. I. Title.
PS3564.E962T47   1995
813'.54—dc20   94-32463
                                                                CIP

Printed in the United States of America
Set in Palatino

PUBLISHER'S NOTE
This is a work of fiction. Names, characters, places, and incidents either are
the products of the author's imagination or are used fictitiously, and any
resemblance to actual persons, living or dead, events, or locales is entirely
coincidental.

things
to be
lost

c h a p t e r

1

Alibis? I have none. Don't need any. It was just me and my old man at the scene of the crime and he ain't talkin. Even if he could, he wouldn't—he loved me. Had it gone to a court of law, some buttoned-down lawyer might've said something about me being a sick kid, and that would've been the weakest defense imaginable. See, I know as fact that the water running through the mind of a child is crystal clear.

I was just turned twelve when it happened—the feel of the metal raking his teeth, his eyes half closed and his head rolling to one side in acceptance, the resistance before the jerk as I squeezed off the trigger, the bang, then the burst of blood spraying me. It was somewhere between action and result that I was claimed, though it's taken a full decade to understand my punishment.

After the discharge there was quiet. My hands were trembling and I stopped short, my finger still on the trigger, and framed the room and the separation between us, the length of the barrel. The blast had pushed the wheelchair back about a foot, his body still seated and slumped to the side. The bullet had made a clean entrance through the roof of his mouth, but the left side of his head was completely ruined. The blood was dark and thick with bits of flesh and tissue and maybe even part of his brain.

I whispered in his ear, "Upon this rock I shall build my church . . . ," but his mouth was dry and the blood was caking to stone.

I laid the rifle down next to the cane, the way we'd planned, then went to the bathroom to clean myself and put my clothes back on. In the mirror I frightened myself and was certain the cops would know. I was almost hoping they would. I wanted to end it, to back away, to run. That's when I started to cry.

Not too fast now, and not too tidy, this cruel thing, my triumph. It's a mess to be proud of, though I'm a little embarrassed about splattering blood all over the first page. Except I don't want you to miss it like I almost did.

I've got a trio of oils being shown at one of those swanky galleries down by the river where it's considered chic to drop five grand on a piece of art. Ma and Yogi even showed up for the opening with Sonny's toe-headed husband, Gil. Sonny didn't bother coming. I'm not sure whether she's boycotting or perhaps she hates me. For my sins, neither would be a stiff enough penalty, but who's complaining.

Before the exhibit Gil treated us to lunch and I asked him straight out, "You fuckin' around behind Son's back yet?" and Ma just about jumped down my throat.

We're at this little sidewalk joint along the esplanade and Gil's wearing a bow tie with suede elbow patches on his sports jacket. He's got a mulatto-ish complexion, wavy brown hair, and funny eyes that change color. I've never been able to picture him growing up in the projects, though he swears he did.

"Can't you be civilized?" Ma says. "At least in a public place."

I blow her off. "So Gil, are you voting Republican yet?" I ask instead, and Mommy dear pops me on the wrist with a spoon.

It's been seven years since I've seen my moms, our correspondence including only the note she sent after Son had the stillborn. It read like a short article in the morning paper, just the facts, though she was kind enough to sign off with her personal signature, a slim elegant script, followed by a perfunctory "love always," an afterthought perhaps.

She hasn't exactly disowned me but the strain of being in my company is evident on her face. Every time she blinks, her eyes stay closed for a few seconds as if she thinks things might be different when she opens them. In fairness, she's made an effort to keep me in line, and I've pretended to let her, 'cause when everything's said and done it's very likely she'll have buried us all. She's self-centered enough to endure most anything, which doesn't make her a bad person, just the mother of unruly children.

"Ma." I lean softly against her. She glances at me, then shakes her head and closes her eyes again.

"Aw shit, Ma. It can't be that bad."

"If you bore only one son," she's visibly upset now, her posture stiffening, "by the only man you ever loved . . . ," and I can almost hear a string orchestra start up in the background. What am I supposed to say? "I'm sorry" is the best I can come up with.

"No," she snaps, steadied by the chance to tell me about myself. "The only thing you care about is smearing blood on canvas. That's all that matters."

She's right, so I let it drop and turn to Gil, who's got his face buried in his salad. As a rule, our family makes Mr.

Toehead uptight so I can't help but needle him, and he tolerates it. Funny thing is, I see more of Gil than of my immediate family. Yogi never liked me much anyway, and once you set the precedent of offing your dad, your moms won't ever look you full in the face again. She won't take her eyes off you either; there's always the leery side glance 'cause she knows you're capable. After that, motive ceases to matter.

I look across the table at my sister Yogi, sipping her wine, smiling at the three of us, perhaps mellowed by some new organic vice. She's looking more feminine than I've ever seen her, ringing her finger around the rim of her wine glass. Her hair is done up in an outlandish style that looks like she just rolled out of bed, a kind of whooshing Don King effect. She's bare-armed despite the breeze. I can see my oldest sister in her and it almost makes up for Son's absence.

Finally, Yogi turns her eyes on me, cold and direct, her knowing smirk jabbing me like a stickpin, then the familiar burst of derisive laughter that makes me smile, makes me feel like her little brother again.

"What's gotten into you, girl?"

Yogi finishes her wine and starts on Gil's glass. "Randall's gotten into me," she says, causing the in-law's head to pop up from his salad, a dab of dressing on his nose. How anything coming out of my sister's mouth can startle him, I don't know.

"So where are you working now, Yolanda?" I ask, using her formal name. It seems to suit her more than Yogi now that we've grown older and farther apart.

"Driving a school bus part-time," she says, her left hand disappearing under the table, another surprise for the in-law. The hand reappears and the toehead seems flustered. "Something permanent in another few weeks," she tells me casually.

"And how long have we been hearing that?"

"Oh, Mother, please! You think it's easy to get good work with eighteen months of reform school on your résumé?"

"You made your bed, now you have to lie in it."

Yolanda looks at me while directing her spiteful insolence at our mom: "Check out her choice of words. Like it was my bed I was trying to put in order."

This bows Ma's face for a full ten seconds and I can see that the wounds are still fresh. "You—just—don't—understand," is her only excuse, proof of a greater bond with him.

I circle her shoulders with my arm but she pushes me away, mistrustful of my concern.

"It's no use." Yogi signals the waiter for more wine. "Our mother has completely lost her mind. Are you proud of yourself, Randall?"

"That sort of talk does nobody any good."

"We'll take that as a modest 'yes,' " Yolanda smiles, and I watch while the wind does a magic trick with her hairdo, fluffing it up and angling part of it into a different direction. Yogi's hair has never known a perm, no hot comb, nothing. Ma never believed in beauty parlors and fashion magazines. We only had two mirrors in our house, that's how confident my mother was, how beautiful she still is, though her confidence has been completely broken down.

I let my hand fall from Ma's shoulder to the curve of her waist, her back, and this too strikes a raw nerve with Yolanda. As family reunions go, our little get-together lacks even a trace of warmth.

"Check you out. When Dad was alive, you were a devoted daddy's boy. Now you're a mommy's boy for some strange—"

"This can be said in private—"

"Like hell it can." Yogi moves her glass aside and leans in. The table next to us has stopped eating, but nothing's going to stop her. "Now you're a mommy's boy for some strange, warped reason. Should I be jealous? Or should I be patient and wait my turn?"

"Give it a break."

"Not yet. No, no, brother dear, not yet I won't." Her eyes are bright and hard. "You see, it's your game to win, and everybody else's to lose. And now you want us to be happy when you sell a few of your morbid little paintings. Why should we be happy for you?"

I look at Ma, then back at Yolanda. They're waiting.

"Dad trusted me," I tell them. "Isn't that good enough for anybody? I feel uncomfortable. OK? I feel uncomfortable that you don't love me."

I watch for their reaction. They shake their heads in disbelief. All three of them (Sonny and Gil have become interchangeable), they're just one person. They're a coincidence. I don't know why I even bother.

"Lookit, I'm not asking you to thank me for it, but at some point you have to let go of the horror."

"Horror?" Yogi laughs and mugs a face. "You pretentious little punk. I told you, Gil, he thinks he's a wizard."

Gil shrugs. He's about ten peas short of an empty plate, and except for Yogi's infrequent lap-dives, he's managed to eat himself right out of the conversation. Gil's never been one to dillydally with his food. He grew up a have-not, and now that he has, he appreciates. You could call him an overachiever, and I respect him for it even if I don't understand it. He's from a broken home. Earned himself an M.B.A. while supporting his mother and three brothers. First time he met our family, he made a goofy little speech about how we were the epitome of all that was righteous within the black middle class.

Yeah, right.

He knows better now, and if it weren't for his blind sense of boy-scout loyalty, he wouldn't be sitting through this. But me? There's plenty I never learned to appreciate, which is why I have to be here, which is perhaps why I have to tell you this story.

I slide closer to Ma, but she's shaking her head no. I

stroke her back, trying to soothe her. After ten years she can't still be in a state of denial. Or maybe it's a place she revisits: a wild notion that if they gave me life, then somehow the favor can be returned.

"He's dead." I state it as simply as I can. "And you have nothing to feel guilty about. You don't have to answer to anybody for anything. None of us do."

"Ain't that convenient," Yogi quips, "with Dad turned to dust six feet down under."

I cover Ma's face with my hand to keep her from speaking. She's shrunken over the years, an old helpless woman struggling against me, her eyes pleading for what I have stolen.

"Shhhhh." I put my mouth against her ear, quieting her. I hold her tightly in my chest till she goes limp, and for the first time I can remember, she is holding on to me for support, my father's wife. The pervert in me is satisfied.

I pour some cream in her tea, then gently take hold of her hand, the way I'd seen Dad do it. Goose bumps rise all over my body. I'm still hers; she can't ever deny me that, although I wonder whether it's occurred to her that she knew him three times longer than I did, whether she's asked herself what gave me the right to take him away.

It's October, sunny with an easterly breeze that has set all the autumn colors in motion, and I feel at peace with myself for the first time in a long time. It's 'cause I'm with family, though there's so much I'm not certain of, including why none of them ratted me out. The cops weren't too convinced about the "self-inflicted" story either, but I was never worried about them. It's Ma and the girls I want to square it with: their sacrifice and my profit.

I'd like to tell them I'm paying for it, standing in front of the only window in my apartment. That's where I am now, with a cup of Aloeta tea that's glowing a lovely greenish blue in the darkness. It's a hybrid root, thick like honey so as to give me the shits by afternoon—sweet in my mouth, bitter in my stomach, exacting a price for my pleasure, a debt to cancel out everything else. There is no judgment passed down on little boys who shoot their daddy. The crime and its punishment are forever linked. But hear me at full length: we all get claimed. It's how it happens that matters. For me, I had to go through my dad, and I'm not the least bit ashamed, not of anything I've done, and especially not of them, these five people I used to know, the Roberts family.

c h a p t e r
2

Outdoors at a Sunday afternoon barbecue, a block party ten years ago, the Daniels' house at the top of the street. Let's call it the last perfect day of summer and I've gone completely tense.

It's the people. So many people, and all of them happy to be here. I'd like to think it isn't so, that they're just pretending. I'd like to think that I'm the only one not scared of the truth.

But no. These folks wanna be here, they're enjoying themselves. And for today that will be the simple truth, sitting here at the root of the tallest tree in the world. Not a tree for climbing through the sky, its thin branches starting about halfway up the trunk, well out of reach.

Next to the garage are fellow captives, two rottweilers, the Daniels' pets. They aren't the barbecueing type either. I've tried making friends but they only show me their teeth and snarl. They probably figure I couldn't possibly understand what it is to be a fat-headed dog hampered by stubby little legs, chained to the fence with nothing to do but bark at the children playing dodgeball on the front lawn. But I can see what they see and it ticks me off just as much, all these neighborhood people laughing and talking, the music and open grill aroma blending on a lazy summer breeze.

Yogi and Terrell Daniels are sitting on the hood of a Benz parked on the circular drive, taking turns feeding each other from a bag of Cheetos, their all-male crew stretched out on the grass before them like lawn ornaments: Mike and Skipper and Naldo, and then two other hangers-on I don't know. They're from Freeport or Hempstead maybe: a biker and a wannabe pimp flyboy, overdressed for the occasion, his hair gleaming with Jheri-Kurl sauce.

Yogi and Terrell are on hold, waiting for the sun to go down so they can lose the dead weight and make tracks for the City. Last night I heard them making their dirty little plans that didn't include any of these guys, not even Naldo, Skipper, or Mike.

I shuffle past them, chin tucked, and scan their faces.

I'm invisible, my arms and legs stiff, my steps shortened. But Yogi knows this hoax. "Come here, mongoloid." She pulls me over, forcing me to listen in on their cheerless conversation.

"Duleo got his ass hauled last week," the guy straddling the Harley is saying. He's got mirrored shades and a crucifix dangling from his ear, centerfold for some "crash and burn" magazine. "You hear about it?"

Terrell nods and brushes a few crumbs from Yogi's mouth. "What happened?" She sighs.

"The concert over at the Vaud," the biker says. "Somebody popped the cork on that mothafucka and the brothers started goin crazy, tearin shit up. One second Sanity is rockin the mike, next second there's a riot. Shit spilled out onto the boulevard too, people lootin and whatnot." He waits to see if anyone cares.

"Yeah? What you take?" Naldo asks.

"Me? I was just coolin."

"Punk," Naldo mumbles.

"Naw, I was gonna—"

"Yeah, you was gonna," Yogi mocks him.

"I was, but 5–0—"

"So what? Cops got an agenda, so do you."

The biker shrugs. "I knew there was gonna be trouble. Always is. T.J. got collared too, and Sly and Earl, all of 'em. Got tossed into the back of a paddy wagon."

Yogi stops the feeding for a moment and looks off into the distance. This is quite rare: she's thinking. I can tell by the little pout and by the way her body starts to rock slightly as she squints into the dense fog for signals from her brain. I guess she's considering good old T.J., a spray-paint vandal from the high school. He used to come around the house for her, but Yogi don't like boys much unless it's to slap them around.

She's giggling now, and on cue, Terrell starts giggling too, a cheap trick they play on the rest of the world. "T.J.," they say in unison.

"T.J.," I echo and try to move on, but Yogi won't let me. "Open up." She shoves a Cheeto in my mouth. She still hasn't looked at me. "I see too much of you as it is" is what she's always telling me, never mind that we live in the same house. But for my liking, I don't see nearly enough of Yogi.

Truth is, I spend a great deal of time staring at my sister 'cause I like animals and she could pass for a coyote. Or a bird of prey, a falcon or an eagle, all talons and beak. My oldest sister, Sonny, she's an animal too, but she's more domesticated, something well-bred and housebroken.

I reach for the bag of Cheetos but Yogi slaps my hand away. I can almost hear the bad air seeping out of her ears, the light in her eyes dimming.

"Dumbass T.J.," she says and pats my head absently.

"Yeah, well, ain't nobody gonna miss T.J. Fisher," Terrell

jeers, her top lip curling. "There's enough garbage running the streets. Naldo sees to that, don't you, baby?"

"Shut up, whore," Yogi says from out of the blue, her face blank. Terrell laughs and bites her neck. Yogi barely flinches. "A poem," she decides, "by Yolanda Roberts." The others groan. They're used to my sister's attempts, her hand falling limp from my shoulder, her eyes crossing.

Why Yogi bothers with poetry confuses most people, annoys and baffles them. For the record her explanation is double vision. She says that when life appears to her in duplicate, it's a reminder that she should share her view with others.

It's an explanation and an excuse—Yogi's personal version of a family embarrassment. At her eighth-grade graduation she interrupted the consecration prayer with birdcalls, a senile whippoorwill she told the congregation, then recited something rhymeless from Giovanni. Ma didn't think it was too cute though and smoked Yogi's ass good after dinner that night. Could've been the last good spanking Yogi's gotten, and a fat lotta good it's done. Excuses and embarrassment, my sister is full of both.

Today's poem is a rerun, *The Great Fire of Onabee Bridge*, "charring trestles in pillows of choking flames gray," she begins as I make my way slowly toward the house, my head down, avoiding but not completely ignoring the neighborhood kids playing dodgeball in the middle of the sodded lawn.

Most of them are my age, eleven, but I'm taller. I got them coltish kinda legs just like my old man. Anyway, that's how come the other kids don't like me, 'cause I'm bigger and sometimes I'll bully them just to ruin their stupid little games. Then there's my eyebrow, which they're always making fun of it. I have only one. It goes clear across my forehead with no break in the middle. I've begged Ma to let me shave a path through the center but she says No. She says the continuity will make me appear scholarly one day.

I stop to watch the dodgeball game. Zayda Phillips and Donnie Masterson are playing the whip, which means they get to aim the ball at the pack of kids in the middle. If you get hit, you're out. Last one still in is the winner. Dumb game, right? But these chumps wouldn't know the difference, except for Zayda and Donnie.

Zayda I don't know too good, but Donnie I known for too long. He got one of them rock'em-sock'em crew cuts that's shaved clean on the sides, sorta like an ex-con war hero living out of a garbage can down on skid row during the depression. I seen it in a social studies textbook once, no foolin, back in fourth grade when we studied Roosevelt's New Deal.

"Randall, ya blockhead, get outta the way!"

That was Donnie the white boy yellin just now. "Blockhead" he calls me. He ain't too clever anyhow.

"I ain't kiddin," he says. "I'll blast you with this here ball."

Half of Donnie's problem is anybody's guess, but the other half is that he idolizes his older brother who happens to be a lifer for the Green Berets or the Navy Seals or one of them hotshot battalions that does dirt for the government. Donnie sees life through crosshairs.

"If you hit me with that ball, it might hurt for a while," I tell him honestly, "but it won't hurt for that long."

Zayda Phillips bursts out laughing, then stops suddenly, her hand flying to her mouth, her eyes widening. Can you imagine it? Zayda's mom telling her it's cruel to laugh at people like me.

"Like who?" I ask her, putting my imagination into words, which I don't know why I insist on doing that 'cause nobody ever knows what I'm talking about, never mind what I might be imagining.

Zayda mouths the question to the others, "Like who?" then shrugs, prompting the usual twittering of group laughter that isn't real. Nobody's actually amused. They just wanna be mean, Jeremy Felton and snaggle-toothed Todd and Felicita and knobby-kneed Cyndi, and of course Lisa McIntyre and her harelip brother Gaylord, seven or eight kids in all. There's even some kids who weren't playing dodgeball; they were over on the sidewalk playing hopscotch or some equally ridiculous game. But when they see it's time to tease Randall, then not even an appearance from the ice-cream truck could keep them from their sneering laughter that just keeps getting louder and louder and none of them are really sure of what the joke is.

I could show them. One day I will, I'll tell it right to their sneering faces, all of 'em. But on top of that, they ain't even in this story. Know why? 'Cause it's mine and I said so. Still, one of these days . . . as soon as I find out what their taunts have earned me . . . one of these days when I understand it, then they'll see what the joke is and it'll be my turn to chuckle, "hahahaveryfunnymothafuckas."

I stand there watching them laugh, looking separately at each face. And, too, there's Zayda, who she isn't in this story either except for just this once, although if I were to tell her she'd probably say she didn't wanna be in my stupid story anyway, and she wouldn't be lying. For the others teasing me is just a game, but Zayda dislikes me for real.

One time she says to me, "Being one against the rest of everybody else doesn't make you any better, Randall Roberts."

Get that. The nerve. Standin there wearing bobby socks, this girl, telling me what's what. Unbelievable. Everybody calls her Zayzay. She's very popular, you see. All the time it's "Zayzay says this" and "Zayzay says that." Anyway, she knows to keep her distance, her and her dopey little friends, the bunch of 'em waiting patiently for another reason to razz me.

It is all I know of my anger, that it's controlled by the faces of certain people like Zayda Phillips. I think she has some idea about this too, though neither of us has any control of my anger because neither of us knows exactly what it is in her face that sparks it, a rush that comes hot and sudden and harmless and yes, this really could be very funny, me closing in on Zayda, my eyes locking into her chin, trapping her. Looking away from me is a dare she can't handle. She's slave to the most sinister possibility—she wants it right now—she wants to get it over with, her punishment for being so cruel as to laugh at someone like me.

I hold my hands out at my sides, palms up at first before turning them over and flexing my fingers. "It won't hurt for that long," I say, taking a small step toward her.

And check this out, all her little friends just standing there. It's so typical, isn't it? If I'm going to do anything to Zayda, they don't want to miss it. If given a choice between protecting her or waiting for the damage to be done and rushing to the house to blab to all the grown-ups that Randall went nuts and tore Zayda's eyes out, they'd choose to watch the gouging and then do the blabbing. Even Donnie is waiting to see whether I have the guts to make blood flow.

"Run," I tempt her, knowing she can't. Her eyes flash from my face to my hands and then back again. It's a toss-up as to which frightens her more. She turns to the others. They're attentive, arms folded, little harelip Gaylord peeking at me from behind his sister's elbow.

"How come you never answer when I say your name like the others, Zayzay." I whisper this in a hoarse voice and reach for her, but not so quickly as to make her scream.

It's a small thing, the difference between reaching to help and reaching to hurt. In an instant she's startled frozen except for the trembling in her voice. "Nnnooooo," she whimpers and I'm certain that it's true, what I imagined her mother might have said.

I back away and start to laugh. "If I was ever gonna, I wouldn't waste any time doing it."

"That's the sickest thing I ever heard," Zayda says, and again I see the weird mix come over her face, pity and caution and dislike as well, and then some other stuff I can't describe even though sometimes it will appear to me abruptly in the dreaming that comes just before sleep, a sharp anger that hurts me when I recall the dislike on Zayda Phillips's face.

"Randall's staring again," someone says from behind me in a bored singsong voice.

Now that they realize I'm not actually gonna do a Sharon Tate number on Zayda, my classmates have surrounded me. Or maybe it was me who walked into the middle of their game. I'm never quite sure how it happens, being unpopular.

Just over their heads I can see Yogi sitting on the blacktop driveway. She's done with her recital and has been watching me while her friends talk around her. From out of her haze I barely catch her smile. It's as close as she'll come to actually being amused by something I've done. She says it's a matter of principle that she treats me like shit.

"Randall, you're such a kook," Donnie the white boy says finally, as if he's made a decision for the whole group.

"Uh-huh." I nod slowly and brace myself as he slings the ball straight at my head. At the last second I reach up and catch it.

"Moron, ya give it back, ya hear?"

"I didn't want it nohow," I say, but still I keep the ball just to see Donnie get mad.

He goes something like, "Youse make me ask for that there ball again, Randall, and it's gonna be a sorry thing to see."

"You were gonna take it back, how come you gave it to me?" I ask, twisting the words so they'll make sense for him. He's wearing Doc Martins and a T-shirt with the sleeves rolled up to show off his wash-away tattoo, the kind you get sometimes in a box of Cracker Jacks.

He walks right up on me, bumping me with his chest. "I'll sock you if you don't give it back," he says, his chin cocked to one side.

c h a p t e r
3

Long Island, where we live, my family. It's still "we" and not yet "I." Our faults are spread thinner that way.

In time I'll grow away from them. That's how it happens, right? A short journey on a road much wider than it is long, a road so wide and I can't help but wander off in zigzags. That's how come I'm not making any progress: too much daydreaming. Or sometimes I spend all day trying to persuade you to tolerate the things I've done, the things I will do. But see me as I was, please, this boy. I need your attention. I am young and I am hopelessly lost—not misinformed, but willfully and delightfully lost. I take pleasure in it, it's true, I confess, and we'll agree that judgment and guilt are the same.

Lookit. All the way out east to Montauk Point, then to the west and the City, then see me apart from my family, watching them from a distance at chatty little late-summer barbecues.

I am eleven. I have no friends.

There are the friends of my sisters and parents, and then there are the people who want to be their friend, plus the ones who pretend to be their friend for no particular reason except make-believe is easier than the truth.

Sometimes I'll strain my eyes, looking for a reason to deny any resemblance to my family, but I don't mind that I can't. Am I supposed to feel threatened by that? Me, I'll just play it cool. I'll leave all the others to be disappointed that such a perfect day as this can actually come to an end.

Imperfection doesn't necessarily lead to regret, my mother has told me more than once. Not unless you want it to.

"Health and an education. Don't ever take them for granted," Ma tells me and my sisters almost constantly, her voice an angry whisper. It's her way of translating Dad's "Train up a child in the way he should go . . ." lecture. The picture is very clear, all the things my parents expect. It might make it easier if they both expected the same things, but that's beside the point.

When people see me, they see my parents, my two sisters.

"It could be worse," Ma's quick to remind me. "Imperfections don't necessarily lead to regret."

Our neighborhood is maybe fifteen years old, a maze of homes covering two square miles, carved out of a woodland that slopes down to the reservoir. The homes were built in the early seventies, right after the rezoning that split Massapequa in two. Most people call our neighborhood the sticks, 'cause all the streets are named after trees. Our street is called Spruce, then there's Elm, and so on like that. The Daniels live one street over on Oak. That's how we became friends with them, 'cause our backyard combines with theirs with no fence between, just a row of trees.

The Daniels, you never seen people party so much. Mr. Daniels is a marketing rep for a Belgium software consortium that owns real estate in the U.S.

What does that mean?

Yogi says it means Mr. Daniels don't do shit 'cause his boss is in a different hemisphere—it means he's probably a front man for dirty money—it means he throws a buncha parties to prove how well off he is. Ma says some black folks don't know how to act when you give 'em money, but I don't see nothing wrong with going out like a champ so long as you got the capital.

Just get a look at the classy paint job in their front room, hot-lava pink, then the living room turns cool lavender with varnished teakwood furniture and a cabinet full of shiny unused china. Farther down the hall is a drawing room that smells of clover. It's been decorated at gunpoint maybe, the walls sick with a million paintings. They could charge admission for this. Party balloons in the shape and colors of oversized billiard balls are strewn across the shag carpet.

The air in the drawing room is heavy like in a funeral parlor, dead air, like when your dad drags you to an auto show way the hell up in the Bronx at a stuffy warehouse that's been converted into a display room with a buncha cars parked at different angles, but there's no windows in the warehouse and the the air is so thick with dust it seems as though somebody's nuclear reactor just went belly-up the way it happened to the Russkies at Chernobyl, and the cars, they're parked all over the place with little signs that give you the price and specifications like how many miles it gets to the gallon but all you can do is wonder how in hell they got fifty zillion cars into a stuffy windowless warehouse showroom that's on the third floor in the first place.

But this here in Ms. Daniels's drawing room is all class except maybe the air is a little stiff. The drapes are layered silk with velvet ropes to hold them open. There's hardly any furniture, just two long couches at either end of the room, then two more couches facing each other in the middle of the room with a snack-food buffet between them. I think the hi-fi in the corner is on but all I can make out is a thin hissing sound. Maybe they don't have the station tuned. Nobody seems to care.

This is where Ma is hanging out with most of the other women. She's sitting on one of the couches in the middle, listening while Ms. Daniels plays the proud host, telling one of her stupid little stories about a European vacation. She must think she's white, with all her gondola rides by moonlight. Ma's expression says Ms. Daniels is lying through her teeth.

I lock in on my mother, certain that I can see her better than anyone else can. I can even see her better than Dad can. Her hair is cropped close to her head in soft baby curls, the short length giving boldness to her forehead, the set of her jaw. By sight there's a hardness about her, but not to the touch. Most people don't know that, but I do; I've touched her. Swear to God, she's delicate and her skin is smooth. To touch her face you'd figure the bone would break easy and her skin would bruise or cut easy. But just from looking at her, you could never figure her to be fragile.

Last Christmas Sonny gave me charcoal and an erasable porcelain canvas so I could experiment with tracings. But I'm not good with charcoal yet 'cause you gotta know when to use it flat and when to use the edge. That's how come when I did Ma's portrait, her cheekbones were all wrong and her mouth wasn't full enough. But she already knows she's beautiful, and her confidence is what convinces everybody else. I've never even seen her comb her hair. It all takes care of itself for Ma, that's what she's counting on.

I move toward her now, almost tripping over the eight ball, anxious to see her more clearly. The others are mostly teachers from the high school, Ma's people, the lot of them standing around, waiting to be amused by the first word she utters.

My oldest sister, Sonny, is here too with her husband Gil, his head on a swivel like he's searching for someplace to take a leak. The wedding was just two weeks ago and already he's got that look. Nobody warned him, now he's trapped.

"Was that from your first or second marriage?" Ma finally breaks in on Ms. Daniels's story, the gentle Southern accent taking the sting from her words. It might as well be Ma's drawing room. "Or perhaps it was your third marriage," she adds after a moment's pause, the way she usually does for effect.

These two have been at each other's throat all day. Ms. Daniels started it with a crack about an outdoor wedding in the rain (Sonny's) being the first step toward annulment, and now Ma has repaid the insult, leaving the hostess speechless. I take the opportunity to move in closer to my mother, forcing myself into her range of vision. Finally she focuses on me without acknowledgment, as if she knows I want her ownership to include me as well. She tinkles the ice in her glass of lemonade and takes a sip.

"Did you eat yet, Randall?" Sonny speaks up to gloss over our mother's tactlessness. "Here, take my plate," she says. "I'm full."

I take a barbecued rib and pocket it, then wait to hear my mother's voice.

"Randall Roberts." She isn't angry though. I step closer to her but a little to the side so that Mrs. Daniels won't miss anything.

My posture is good before this audience. Ma's told me about my public carriage. She don't like my private carriage either, but in public I'm supposed to stand taller and be proud of my height. She says one day it'll make me appear scholarly, but from the look on her face, it hasn't quite happened yet.

"Aren't those your good pants, young man?" She reaches into my pocket for the rib and puts it in a napkin, then looks deep into my eyes for a response. I take the rib and nod.

"And who washes your good pants?"

I nod again, and she meets this with a smile, her hand raising to my face, wiping at my eyebrow.

"Is he a mute?" Ms. Daniels chuckles. She's all open cleavage and watermelon thighs.

"He talks just fine when he's a mind to," Ma tells Ms. Daniels without looking at her. My mother's got eyes only for me, a look that I take firm hold of, and the moment. I have scrapbooks filled with such moments, her hand moving down the side of my face, my neck. My silence has pleased her so I leave it at that, dismissing myself for another tour of the house.

chapter
4

Downstairs in the game room it's crowded, the rowdy laughter of men drinking. There's a large-screen TV in the corner. It's well-lighted with paneled walls. Next to the bar, a moose head looks out over a display of trophies.

Today the game is Ping-Pong and Mr. Daniels has got his shirt off, working up a pretty healthy sweat, talking as good a game as he's playing. Looks as though he's been having his way on the table, taking on all comers, his head fashionably bald with a paintbrush moustache.

The room falls silent as another serve is put into play. I think they're betting on the games, or maybe they're betting on each point. Enough liquor has been downed for them to bet on damn near anything, a half dozen bottles lined up along the bar. No soda or mixers, just straight liquor.

The host and his opponent trade a volley of smashes and retrievals, the ball making that hollow sound off the table, then finally Mr. Daniels gets his man and the noise starts up again, the trash talking that's taking more time than the game itself.

I spot my old man sitting over at the bar, still dressed in his church-going suit. Dad's a deacon at an Episcopalian church in Bellmore—leads out in Wednesday night prayer meetings, gives Bible studies, doesn't eat meat. That's just the way he is, my old man, a Holy Joe. He isn't of the born-again variety, he was always holy. His father was a minister. Me, Son, and Yogi have never been forced into being religious though. The only things we're forced to do is what Ma tells us, and she is neither a vegetarian nor a big fan of God.

"The voice of authority sings solo," she told Dad once. He was trying to get her to attend the communion ritual one Easter.

So Dad goes, "Solo?" all confused and whatnot, a lamb being led to slaughter. He had to know she was setting him up.

Ma's like, "Exactly, Frank. I only do solos, and I won't tolerate competition from on high."

Yeah, I know, you're probably thinking my moms is a bitch, and she is. But no one seems to hold it against her. Yogi calls her a strong-arm, the way she forces people to sign petitions and march against Shoreham. She even set up a neighborhood crime watch on our street that's constantly on red alert. If a neighbor doesn't wanna cooperate she'll give them that old "if you're not part of the solution" routine.

She's heavily into your typical local crusades, the stuff that gets smeared all over the editorial pages of *Newsday*, prompting the masses to picket City Hall. Moral outrage they call it. Righteous indignation. Yeah, well, my ma might be filled with outrage and indignation, but she ain't foolin me none. She isn't righteous, and she isn't all that moral either. She just likes pointing out what's wrong.

Last week she took part in one of them radio roundtable discussions, some to-do about condoms in school, a seven-chair panel of Ph.D.s and politicians, you know, the egg-heads who are always pretending to solve problems. Anyway, they must've had just one microphone cause Ma absolutely ruled. Then when some councilman wanted to disagree with her, Ma starts quoting law. She's got a degree in that too, just so she can bully people with the goddamned Constitution. She knows it from the preamble to the amendments, the Bill of Rights, all the bullshit not even the Supreme Court can figure out.

Yogi says half that law shit Ma makes up, but you think anybody on that roundtable was gonna challenge her? No way, man. People like having somebody who will take charge, then they can sit on the sidelines, bitching and moaning about how she's a grandstander. But when she says jump, they ask how high. People swarm around Ma cause she gives them a target for their hatred, and more than anything, people love to hate.

Dad's altogether different. Maybe he recognizes stuff that ain't right, but he'll stand back and marvel at it. People swarm around him too, but it's on account of him letting them be whoever they are. He doesn't strong-arm nobody, he accepts. Dad's the source of what little wholesomeness there is in our family.

OK, so you say we're twenty-five pages into this, and pretty much all you know about my dad is that I blew his brains clear through the top of his skull. But don't be quick to judge. He's the coolest. Check him out, sitting by himself at the end of the bar, watching Mr. Daniels play Ping-Pong. Dad's easy to impress.

People have always said I look like my dad and walk like him. For some reason I've never taken that as a compliment. It ain't that Dad's a complete jackass, but he's never been too graceful, and generally speaking he looks better sitting down, being observant, like he's doing now.

I take the glass from his hand and sip it. Ice water—he's sober as a judge, taking detailed note of his surroundings and trying to come to a conclusion. Everybody knows he's wrapped too tight.

"You make life twice as complex as it really is," Ma's forever telling him, but he won't never respond when she says that. The things inside him, the things he hides, only he's got a stake in them. That's why we both love him, me and Ma, 'cause we ain't sure whether he's the smartest guy alive or completely off his rocker. What we do know is that he needs us, and even though I've never heard Ma say it, she swears he needs her more than he needs me.

No. She's never come out and said it, but if she ever does, I'll tell her fast and hard: "THAT IS A LIE!"

I spin a complete circle on my barstool and almost fall off laughing, but I can't take Dad's attention from the Ping-Pong. He's been ticked at me lately on account of me getting tossed outta some goofy upstate boy's camp. That happened in early August and for about two weeks I've been holed up in my room, coming out only to eat. That's why Ma forced me to come to this stupid barbecue—to help me come out of my shell, to make me less antisocial.

Dad's eyes slowly scan the room, stopping on a guy standing a little apart from the others. A tall guy.

"You know him?" I ask.

Dad nods. "He's the new gym teacher your mother hired. Would you like to meet him?"

"Not today."

"Then maybe I'll introduce you one night when the world is asleep."

I lower my face and shrug. "I don't want to play that game anymore, Dad." It's his journal he's talking about, the one I'm not supposed to read late at night.

"What game, Randall?" he says softly.

"The game where I gotta start talkin weird 'cause of the stuff I read."

"Are you going to stop reading it?"

"No."

He nods again, satisfied that I won't try to pretend about things we both know. My hope is that if I don't lie to him, he'll never lie to me.

I try to put the glass of ice water back in his hand but he won't take it, giving me his menacing I-don't-want-to-be-bothered look that never works.

"*Eloi, Eloi*," I whisper, "*lama sa baeh thani*," and he can't help but smile. Translated it means, "My God, my God, why hast thou forsaken me." Jesus made that prayer after the Romans stapled him to a tree. The Bible's been Dad's favorite book for as long as I've known him. Either it's a long story or he's a slow reader.

Today he looks beat, even with the festive goings-on all around. Hasn't been eating or sleeping too good. He gets that way sometimes, distant from me, tolerant of my company. He'd never call me a nuisance, but it's written all over his face. I've always imagined it's the way he looks in the company of strangers, but lately he's been like that around friends too, and it appears to me that he's not my dad right now, but my father instead. It's a small difference, but it cautions me.

Still, I can bring myself closer to him. Watch.

"So . . . ," he says in that drawn-out way, as if to tell me he doesn't really have anything to say, which is fine with me. He's the best listener in the whole world. He's so good, people pay him for it.

He's looking at me with blank eyes, trying not to smile. I think Ma made him promise to be short with me 'cause she's always saying how I think I can get away with murder.

"Soooooo," I mimic him and bite at my thumbnail, secure in the advantage of being a dependent on his annual tax forms. "You still mad at me?"

"Why would I be mad?" he returns a question, and I figure he wants me to go through the whole confession bit, which ain't so bad really.

"I thought you might be mad 'causa my conduct." That's a word Dad likes using, "conduct." Either that one or "behavior." Ma prefers the word "hardheaded."

I says, "I figure you're mad since you know I rolled around in the poison ivy on purpose, just to get out of that dumb summer camp."

He takes a closer look at me at the mention of sickness, concern lining his face. He moves his chair close enough to brush the tips of his fingers along my arm.

The morning after my baptism in poison, the rash had bloomed in big red splotches all over my body. The camp nurse, Ms. Hagwood, put me in quarantine so I wouldn't contaminate all the normal kids. She sent me to the infirmary, which just happened to be downwind of the latrines, and I'm lying there all whited up with this powdery balm that didn't do anything but make me itch even more. But Ma didn't have an ounce of sympathy when they came to pick me up.

She was like, "And don't think you're fooling anybody, Randall Roberts. . . . I knew you before you knew yourself. . . . You don't run this world, little boy, I do. . . . You'll be right back in this camp next summer."

Big deal, right. She's always yelling at me anyhow, or yelling at Dad that he should yell at me more. My moms knows all there is to know about deviance, its causes and cures. But now the whole adventure has gone full circle, with Dad leaning his face close, his hands on my skin, the others in the room disappearing. It's just me and my dad. He's so close that I can smell him, the same cologne I remember from when I was small enough for him to hold me up over his head and blow raspberries on my bare stomach.

He lifts my T-shirt to look at the rest of the rash, moving his hands over me slowly. I could close my eyes and I'd still know my old man's touch. If something was ever seriously wrong with me, he'd recognize it right away and then I'd be healed. It's true, no joke. He's a doctor. Runs a

whole ward at the Samuel P. Jacobs Sanatorium in Queens.
On the side he's got a private practice for "specialized therapy," whatever the hell that means. I've visited him at the
Sanatorium plenty of times, but his private office in Midtown he's only let me see once.

"It's just about dried up," he says and shakes his head.
"Poison ivy, Randall? What am I going to do with you?"

"We could go to Friendly's for a sundae," I laugh, but all
Dad's willing to give is that tired old smile.

He loosens his tie, taking it off and putting it around my
neck. "Watch this." He ties a fat knot, looping the cloth over
so that when he's finished, it's ridiculously short.

I look at myself in the mirror over the bar and laugh. "I
can do better than that."

"Sure you can, son. But the camp, what was that all
about? Most kids love camp."

"What's to love? Ceramics? Bird appreciation? Gettin bit
by giant swamp mosquitoes every night? Then on Wednes-
days we took a five-mile hike before sunup. They don't ask
you whether you want to either. Wasn't any different from
school as far as I could tell."

"Didn't you make any friends?"

"Just this counselor named Dino. His real name was Ar-
thur, but everyone called him Dino 'cause he had a neck
like a dinosaur. He's the one who told me how I could get
sprung from camp."

Dad sees what I want, a chance to make a picture for him.
"Show it to me," he says as we get up to leave. We don't
belong in this din anyway.

"It was one night after curfew," I begin, making sure to
hold his hand as we pass the drawing room. Out the corner
of my eye I see Ma barely glance at us. Not that it really
matters, us leaving early, but she don't miss a thing.

Outside, the party seems in slow motion. There's precious
little daylight overhead; the moon has appeared, a perfect

circle. It's the color of vanilla ice cream, and the sky, it's that funny light blue color.

"Azure," Dad tells me before I can ask, and this cautions me as well.

There are things to be lost on such a beautiful day, walking in twilight, hand in hand.

c h a p t e r
5

Late afternoon, a week into the school year. I'm not supposed to be home yet, but the driver on the school bus doesn't seem to know which kids belong on his route and which kids don't. So I hop on like nothing, then get off just past the water tower and walk the rest of the way home.

Ma'll be ticked. She won't do anything though.

"You just want attention" is the line she's been running at me lately. "One day something's going to happen, little boy, and then you won't think you're so clever. Then you'll have more punishment than you'll know what to do with."

This last bit she says hesitantly, and I can see a small fear in her eyes before she turns her face from me. Sometimes she'll turn her face away for a full week till I do something else wrong, just to get her attention, just to see how much the fear has grown.

I climb through one of the windows in back and check each room in the house. It's empty. Upstairs in the kitchen the sun bursts brightly from behind the overcast, and rays of light filter dully through the orange curtains over the sink. I stand in front of the window with my eyes closed, the dark red warmth of the sun on the inside of my eyelids and throughout my whole body. It's a nice color, the kind you can't find in a crayon box.

Stretching my arms forward, I feel the quarter-inch-thick hum that envelopes the refrigerator, adding streaks like bluish veins through the dark red color, vibrant and alive. With care I tear free a swatch of the color mix to store in safe-keeping, then stand basking in the glow of the sun against my closed eyes, waiting for the room to stir. The house is shifting on its foundation, the walls moving in closer to touch me. I sense the furniture sliding to one side to show me what the rest of the family cannot see. Our house always knows when I'm here alone.

My dad had it built before I was born and it's the only place I've called home. The others can't say that. Sometimes when everyone is here together, I am aware of its cozy deception. It's a flexible house that holds the peaceful joy of Christmas with the same comfort it supplies during the active days of summer. We've molded it to our wishes, but still, it will outlive us. It's not really our house, only the place we live, the tribal confines we've set in hopes of making our love stronger.

I take a bowl of Fruit Loops down the stairs into the game room where the parts of a 1,600-piece jigsaw puzzle lay out on the floor. Yogi and Dad have been working on it for a few months. About half the pieces are fitted together. The rest are in separate piles of like colors. I sprawl onto the rug next to the puzzle, choosing the silence over TV, waiting still and quiet for a dream from the night before.

It's an old one. I've had it maybe five times, but it disappeared for about two years until last night. It's so old that it's blurred and curled around the edges. It frustrates me.

In the dream I can see the car coming from a far distance

up the street—closing the distance, hitting the brakes, making the car skid. I picture the car. It has four doors and a squared front and I see all four sides and smell the leather interior.

The dog lopes out into the middle of the street and doesn't hear the screeching wheels over the noise of the lawn mower. The dog never looks at the car. After impact, I see its neck and back snap while in the air, its eyes wild with terror, the frame falling twisted and rigid in the middle of the street, his big sharp teeth stained with blood.

There's a commotion upstairs, doors slamming, voices chanting some spliff-key Rasta beat.

Like fallen angels, Yolanda and Terrell come tumbling down the steps a million miles an hour, banging their fist against the wall. They're hell-bent and nothing will slow them. Just hearing them gives my heart a rush and I still myself at the sight of them.

Yogi flips on the television and the two flop down on the couch with some poor guy's wallet.

They're filled with energy, their eyes and hands frenzied. They can barely keep still, rewinding the lyric and letting it spill out as if from one body, over and over till it seems they don't know they're doing it. Demons on automatic pilot. I'm not sure they even realize I'm here while they count the money, four twenties, two tens, a five, and a host of singles. There are credit cards too.

Yogi takes one of the bills, balls it up, and tosses it to me. I smooth the crumpled money. It's the five, a bribe to keep my mouth shut. She waits to see if I'm bought and I ball it up and toss it back to her. She takes another bill and does the same thing. I open up a ten. I was hoping for a twenty, but the ten will have to do, the only choice left being a black eye.

"You think Naldo does these?"

"We keep 'em. I've always wanted a Discover card."

"Cash is better."

"Whatever." Terrell absently rubs the suede wallet against her cheek and smells it. She's still turned on from the take. "I know what my stepdad's gettin for his birthday," she laughs while Yogi lays out the photos from the wallet.

White people, blonde hair and rosy cheeks, colored eyes, the bunch of them smiling like they don't know what a steer their dad is. I wonder what the con was but don't bother asking. They've got trade secrets, these two.

"Where's Ma?" Yolanda turns to me.

"Teachers' meeting."

This gets an immediate reaction from them. I've heard them say the words a thousand times: RIPPIN OFF COMES BACK-TO-BACK.

On weekends, at the Sunrise Mall, they'll use me to case the stores to see if any security guards are hanging around or if there's a nerd working the cash register. They don't feel comfortable casing a store, then leaving, then coming back to steal. So I do their homework, and afterward they'll checker the stores, which means it's every three stores they hit. One'll work upstairs and the other downstairs, and it don't make a damn's worth of difference about what the store sells. It's not about merchandise with them; they couldn't care less.

"In the teachers' lounge at the high school," I offer them more information about Ma's whereabouts. I'm bored stiff. I want in on the next scam.

"When is she due home?" Terrell asks. She doesn't bother asking about our dad, but if Ma gets wind of any devilment, she'll beat anybody's hind parts like they're her kid.

"Talk, boy," Terrell slaps my arm. "Your ma? When?"

"Couple hours. Whatever ya'll gonna do, you better go ahead." I look to Yogi. "Can I come?"

"Naw," Yogi shakes the idea off. "It's chill. We're not taking any more tonight." She leans back on the couch. "For this score, winter is better anyway. When it gets dark early."

Terrell leans back on the couch too. "Where'd he park it today?" she asks, her head on Yogi's shoulder.

"Same place, around in back."

"Damn, he stupid. With a jeep like that, all we gotta do is cut through the canvas roof."

"The sound system alone is worth a mint."

"We should take it out to the Point. Have it stripped. He'd never know what hit him."

They're talking about that tall guy from the barbecue, the one Dad was staring at. His name's Eric Hazzard, the new gym teacher at Pinelawn High. Terrell's always talking about him, which could mean any number of things, all bad.

"Whose jeep?" I ask just to hear how they scheme, but they ignore me, the focus coming slowly back into their eyes. In a minute they'll realize they don't like the scenery and be off in any given direction.

"Would you fuck him?" Terrell crosses her legs and tilts her face up at my sister. Her boots are tan, steel-toed, and pointy with gold spurs on the heels.

"Who? E. Hazzard? I wouldn't touch him for a million bucks."

"Yeah, you'd rather his old lady," Terrell giggles, and I see Yogi stiffen. This secret I'm supposed to pretend I don't understand.

"Would you?" I ask Terrell. "E. Hazzard, I mean."

She pauses as if there's any doubt. She's got a small copper ring in her left nostril, a new barbarian twist.

"I'd fuck him," she nods and flips the lenses up on her sun-shades so I can see her eyes. She's stoned, but there isn't any haziness. She knows exactly what she's saying.

She's still looking at me, the scariest bitch in the world. In a fight though, Yogi could lick her easy. It happened out on the softball field once, something about Terrell cursing our moms, so Yogi kicks her in the stomach and makes her eat dirt. We must've been coming home from somewhere, crossing over through the park, just me, Yogi, and Terrell. I wasn't gonna break it up either.

Yogi kept letting Terrell up and knocking her down, then letting her up to run but Yogi would catch her and slap her some more, nothing but backhands.

I'm like, "Hey Yogi, let her go," but Terrell had it coming, and we both knew I didn't really want her to stop. Any slack you give Terrell Daniels, she'll take twice as much until you put her in line.

"Lemme get a spoonful of Loops," she says, leaving Yogi's shoulder, moving down the couch close to me. And of course she gotta touch me. Whenever it happens that I start liking girls, Terrell will be the first to know. She's already promised me. She's promised me stuff I don't even know what it is.

"Come on, Randall," she teases. She's got a heartshaped face and a head full of dreads wrapped in a purple scarf.

I hand her the bowl, knowing I won't be getting it back. Her nails are tie-dyed, the stains overlapping and making new colors, like the colors in a sunrise that match the ones in my bowl of Fruit Loops. She feeds Yogi a few spoonfuls while looking at me. There's a sick pleasure Terrell gets from this thing she has with Yogi.

"Hey," I punch her in the leg. "My Loops, give 'em back," but she just flips her shades back down.

"Get lost, Randall," Yolanda says, then Terrell goes, "No, stay, Randall." She's a balance between us, a threat.

"Go," Yolanda says more firmly, and I get up to leave them. Terrell's probably promised Yogi plenty too.

"You'd do it with that guy, E. Hazzard?" I ask, just to hear her say the word again before I leave them.

"Yeah. I'd fuck him in a second."

chapter
6

A coincidence, we're having dinner together, a Friday night. That hasn't happened since Son got married and moved out. And it wouldn't be happening this evening except Dad is home early from the hospital, again. From the looks of him it could be the flu, but I know better. Something's gotten ahold of him and with each week it is changing him, little by little.

It started after Sonny's wedding, and even before the engagement there were a couple of arguments. The whole mess was sort of pathetic, the way Ma and Son had teamed up against Dad on Gil's behalf, and Gil ain't even family. Poor Dad didn't have a chance. Then there was Gil, the cowardly in-law, who was willing to agree with both sides until Ma explained to him that that wasn't possible. So when Gil finally made a stand and formally proposed, Dad was the one who came off as being unreasonable. He kept saying, "Why is this different from taking an arm or a leg?"

Nobody could give him a straight answer, as if they were

embarrassed that he wasn't making sense. I wanted to rush
into the dining room and explain it for him, but it wasn't
clear to me either. It doesn't yet make sense, the handwriting on the wall.

The day Son moved out for good it was like furniture
being repossessed. Dad wouldn't even help her pack the
luggage into Gil's car.

"He'll get over it," I heard Ma whisper into Son's ear.
The toehead looked guilty as all hell.

I glance over at Son's empty spot at the dinner table, then
look into Yogi's face to see if she's noticed that all is not
well. She's rolled up into one of her moods though,
slouched in her chair. The only thing she's said all day is
"I don't care," as if that's supposed to make the world stop.

She doesn't care. Well, maybe not, but she will. "Sonny's
betrayal will be contagious," that's what Dad said in his
journal, "before the cock crows thrice . . ."

I glance over at Ma and there's no question, she sees it,
she sees the old man is being fed on.

She ladles him up a healthy serving of lasagna and green
beans. There's corn bread too, and collard greens, and roast
beef, and mashed potatoes, and macaroni and cheese . . .
enough starch to fuel a car engine. It's way too big a spread,
all his favorite dishes.

"Say when," she says cheerily, piling the food up under
his nose. Finally he nods. "Looks good," he says, and mumbles grace.

I'm starving and don't waste any time diving into my
plate. Yogi's got a plateful too, but she's just playing with
it, building a tower with the lasagna and making words
with the green beans and corn on her napkin.

"You put it in your mouth," Ma glares at her. "And take
off that silly hat."

Other than Ma's scolding, there isn't much talk around
the table. It's putting a bug up her ass. "You didn't make it
in to work at all today, did you?" she says to Dad.

"Felt a little run-down," he says quietly, picking through his plate. He's got food tucked in his jaw to make it look like he's eating.

"A little run-down," Ma looks at me. I shrug. It isn't much of an excuse. Excuses are for the weak as far as Ma's concerned.

"A little run-down." She lets her voice rise and fall over the words, like she's trying to construct something. Then again, "A little run-down," with a different inflection, her fingers drumming the table.

She grew up with three older brothers, a father, and no mother. That's gotta mean something. Like say, maybe she got a mean streak. Doesn't take bullshit. Everything our family owns has her touch: the cars we drive, the color of our drapes, the linen, the silverware, the schools we attend.

Sometimes, in the morning haze that lingers before I'm fully awake, my mother can become the thing she was at the moment of my birth, a larger-than-life image who has made the decision to allow me to exist. Mornings, lying in bed with my eyes closed, I can reenter a warm shapeless place of dense fluid, anticipation, the faintest outline of her face looming above me, drenched with the perspiration of her effort that is resulting in me, and suddenly the two of us are staring into each other's eyes for the first time. On other occasions I'm crawling to her side while she sits in the upstairs library reading. I begin to climb up on her lap, but she won't help me. If I make it up on my own, she will read to me. If I should fall, she will only watch to see if I will try again.

One time I asked if she remembered these things: the first time we met, the dim lighting in the operating room, the number of nurses surrounding us, her hair pressed to her sweating head in ringlets. I even described the doctor, a short, balding man with wire-rimmed glasses and goat's breath. She listened to my recollections and laughed, but she wouldn't confirm that my memory was true. It was sort of like it didn't matter. Not to her at least.

Ma's mother ran off with another man when she was seven years old. Her father never remarried after that. I've never asked about her mother, and of course she's never volunteered any information. She told Son about what happened though, and Son told me and Yogi. Ma confides in Son a lot 'cause she's the oldest, and 'cause they're kind of alike, although Son isn't as hard-assed.

Ma's father died of TB before I was born, but her brothers I've seen maybe four or five times, and always together. Yogi says it's 'cause they're scared of Ma. Yogi likes bragging about Ma, but never around anyone except me and Son. Son's proud of Ma too, but Yogi worships her. She thinks that maybe she can copy something. Sonny looks like Ma so she doesn't have to copy anything, even though she never earned it, the way people notice her height when she walks through the mall. Yogi's tall too, but she tries too hard, and then other times she doesn't try at all and it's everybody else's fault.

"A little run-down." Ma keeps after the old man. The more she says it, the more ridiculous it sounds. "All night you were reading, Frank, out in the car under the dashboard light you were hunched over in the front seat reading. Like some kind of homeless savant."

"Don't do this, Georgia," Dad makes a small plea. "Not in front of the boy."

I reach for a roll and stuff a slab of butter into it. I don't wanna watch what's going on in front of me. They aren't arguing. That wouldn't be so bad, if it were just arguing. But this is so one-sided.

"Why do you always have to be mysterious, Frank? Why can't you just turn on the night lamp if you want to read?"

"You were asleep. I didn't want to disturb you."

"Good!" Ma's voice rings out, snapping Yogi to attention, her eyes wide with awe.

Ma goes, "You didn't want to disturb me, Frank? Well, isn't that thoughtful? Because there is not room for two disturbed people in this house." She gives him a chance to reply, but Dad won't fall into that trap. "Will I have to feed you as well?" she finally pops off, and I slide my chair in closer to the table while Mommy Dearest does a slow burn.

Dad's only response is to shovel up a forkful of mashed potatoes, something he won't have to chew, and swallow it in one gulp. He's wearing his robe and slippers, his eyes streaked with little red veins.

"Such wonderful etiquette, Frank." Ma's lapsing into the rapid eye-blinking mode. I've never seen her hurl furniture, but it's her favorite threat.

"Don't tell me that's all you can eat after I've gone through this much trouble . . ." She stands over him for a second, then takes his plate.

"A poem," Yogi announces, but Ma's having none of it. "Make that three disturbed people." She takes Yolanda's plate too. "Good night," she dismisses them both before marching off to the kitchen. She gets an attitude about food that's been rejected and it's straight down the garbage disposal. No leftovers in her fridge.

There's a noise like World War III in the kitchen, clattering dishes, and then she returns, the insult taken care of. I don't look directly at her, choosing instead to follow her from the corner of my eye, hoping her wrath won't be directed at me.

"Your appetite's just fine," she says. It's just the two of us now. Until recently, I had assumed that being from the South meant Ma liked to cook and eat, but that's not true at all. She's only a so-so cook and has never taken kindly to compliments about her meals. She'll mostly undercook stuff, seldom does she burn it. For example, her breakfast eggs are usually runny. She doesn't have the patience for breakfast I guess, waiting for the skillet to get hot or what-

ever. Her potato salad is uncommonly heavy, and she's no-
toriously generous with salt while she's likely to parcel out
sugar grain by grain.

My dad?

Well, he's from Ohio, which leaves my canvas blank, until
he gets specific and tells you it's Cleveland. A dog's town.

I finish my plate and go for seconds, allowing Ma to do
the honors. She heaps the helpings on but not quite as much
as the first round. I think she knows I'm doing it just to
make her feel good.

"And no more juice until you're finished," she recites one
of our dinner-table commandments, something to do with
proper digestion.

She's got her elbows up on the table, her chin resting in
her hands, which isn't correct table deportment, but I know
better than to inform her about manners. She sighs comfortably. Doesn't seem she's got anything better to do than
watch me eat, and to be truthful, I could do without this.
She maybe carted me around for nine months, but we aren't
all that close. In the beginning, yeah, when I was real small
and had to depend on her to tie my shoelaces. But them
days are over.

"You rode a palomino when you were a kid?" I ask nervously, a defendant before the judge and jury.

"Yes, Randall," she sighs again. "I rode a palomino when
I was a child."

She's not one to tell a story more than once, about how
her dad owned twenty-five acres outside of Richmond. It
occurs to me that her name should be Virginia instead of
Georgia, but I already know what she thinks of that joke.

"What do you think Dad did when he was a kid? I mean,
he didn't look after horses or ride them in the rain like you
did, did he?"

She shakes her head. She sees where I'm heading. "Your
father was a straight-A student. Always had his head in a

book," she says, as if she's told me this twelve dozen times, which she has. I spear a group of green beans, one for each tine on my fork, and helicopter them over my plate.

This gets a tiny smile.

"You think he's OK? I mean, maybe he needs some kinda checkup."

"He just had one," she says quickly. "Got a clean bill of health."

"Then what's with him? Seems like—"

She has no answers so she cuts me off, "He'll be fine," but the words don't offer any comfort to either of us. "Let's not worry about your father, though. You've got enough to be concerned with."

"What's that mean?"

"Your teacher, Ms. McElroy, gave me a call the other day—," and before she can go on, I'm thinking up an alibi. I've got a million on file.

"I didn't break that window at school," I blurt out, and for once I'm telling the truth. "It was Donnie Masterson and them guys. They were throwing a baseball around inside the classroom. They shattered that window. I had nothing to do with it. Even if I wanted to, they wouldn't include me in their stupid games. And even after that, I get blamed."

Ma's nodding her head, a trace of amusement. "Did I say anything about a window getting broken? Well, now. Isn't that interesting the way your guilt just comes tumbling out? Wonder why that is?"

"I'm just sensitive, that's all," I mumble, and out of nowhere, she's laughing.

With Dad, I can usually make him laugh when I want. But Ma, she don't never laugh when you're trying to make her laugh. I watch her to see how beautiful she is, the crinkling around her eyes, perfectly white teeth, and dimples on both sides, the works.

"Randall, Randall, Randall," she says my name like music and I remember somewhere in my diapered past that I loved her. When she wants, she can make me hate her too.

"What is going to become of you, little boy?" She begins cleaning off the table, then heads back to the kitchen. I follow. "Come, come baby boy and let's wash the dishes." She offers me another smile for my clean plate. "And you can tell me all about how the whole world's against poor little Randall."

c h a p t e r
7

There's stuff that lives in darkness. Lots of people are aware of it. Then there's stuff that needs both stillness and dark. Usually you come across these things by mistake, like stubbing your toe, knowledge and pain. Knowledge doesn't want to hurt you. It'll even hide from you, but if you keep feeling your way still farther, you'll learn stuff you really don't want to know.

Some stuff you find out only when somebody else tells you. Usually people won't tell you stuff you're not supposed to know 'cause most times they don't even know it. They don't wanna know.

But I wanted it. That's what Dad held over my head. And it wasn't like he knew it either. He might have been the conductor, but the spirit was within him and he could only act out this evil thing we both wanted to know. His last twelve years, my first twelve, they were best.

He was always weird. Didn't seem much harm, and people liked him that way. They could pull him aside and tell him all the things they would never admit to anyone else 'cause he was kinda goofy anyway. They used him to cleanse themselves.

"If your father goes to heaven, then that'll be the same as us all going," Ma used to joke, but it really wasn't such a funny thought, his sacrifice. A man among heathens, his own family.

Early morning hours and the darkest night sky, a time I'm committed to discover. The others are asleep and I find myself creeping down the dark hallway toward the library. For a moment I must've been sleepwalking 'cause I don't recall climbing from the bed or leaving my room. The first thing I feel is my coonskin on my head and my bare feet on the cool varnished wood floor.

I'm not startled to find myself this way. It's happened before. Sometimes my body will wake without an OK from my mind. The mind, even my mind, it won't OK some things. The mind realizes the body will put itself in danger 'cause it doesn't know any better.

Even so, I trust my body as much as I do my mind 'cause my body can withstand more than my mind will give credit for. That's how come when my body wakes without getting clearance, I'm pleased to find that it has gotten its way, sidling softly along the hall for the first five steps and then my mind awakes and sees that it's too late, the body is in control.

There's a creak as a floorboard gives slightly beneath my weight. I halt, poised on tiptoe, and move to the side, closer to the wall. None of it matters. I live here, after all. But sneaking around gives me a chill that tightens my chest, my eyes closed, dependent on radar.

Dad's always telling me that things of value are not handed to you; you have to first expose your mind to allow access. First time he said that to me, I pretty much teed off on him.

"Hey, Dad. You don't think for one second I know what you're talking about?" I says to him. Sometimes he flips out and you have to remind him that you don't speak Latin.

We were coming back from the City, stuck in rush hour traffic along the Southern State Parkway, and Dad's acting like he didn't hear my question, which is another one of his weird little habits, making you ask questions twice just to be sure you really want to hear the answer. Then he'll hand you some open-ended answer, "All good things to those who wait," or "The early bird may catch the worm, but hunting for lunch and dinner takes more than punctuality. It takes diligence and resiliency and perseverance."

Yeah, Dad. Whatever you say.

I'm not sure if he's ever talked this way to Son or Yogi. He's never done it to Ma though; she wouldn't tolerate it. One time she overheard us talking crazy in the living room. We were playing the game of relations where he'll say something, then I have to take the same idea to an even more ridiculous level. Sort of an "A is to C as B is to D" competition. So Dad said something like, "A picture of a fast car isn't really very fast at all," and I replied, "On the reverse side of leather there's suede. Cows are very modest people."

That's when Ma walked in with her hands on her hips. "What kind of nonsense are you teaching this boy?" She doesn't have patience for riddles. And she could never understand creeping down a dark hallway in search of truth either. She's logical. If she's looking for something, she'll just turn on the damn light.

Farther down the hallway, Yogi's door is cracked open. I take a peek in at her, a huddled lump under her blanket. I ease into the room, making my feet go flat against the floor to muffle any sound.

The room is a mess, with clothes on the floor and four jelly donuts on the dresser. I help myself to one, sucking

the grape jelly out of the middle and licking the white pow-
der from my fingers. There's orange Nehi too but it's piss
warm.

Kneeling beside the bed, I peel back the blanket to find
Yogi's feet where her face should be.

"What are you doing, retard?" The voice comes from the
foot of the bed, her head appearing. She sleeps like a hur-
ricane, all elbows and knees. Her hair is swirled and spiked.

"What you doin down there?" I ask.

"What are you doing in my room?"

"I dunno. You heard me come in?"

"Of course," she says and sits up. She's naked. Pajamas
are too civilized for Yogi. "You got feet like cement." She
digs an elbow into her pillow. "Now what do you want?"

"Dad. What's wrong with him?"

"He's a nut, just like you. Anything else?"

"But he's been skipping work."

"Randall, he's our dad. What we're supposed to do is
whatever he tells us. And anyway, he's paid his dues to
that hospital, his whole damn career is all. What're they
gonna do, fire him? Not a chance. He wants to skip a few
days, then fuck it, he's earned it."

"But his journal, he ain't doin that right neither. He's
writing about himself as if he were somebody else. He keeps
calling himself the victim, like he's talking about one of his
clients or somethin."

"Maybe he is."

"No. It's him he's talking about. I can tell."

"Well, what are you doing looking at his journal anyway?
You know you're not supposed to."

"Hold still and I'll go get it."

"I'm not gonna read his journal. It's wrong."

This almost makes me laugh.

"It's wrong," she says again, "and you should be
ashamed of yourself."

"Well, I ain't. Besides, I think he wants me to read it."

"No, Randall," she says and cuffs the blanket under her breasts to prop them up. I've known Yogi's breasts since we were small, back when we used to take baths together. They're the same size as when she was seven. Terrell's a whole different story.

"Dad doesn't want you reading his journal." Yogi slides farther under the blanket. "You're just nosy. Now get out my room before I tell Ma."

"Wait. Can't you see it—"

"Quite frankly, no, goddammit." She kicks me in the head but the blanket softens the blow.

I grab her leg. "Ever since what happened with Son, can't you see the way he's been?"

"She got married. He knew she would."

"But in his journal he says he can't stop the bleeding. He says the blood is rushing to his head."

"Randall, you're not making any sense."

"Dad. He don't think it's fair, Son marrying the toehead. He says the wound of trust betrayed can never heal. Think it's poetry?"

"How would I know?"

"Well, whatever it is, he says it's just the beginning."

"Beginning of what?"

"That's what I'm gonna find out. I'm on my way to the library where he keeps his journal. Wanna come?"

"No." She turns over and pulls the blanket over her head.

"All right. But don't say I didn't warn you."

We all have to keep a journal, a rule Dad made in hopes of rearing a well-adjusted family. Obviously, it hasn't worked out so well.

Dad knows I read his journal. He chooses when, and each night I make my way up the dark hallway like a thief, hoping I won't be disappointed. When this started, I can't really say. At first I thought I was being slick, reading things I wasn't supposed to. But he isn't so careless as to leave his journal lying around, and even if he was, it wouldn't be only once a week.

The library is large, the size of the dining room downstairs with the same hardwood finish. There's a draft in here. It flows cool and steady from the window to the door. The room is narrow and long, about thirty paces front to back, its center in perfect line with the oval window, the study desk, and the Kentucky rifle. The sun and moon fit fully through the window and sometimes when the sun reappears after a thunderstorm, the moisture on the glass will make a rainbow.

I can never feel alone in our library. It even smells like him, his pipe tobacco. On weekends he spends full days here. If he goes into the library early in the morning it's like he can't leave. If he's here early, he's staying. I hate it when he does that 'cause I wanna be with him. It's where I belong, especially late at night, settling in his chair to read.

September 3—sundown—midtown office

The victim kneels at the corner of his desk. It's how he was brought up, prayer, an opportunity and a need.

The office building lies in the middle of a fork in the road where Broadway and Columbus come together. He's seven floors up with a view to the Hudson and Riverside Drive. His wife had insisted on filling the office with cheerful "mood colors," proving how little she understands about the demons he entertains there. Tropical plants in large earthen jars line the wall-to-ceiling window that faces the river. The couch and chairs are upholstered in soft kidskin leather. Above the bookcase is a pastel painting of women hanging laundry on a windy day.

After his last session he sits idle. A headache is lodged at the base of his skull, an uneven barbell that's weighted more heavily on the left side, causing his head to tilt in the manner of a man constantly perplexed. No good deed goes unpunished, not even for a public servant in tune with the ear of God.

A glance out the window and he realizes that night has fallen in an eye blink, leaving him unsure of where the afternoon went. One moment sunlight washes out the corners of the office, putting everything in plain sight; the next there is only darkness and a thin, shrill scream that echoes before fading with impassioned vibrato. A demented seagull. With binoculars he searches the horizon for a warning. Nothing.

For a long moment he is patiently aware of another suspicion behind him, moving closer. He will not rush, however; he will sit perfectly still, expectant, holding his breath, hopeful of the worst as he turns abruptly to confront only his paranoia. He is alone; his time has not yet come. It has occurred to him too often for it to be a complete lie, that he's straddling a line between life and death, still unworthy of the latter.

With half an hour to kill before his train, he wanders out along the sidewalk empty-handed and waits out three light changes at the corner, unable to move when the sign flashes WALK. The rush hour sounds are rich with confusion and he closes his eyes to amplify them. The result is no surprise. He's done this before in an effort to simulate the Second Coming, the thing he is willingly moving toward even as he understands the destruction it will involve. The paradox is pure, its riddle being solved by faith.

Helpless, he stumbles across the street and up the sidewalk toward the train station.

So much time to endure, a mandate for the faithful, a billion steps to glory. With a view from above, he spots his aging figure caught in the middle of the midtown bustle. No one notices his struggle, the rugged cross that burdens him, the crown of self-delusion, a dividend for his good intentions. Stubbornly, he pushes his stride beyond the pack of pedestrians and boldly leads out into a busy intersection.

In a loud voice he commands them, "Follow me and I will make you—," but before he can finish, it is obvious that he has chosen the path to destruction, out in the middle of the street against *the lights, the cars whizzing past. A leader without charisma, a prophet ignored.*

His wife had given him the cold facts. "Who do you think you are? You don't have the forum or the voice. You're a doctor, and a damn fine one. Don't start overestimating yourself."

He'd come to her with some lame idea about community service, free food and shelter for the homeless, a chance to make someone listen. "Why can't you be supportive if what I'm doing is right?"

"Because I can see what's happening to you."

"But what does it cost to try?"

"From what I can tell," came her simple reply, "your sanity."

Finally, a break appears in the traffic and the passersby edge past him a bit cautiously, faces of a mob that's waiting to happen. "Give us Barabbas," their lips are prepared to say. What it is they need, the victim knows, but to help, to reach out, to offer up the words of salvation, "And with His stripes we are healed," would only scatter them further, their faces flashing open contempt.

I slam the journal shut. There's more, but I don't want to read it all, not yet. And he can't make me. None of this can happen by force. He can't make me see it, his words becoming scrawled, the letters getting bigger, almost childlike. There are splotches where the pages are yellowing. He keeps spilling something, but still the words will not fade.

I hush myself and stare at the door. He is on the other side. He is my father, and that gives him the right to frighten me.

I part the pages once more to peek into the future without reading the words. Not yet, I can't read them. And I cannot move, laying the open pages atop the desk and leaning back into his chair, waiting for him.

c h a p t e r

8

Steadily he is moving farther from her.

It's Tuesday evening, about 8 P.M., and I'm in the dining room matching a word puzzle when I hear the explosion. It isn't so much the loudness of her voice, it's the strain. Pleading isn't something she's used to doing. Patience has never been her strong suit. She's close to going ballistic. From Dad there is nothing.

I can picture him, sitting up in bed with the bowl of split-pea soup I made for him when he got home early. Ma has come home late, a meeting at school probably, and when she arrives to see him in bed so early, it irks her. It's something that's been building for a while, and he seems to be giving her every opportunity to sound off on him.

She does her bit, a quick eruption complete with demands, ultimatums, and a few "goddammits" for emphasis. Then suddenly it goes silent. She's in the shower.

I drop down flat on my stomach to inch across the carpet,

using my elbows to pull my weight like oars on a boat. In the living room I pause to check the terrain. Good cover, the lights are out. I peel an imaginary banana, for protein, then take a swig from my canteen. I'm on a recon mission —I'll need my strength.

I'm wedged between the stereo and the piano when Yogi comes through the front door.

"Boy, what the hell you doin now!"

I hop into my praying mantis karate stance, then fall into a soft forward head roll, combat-ready.

"You're almost twelve, Randall. Try getting a grip on puberty."

"You'll give away our position—we'll get shelled." I wave her off, then signal to the other two G.I.s in the corner. Yogi rolls her eyes and heads off upstairs. "Need to get some friends," she says, like she's Ms. It.

Yogi's familiar with my war games, my treks across the Sahara. Twice I've climbed Kilimanjaro and another time I swam the English Channel. You can never impress her though.

I dive behind the couch and look over a road map. The trail is pretty hairy but I've had tougher missions. With an AK-40 slung over my shoulder, I pick my way through a minefield before snaking into the hallway to set up a command post outside my parents' door. Luckily Ma's still in the shower. She has no use for my war games either. Dad couldn't care less.

Finally, the shower turns off and I can hear Dad fidgeting in the bed, hypnotizing himself over the mug of split-pea, stirring it three times around. "Ting ting ting," he taps the silver spoon against the porcelain rim. Ma has returned to the room, that's why he's tinging his mug. He knows the precision drives her crazy, his favorite hobby of late, watching soup grow cold.

Dad goes first: "What'd you think of the Halloween costume I bought for the boy?"

I move in tighter against the hallway wall so I can look crossways into the mirror at them on the bed. A perfect view, except that if I can see them, how come they can't see me? I must be invisible again. It happens that way, quick and silent. It's too early for them to sleep so I huddle my knees in tighter to my chest and wait for the fireworks. Ma's sitting up in bed, flipping through a magazine while Dad plays with his soup.

"The costume. What'd you think?"

"It's a waste of money, Frank. The boy doesn't even take part in Halloween." Her voice is thin. She's ready to argue if that's the way he wants it. "By now you should know Randall will never do anything he sees other children doing."

Dad shrugs and sighs and pokes his feet out from under the blanket. They don't seem to please him much either. "I just wanted to buy him something after we ruined his summer with that camp business."

"Don't forget who the parents are around here."

"You think he's still upset?"

"He'll get over it."

"But why'd you have to spank him twice over some silly summer camp?"

"Because he deserved it." Ma makes a hard crease in the magazine, but she won't be reading anything. "Had the nerve to ask me was I finished yet," she says. "I should've spanked him three times."

"That's just his way."

"But it isn't the right way. I don't think you know that little boy as well as you think you do."

"Do you know him?"

She hesitates and I feel my insides tighten. Confusing Dad comes naturally, he prefers it. He wants to believe things are hidden, that there is something being risked, something to be saved. But Ma should know me clean through to the core. I came from within her. She's got my heart, but she won't give in to that. She has never really claimed me—just in case, she will not come too close.

"He's living out of his suitcase again," she sighs. "Says he wants to be ready."

"Ready? Ready for what?"

"Who knows. I made him put his things back in the chest of drawers and locked the suitcases away."

"Was he trying to be funny?"

"Probably some nonsense you've taught him."

"Don't be so rough on him. He's just a child."

"And he's my child, that's why I have a right to be concerned when he starts acting like a basket case. He's our responsibility, Frank, and if he grows into God-knows-what, we'll be to blame."

Dad takes another dose of the split-pea soup, leaning his face into the steam. Most times he knows when I'm eavesdropping, but this time I can't be sure. There's little I can be sure of anymore, unless he allows me to be.

"Do his classmates ever call him up?" he asks. It's obvious he doesn't want the conversation to end yet. "And what about his teacher? She didn't strike me as particularly alert."

"Of course not, Frank. There isn't a teacher alive good enough to teach your children. I'm surprised you didn't check her fingernails the way you used to with the baby-sitter."

"Never mind that. What's your take on this McElroy woman?"

"I'll have the FBI run a check."

"My God, am I asking too much?"

"Well, what do you want me to say? She's professional. Observant."

He curses himself.

"Now what?"

"Why is he so intense, Georgia?"

"Maybe if he saw his father relax more often—"

"But he's a boy. Why doesn't he get along with other

children?" He puts the soup aside. "Think we had him too late?"

"Not this again."

"Hey, families fall apart all the time. I've got a cabinet full of case studies—"

"And a wife and three children," she breaks in. "Don't confuse the two."

"But you're asking me to ignore empirical evidence that says the family structure is a fragile thing in our society."

"You know, this kind of talk is probably very useful at a symposium, but it does little to impress a woman in bed."

"Go ahead, make a joke of it. I just want to be sure there's as much love in this house as there was when Sonny was eleven." He winces the moment he says it.

"You doubt that?" She turns on him and his shoulders begin to fold into his chest. "I've never doubted my husband or my children. But you have, is that what you're saying?"

"I'm talking about doubting the amount of quality time we spend together," he dodges, "not the amount of love. You can't measure love anyway."

"After all this time, so little you've learned. By a family's combined accomplishments you can measure the amount of love in their home. Love translates into accomplishment, and don't tell me we haven't had some of those, Frank. Don't rob us of that."

Sometimes I'm certain my parents don't like each other. I heard Ma say it once, "You'll never understand what it takes to make me happy." She said it as an accusation, as if Dad didn't understand because he didn't try.

This flap happened after a cocktail party Ma hosted at our house last winter for some Nassau County exec, a white guy named Simon Dupree. He was tall and toupeed with one of them tans he must've bought from a salon, it being February and all. Me, I was pretty impressed with the whole scene since I'd never been to a cocktail party before, although I kept waiting for the food that never came, which ticked me off 'cause I'd skipped lunch figuring I was gonna pig out at the party. But there was just bite-size stuff that was so small you had to stab it with a toothpick before you could eat it. There was plenty of booze though, and Ma had Skipper, Naldo, and Mike dress up in these white valet jackets so they could serve the guest from silver platters that Ma must've rented cause we don't own that kinda stuff.

It was a slick party. Mostly I hung around the kitchen, popping corks off the champagne bottles with the guys. Naldo got pretty blitzed, but Mike didn't drink cause he's a jock, and Skipper was too busy brownnosing all of Ma's self-important friends. Got himself a summer internship too. The guest list included sixteen very influential people, at least that's the way they presented themselves. Ma's guest list is always limited to sixteen for reasons that only a phony socialite would understand.

Anyhow, this Simon Dupree character showed up late for the party and barely stayed an hour. He had his wife with him, an old bag who stood at the door like she was too good to schmooze with all the other phonies. So me, taking it as a personal insult that she was dissin my mom's party, I struck up a conversation with her for the sole purpose of telling her in so many words that I thought she was a stuffy old bag.

Check me out, moseying on over to this dame, suave as an eleven-year-old is capable of being. "I'm the man of the house," I tell her, then give one of them sophisticated chuckles like I'm the cleverest SOB she's ever gonna meet.

It's a joke, right? I'm just kidding. But this dumb broad, who happened to have a dye job straight from hell, a sort of weird purplish-puke color, she up and gives me a look as if she thinks I'm gonna try 'n snatch her jewelry or something.

So I go, "You from Westchester, or what?" which I didn't

realize anybody would take that as a putdown, but this babe is totally indignant and whispers something in her hubby's ear. Before you know it, they're scootin out the door to hop into their stretch limo, except me and Naldo had already slit the back tire while the chauffeur slept. What the hell was a limo parked outside our house for in the first place? Too much, man. The way these guys take themselves so seriously, a chauffeur no less.

Wasn't like anybody noticed the toupee and his snotty old bag of a wife left early anyway. All the other guests were busy networking, which I think that means they were making plans to help each other make money or steal money or if worse came to worse, make sure the money didn't end up in the hands of people who had less than they did. It's the whole "status quo mandate" that Dad explained to me last election year when I asked him what an incumbent was. Status quo is what Ma's friends are all about, and Ma fit right in like Ms. Congeniality, mingling and whatnot, all charm and sparkling smile, then when everybody had left, that's when she turned into the Wicked Witch and sounded off on the old man on account of him not bothering to show up. He was in the house all right, stuck up in the library. "Like a bat in the attic," was how Ma started in on him.

She marched right up to the library where Dad had locked himself in. He'd been in there maybe twelve hours straight. So Ma goes pounding on the door, "Franklin Roberts," she says, "how could you possibly embarrass me that way?"

Dad mumbled his usual complaint about not coming to the party 'cause Ma's friends were pretentious phonies. I was tucked in my room, peeping down the hall at Ma through a crack in the door.

Ma's like, "What are you, a child?" She was wearing black velvet with a red satin sash and those stockings with mirages weaved into the netting. "Only children complain about things they don't like to do." She stood there a second, her feet slightly apart and her hands on her hips. She looked incredible. She says, "There are some things you do as a matter of responsibility."

"Responsibility to whom, Georgia? I don't know those people. And I don't owe them either."

"What about me, Frank? Did it ever occur to you that your presence tonight might make things easier for me?"

"No!" Dad had shouted. He sounded pretty brave behind a locked door. "As a matter of fact, I've never imagined anything I could do would be something you absolutely couldn't live without."

That one had stunned Ma for a moment. Maybe it even hurt her, 'cause after that she went for the killer line: "You'll never understand what it takes to make me happy."

She had said it timidly, almost hopelessly, which of course caught Dad totally off guard. He was speechless, and it seemed to me that she was right: he had no idea what it took. He didn't even understand what it took to make himself happy.

That little explosion happened in the winter and turned out to be the intro to a series of arguments that may as well have been scheduled for every other week. Dad was staging them too, and don't think Ma didn't realize she was being goaded. But she couldn't help herself. She might not have liked him, yet she still loved him. There's a dangerous difference between the two. Liking stops just short of obligation; loving is a debt.

That's how it sounded to me that night while they argued about the amount of love in our house. I went upstairs to lie in my bed, directly above the master bedroom. I could still hear the back and forth, first him then her. As usual she was responding to his doubts. Finally, I shut them out and propped a book of colored pictures up on my stomach, looking for the best picture, one with few details, something strong and singular—something I could hang on my wall before I went to bed.

Solitary games are best. I learned that long ago. They're best especially if you got only sisters to play with, or if you're tall for your age and all the kids in your class are smaller than you. My classmates were happy when I didn't play with them. It wasn't like I planned on not getting along at school. It would just happen, and all of a sudden I wasn't included. Every year I'd get another chance too. There'd be some new kid who didn't know any better, and he'd try to be my friend until I taught him something unkind. In second grade I stapled Sean Ferguson's finger to make him get lost. Man, I got in trouble big-time for that one.

"The other children are only curious because you won't play with them," my second-grade teacher, Ms. Weidle-meyer, would lie to me, when all she wanted was for me to fit in and be like everybody else. Teachers like it when all their students are the same 'cause it makes their job easier.

"They like you," she said.

"Everyone just wants to be liked," I replied.

"Exactly," Ms. Weidlemeyer nodded. "It doesn't feel so nice when you aren't liked," she said.

She was very understanding about the stapling, although a couple of my classmates cried at the sight of the blood, and of course Sean was pretty upset about the whole ordeal.

He kept asking, "Why, why, why?" the tears streaming down his face.

"I don't know why," I told him honestly, but it didn't seem to satisfy anybody much. All my classmates were hud-dled around, giving me nasty looks.

I tried to be frank and forthcoming, "He ain't gonna die," but that only made them hate me more. That's when Ms. Weidlemeyer took me into custody so I wouldn't hurt any-body else.

It's crazy, but a few seconds before I stapled him, I was

thinking: "I wonder if it would hurt if I . . ." I was only eight years old at the time, what did I know? I mean, I knew it would hurt; I just wasn't sure how bad it would hurt. Sometimes you think that way when you're a little boy. I wasn't gonna tell Ms. Weidlemeyer that though. She'd never been a little boy before. I don't think she was ever little at all. "They want me to play with them so they can find more reasons to hate me, not because they like me." It didn't seem to bother her that I wasn't making much sense. "They hate me," I repeated, casting my eyes toward the floor.

"Oh no," Ms. Weidlemeyer said, her voice aquiver with concern. She was pretty old with flanks like a cow and played the organ every year for graduation. "They don't hate you. Children your age aren't capable of hating each other."

We were sitting in the teacher's lounge, sucking peppermint candy. "You're not such a bad boy," she beamed. "You only want me to think you are."

She patted my head and smiled.

I thought about what it would be like if she was at the zoo and climbed down into a cage with a lion or something. "You aren't such a bad lion," she'd say and pat the lion on the head. "You only want me to think you are." I imagined it and smiled and me and Ms. Weidlemeyer were both smiling for different reasons.

"I think I get it," I said, unwrapping another peppermint candy. She had an endless supply. "Us kids we trade off liking each other, and the punishment for not liking is being hated?"

There was an awkward pause while Ms. Weidlemeyer tried to agree with me but the words wouldn't come out of her mouth. She didn't have a clue as to what I was talking about. Neither did I, so I asked another question.

"Does that mean I really don't hate them, I just think I do?"

"Of course, Randall. Maybe deep down you're afraid they won't like you, so you don't like them first."

Her words caught me square and she saw it and touched my arm. I could've cried for her then, that's what they always want. It's what I wanted too, but instead I swallowed my candy first, the whole thing. I started to choke and my eyes started tearing. I don't know if Ms. Weidlemeyer realized that I did it on purpose so I could have an excuse for crying. Probably she did, but if I hadn't made it look like I was crying by accident, then she'd have kept after me. And I couldn't take that. What for? She can't ever know anything about loneliness, not my loneliness, and besides that, she wouldn't want to know. Loneliness is never happy, but it's always freedom.

c h a p t e r
9

A sure sign: Ma does not want the responsibility of leading this family anymore. It's always been her ship, but we're off course. If we crash, she wants to be clear of the fallout.

She's given up. She hasn't spanked me since the summer camp thing and it's got nothing to do with me turning over a new leaf. For the last two weeks she's even cooked breakfast on weekday mornings, not just cold cereal. She's gone to the hugs and kisses routine—discipline is not her concern anymore. It doesn't work. Everything will have to take care of itself.

I've tried to get ahold of her journal to see how much she's admitting, to see if she's surrendered in writing. She keeps it under lock though. She's not stupid, she knows. She understands there can't be absolute privacy, not with what's living under her roof. The lock she uses is more than just good, it's tin-plated. If the tin is scratched, she'll see it.

I'm good with locks. I learned from Yogi, who happens

to be a pro. Once when Dad locked the keys in the car, Yolanda clipped the lock on the trunk, crawled in headfirst, unscrewed a few bolts, and slid into a compartment behind the backseat where she punched through the panel around the radio speakers. She ended up in the front seat. Swear to God, she's a coyote.

But she's never taught me anything so cool. Mostly she's shown me stuff like how to use a coat hanger, and how to fall from heights. We used to practice jumping off the roof of the house until one of the neighbors ratted.

Anyway, little by little we're wearing Mommy dear down. At least Son came out OK, and now she's pretending her job is finished.

Yogi has noticed Ma's relaxed attitude too, and don't think we haven't taken full advantage of the lack of supervision. You wouldn't believe the capers her and Terrell dream up. A few weeks ago, the three of us used Dad's camcorder to film one of the neighbors, Mrs. Davenport, taking a bubble bath. We ran the whole lark just about perfectly.

See, during the afternoon I doped Sophie, the Davenports' Irish setter. Sophie's got a beautiful coat, a sort of glossy deep red that borders on purple when you wet her down. Me coming into the Davenports' backyard to visit Sophie wasn't a problem since I hang out with her a lot anyways. She's a barker mostly. She ain't too bright. Setters usually aren't, and they're trusting to anyone, as opposed to your dobie or pit bull.

Dad's never let us keep a pet after me and Yogi starved the goldfish he bought us one Christmas. Not on purpose, we just forgot to feed them. So what—they weren't much fun nohow. We didn't even give them names 'cause what's the point, goldfish can't hear, and on top of that we couldn't tell them apart. I'm not sure whether they were identical twins or maybe all goldfish look alike.

All things considered, goldfish could become extinct and

nobody would shed any tears. If they could make a noise or something, then we probably wouldn't have starved them. Goldfish are like plants: if you forget to feed 'em, they don't say shit. They just die.

A morning comes around and I go, "Hey, Yogi, are they sleepin?" We both peered down into the bowl at the goldfish lying at the bottom.

"Fuck 'em," Yogi said, and flushed them down the toilet. Dad wasn't one bit pleased though, and ever since then he's refused to buy us a pet. That's how come I'm a close personal friend to all the pets on our street.

I like shepherds most. They're stately and they'll pose for you to show off their body. You won't catch a shepherd lying around with his snout on his paw. They like being in motion. They're sleek and firm and will trot and canter just so you can sit back and admire them. I'd put a shepherd almost in league with coyotes as far as cunning goes, but not quite 'cause they aren't naturally devious the way coyotes are. Not that I've ever met a coyote, but just from what I've seen on the PBS wildlife specials, I wouldn't much trust a coyote to do anything that wasn't underhanded and mean-spirited.

But setters are basically retarded. Take Sophie for instance: she ain't good for nothing except barking when someone starts prowling around in your yard at night. That's why we had to dope her up. I came over the house that afternoon and told Mr. Davenport I was taking her for a walk. The Davenports like me OK. They don't have kids.

"Be sure you chain her back up," Mr. Davenport said. He works for the post office and drives a huge white Cadillac that might could float if you took it out to sea.

He said, "The wife and I are going to visit some friends for a few hours so make sure you feed her too. The Alpo's in the garage."

"Sure thing, Mr. D."

That was at about five o'clock, and by the time the Davenports got back Sophie was snoring peacefully off the dozen Sominex I crushed up in her Alpo, allowing me, Yogi, and Terrell to slip into the backyard after dark with a ladder. The toughest part was setting the ladder against the house and climbing it without it making any noise. We solved that problem by wrapping a towel around the top of the ladder to muffle the sound, and Yogi told us that when we climbed the ladder, we had to plant our steps with our tippy-toes in the middle of each rung. That way the ladder wouldn't sway and creak.

We took turns doing the filming, climbing the ladder up to the second floor to peek into the bathroom window. Mrs. Davenport is a three-hundred-pound whale who thinks she's an opera singer. Needless to say, it made for a lovely film.

The only problem was that we didn't know the Fotomat was obligated by law to file a report after developing any film that's "deemed lascivious in nature." But before they called the cops they called Ma. And get this, she's taken the whole thing in stride. No lecture, no punishment, no spankings. Nothing.

All she said was, "If you kids aren't embarrassed about this little misadventure, then neither am I."

"Are they gonna give us back our footage?" I ask.

"You're lucky if they don't throw you in jail. And I'll tell you something else. If one of you kids ends up in the morgue one day, I won't bother claiming the remains. More than likely you'll have gotten exactly what you deserved."

Terrell didn't get any blame since it was Dad's camcorder, so me and Yogi are taking all the heat, of which there is very little. In fact, all weekend we've been hanging out with Ma, "so I can keep my eye on you." She's doesn't seem to be riled in the least. Instead, she keeps looking at us and smiling. The three of us are sitting around the kitchen table eating Häagen-Dasz, a mother and her two brats.

"Hey, Ma," I say, basking in the rare glow of maternal

attention. "I been in a morgue before. Once when I was visiting Dad at the hospital, I snuck downstairs where they keep the stiffs. They keep it refrigerated so the bodies won't rot."

"Shut up, stupid." Yolanda snatches my butter pecan and helps herself. I'm left with her cherry swirl, which I hate.

It's Saturday evening and we've just gotten back from the circus at MSG. Dad's out in the yard, hacking up the shrubbery. He's been at it all day, a mistake that keeps getting worse.

"So, can I get forty dollars to go bowling tonight?" Yolanda asks, trying to make the most out of Ma's generous mood.

"Since when did bowling cost forty dollars?"

"I gotta rent those bowling shoes."

"Yolanda, don't insult my intelligence."

"What about if I wanna eat something?"

"Make a tuna fish sandwich before you leave."

I have a laugh at Yogi's expense.

"Keep it up," she bares her teeth at me.

"I'm not giving you a red cent," Ma says, "unless you take your brother along."

"But I'm going with my friends."

"So?"

"So, they hate Randall."

Ma gives her a stern look.

"Well, how come he can't get his own friends. My friends hate him."

"No they don't," I say. "Only Terrell hates me."

"And don't you let that bother you." Ma leans over and gives me a cold rum-raisin kiss on the forehead, keeping her face close for an instant, her eyes narrowing as if she's imagining me in one of those slide-out drawers at the morgue, or maybe as a mugshot photo in the post office.

"He doesn't need a lot of friends if he has a supportive family," she says to Yolanda while picking a piece of lint

from my eyebrow. It makes me feel good, having her attention, but not for too long. I've always come just short of
whatever it is she expects.

"Here." Ma takes a twenty from her purse and lays it on
the table. Putting it directly in Yogi's hand would make her
an accessory. "Who all is going bowling?" she asks skepti-
cally. Yogi never tells the truth about her after-dark plans.

"Same run-around bunch."

"I don't follow slang, young lady, and take your feet off
the table." She slaps Yogi's Reeboks off the edge.

"Terrell, Naldo, Skipper, and Mike."

"Good. At least Skipper will keep you in line."

"Yeah, right," Yogi says. "Hey, Ma, just 'cause somebody
makes straight A's, that doesn't make him an angel."

"Let me put it this way," Ma chuckles, "if I could trade
you for him, I'd do it without a second thought."

This startles Yolanda, which startles both me and Ma, seeing the tears well up in her eyes. "How can you say that?"
she moans, and all of a sudden she's a lost little lamb. Ma
moves her chair closer and gives her a big hug. "I was just
kidding, honey," she says in her best Claire Huxtable. "You
know how much I love you."

"You always kid like that and then you wonder why I
rebel."

"Oh, Yolanda. You're just looking for excuses."

Yogi sucks her teeth and pockets the money. "I'm going
outside with Dad," she says in a huff. "He'd never trade
me in."

Come nightfall I'm out with Yogi's lot. I'm the one with the
chef salad and ice tea, sitting in the corner booth at a greasy
spoon diner where Terrell works on weekends. 'Course,
Terrell hasn't done a damn thing all evening except swab
down a few tables and steal other people's tips.

Our booth is U-shaped and I'm at the center with Mike

and Yogi on one side, and Naldo and Skip around on the other. Naldo and Mike are playing hot-sauce poker. They've got bowls of chili and a bottle of hot sauce; for every squirt one guy puts in his bowl, the other's gotta match and put up a coin. Finally, Naldo calls Mike's bluff. If Mike can eat both bowls he wins. Four-fifty in change is the pot and Mike's the sucker.

Yogi. "You ain't too keen, Michael."

"I won, didn't I?"

"It ain't competition, stupid." Yogi rolls her eyes. Mike tries to hold her hand but she won't let him. "Look at you," she wipes his face with a napkin, "sweatin like a pig. Every time, the same dumb trick."

"Ain't nothin. I can eat this—"

"You can jump off a bridge, too."

Skipper just looks on and chuckles. He's eating pistachios, stacking the shells in neat rows across the table, five even rows deep and wide. To be neat you have to be slow. Every five minutes Skip's got his glasses off, inspecting the frame, buffing them to a high shine, the light sparkling off the lenses to brilliantly reflect the redness of the shell stacks.

Terrell comes over with her jar full of tips. "What we doin?" It's quitting time and she's changed into raw leather, a pink choker, and a bullfighter's hat.

"You ain't gettin fucked tonight," Naldo cracks the table up with laughter, "not dressed like that, you ain't."

Terrell doesn't respond. She's too busy counting her money. "Damn. I didn't make piss," she whines, then looks out at the waning moon. "No wonder."

We finish up the meal, pay the tab, then head out to the parking lot where a Ferrari catches Yogi's eye.

"That's Fletcher's ride," Terrell says, smearing her lips red. "Believe that shit? A greasy mick with a ride like that? Started out a short order cook, now he thinks he's Donald Trump."

Yogi peers into the windshield. "He let you hold it yet?"

"Hell, no. He don't let nobody touch it unless it's to wash it."

I'm between the two girls as we circle the Ferrari. It's shiny and new but the guys don't seem to care. They've climbed into Skipper's Hyundai.

Naldo leans out the window, "You leading or what?"

Terrell's got her Mom's Benz and we pull out of the parking lot, leaving a stretch of burned rubber. We're breezing up Sunrise Highway, the girls bopping their heads to some silky Trent D'Arby sex song. No one's said a word about the bowling alley, it was never an option. Yogi and Terrell are proud they can't sew or bowl or bake cookies. Anything wholesome, they want no part of. They prefer Milk Duds and M-80s.

We dip in and out of the traffic, the Benz pushing Skipper's standard transmission to its limit. He can't pass Terrell and he wouldn't try. She's headed out farther east past Lindenhurst, going as fast as she wants to to no place in particular. Finally, she hangs a right and scoots up onto a dirt road that leads to a cemetery.

Several miles up the service road, we pull over to the side and begin walking. A wordless journey. Our destination hasn't been discussed. The night is true black. No stars. I haven't said anything all night and they've just about forgotten I'm along. I let myself fall behind them to see how they look, five kids crossing a cemetery at night. They've got coffee and blankets and a bottle. Naldo's got a sound box hoisted on his shoulder. But it isn't on. There is no conversation between them, there's only the jingle jangle of coins in Mike's pocket. Just we six and everyone else asleep beneath the crowd.

We could be survivors after a nuclear apocalypse—judgment day and we've outfoxed God, a wicked remnant.

For a long distance we're walking in silence and the scenery doesn't seem to change. I figure we're going clear to the other side, though it has not yet come into sight. The word "forever" would echo into eternity; as a prayer it could carry to the heavens. I glance up at the sky and find that the moon is in hiding along with the stars, leaving only a stretch of soft black velvet. A sky without decorations or promises.

I let myself fall farther behind the teenagers. For every two of their steps, I take one. They don't seem to notice. Their stride is determined, the ground sloping and rising in smooth green waves, the steady jingling of coins setting a brisk pace. The lawn is cropped close and is opening before us, expanding into endless rows of graves, growing ever bigger, though each tombstone remains individual. Counting them would take a lifetime.

Somewhere out in the middle Terrell stops along one of the aisles that's lined with dim bluish lights. "Here, this one," she says.

This totally blows my mind. "How come this one?" I come up behind them.

"Shut up," Yogi slaps me in the head. "And don't think I didn't see you wandering off."

Terrell spreads out one of the blankets. "Come lie with me, Randall," she purrs and trades hats with me, taking my coonskin and replacing it with her bullfighter's number. Terrell's got hats you could never imagine: Indian head-dresses and Jewish beanies and one that looks like a sail-boat. She's got capes too, but Yogi says she won't be seen in public with anybody wearing a cape. She says capes are too showy, like Terrell sporting Napoleon's triangle is understated.

"How many you think is dead out there?" Mike asks, settling next to Yolanda.

"You ask that every time we come up here. All of 'ems dead, Michael. They're waitin for us."

"I'm mean in number."

"Couple ten thousand maybe."

"Damn. That's a lotta dead folks."

Terrell pours a heavy shot into everyone's coffee, all except Skipper. "Sambuca," she whispers in my ear. Terrell can make anything sound forbidden. "I'll give you some later." The Sambuca is clear and smells like licorice.

"Does it taste good?" I ask.

She kisses my ear and I take this to mean yes. "In the kingdom of tombs," her words are soft against my face, "the queen must be stoned."

chapter
10

Earlier that morning I had spent some time inside Yogi, thumbing through her journal. The pages were smudged with grape jam and ketchup but the reading was decent.

During the first two weeks of school she was frantic over trigonometry. School's the only thing she thinks she can win at. She says most other times people expect you to do what they want but they don't tell you what it is. She says they make out like "maturity is a state of mind, but really it's the place of the dispossessed," whatever that means, and I don't think Yogi even knows. If she doesn't understand something, she solves it with logic that doesn't make sense. Fair is fair.

Last night she wrote, "everything is scripted: social morais, state and federal tax, mortgages—the type shit people get points for. Being funny doesn't amount to nothing unless you do it for money on HBO." She figures she's got three more years before anything worth anything will have a price tag.

Sometimes Yogi'll ignore all the rules of keeping a journal. She'll forget to put the date at the top of the page. One entry will lap over onto a week's worth of pages. Her confusion has no boundaries. And she'll harp on the same thing, over and over. The trig, for instance, it had her completely buffaloed for ten days, ruined her weekend, plus her and Ma had two huge fights about Yogi wearing dungarees to school every day. They were just blowing off steam though. At the beginning of every school year, Ma and Yogi have the same argument, but by spring everything'll be straight. As long she grades out with A's, Ma don't really mind if Yogi dresses like a boy.

It's on account of education being a big fat hairy deal in our house. Always has been. For Ma, it's her job, but Dad sees himself as a scholar. He can't get enough of books, especially the ones he reads over and over. And still he keeps buying new ones as if they're gonna explain what he doesn't understand about the ones he's already read three million times. He's got books in the garage that are waiting for a space to open up on the shelves in the library. Of course, he would never throw any of his books away either, so I guess you could say the garage is the new wing to the library. I try telling him that it's a fire hazard but he says I just hate to read. And he's right, I do. Most things people have to say are bullshit, so why should I want to read what they write.

There isn't a section in the Sunday paper that doesn't get read in our house. We're assigned a different section every week, and to prove that we've read it, we have to underline the premise and secondary points of the longest article.

"Gird up your loins with truth," he tells us. "Resourcefulness and vision."

Yeah, sure Dad.

Anyway, Sonny went straight-A clear through high

school and Yogi's only made three B's going into her senior year. She'd be a cinch to lead the march come graduation this spring, same as Sonny did, except Skipper Douglass is 4.0, which makes him a shoo-in for valedictorian. Ma will never forgive Yogi for that either. Even if she doesn't come right out with it, she's always gonna throw Skipper Douglass's name into a conversation just to put Yogi in check. That's part of why Yogi hates Skipper, and why she got into such a funk about trig.

There's no way Yogi will ever match Skip's GPA though—her journal admitted as much—but she sees high school as a footrace and she wants to finish strong. She doesn't want to get lapped by the likes of Skipper Douglass.

It took two weeks of hell, but finally she caught on to the numbers and aced the first trigonometry test, then celebrated with T.J. and Terrell, one of their late-night pranks. Over at the Farmer's Market greenhouse in Laurelton, they dropped down through a steam duct to spray-paint all the flowers black.

The pint of Sambuca is just about finished and they've grown restless. It could be a once-a-month routine, coming to the cemetery, a chance to get used to it. Yogi's taken a handful of Mike's coins and is skipping them off tombstones. Twice she's clipped five stones with a penny, which is just about impossible. With a quarter maybe, 'cause they're heavier and you get a clean ricochet. The best me and Naldo can do is three graves with a nickel.

Mike's asleep, his head balanced on his basketball, while Skipper and Terrell make out. Skip's leaned back against a grave with Terrell straddling him, her tongue down his throat.

"Fuck it," Terrell says suddenly, lifting herself off Skipper like she just finished taking a dump. "I'm gonna buy a gun," she says and lights a cigarette.

I look to Skipper for an explanation, to see if there's some connection between tongue kissing and guns, but he's got his glasses off again, fiddling with the frame.

"A gun," Yogi repeats thoughtfully.

"There are some nice ones."

"Yeah? Like how?"

"Like pearl-handled or copper-barreled." Terrell makes the cigarette smoke do a french lick, a thin menthol stream, a tiny whistling noise.

Yogi says, "A silver derringer with an inscription."

"Yeah, but those only got one shot."

"You'd never have the guts to use it anyway."

"Yeah I would. You?"

"In the leg maybe."

Suddenly Naldo flashes a hunting knife from out of his back pocket. "Get up on this," he grins, a surprise he's been saving.

"Booyah," Yolanda shudders and reaches blade-first for the knife.

"Careful, girl. It's real." He flings it expertly into the sod between his feet. Yogi's eyes are just about dancing.

This is familiar. From as far back as the crib I can remember my sister's energy. Before I could walk, she used to carry me around when she wasn't supposed to. She must've dropped me a million times, and there wasn't a damn thing I could do about it.

"Lemme see it," she grabs for the knife but Naldo snatches it first and flings it once more. He lets Yogi try but she can't make it stick in the ground the way he can.

"Here, like this," he rolls his wrist over the same as you would a yo-yo. The knife is so sharp that the whole blade plants in the sod, all the way down to the hilt.

Yogi blindly tosses the twenty down next to the knife, our bowling money.

"It'll take more than that," Naldo says.

"A down payment?"

"Plus twenty."

"Ten."

"Fifteen."

Yogi picks the knife up and folds it against her pants leg, then flips it out with a snap. "Stainless steel," she tells Terrell, who has crowded her face close to Yogi's, their eyes wide with amazement as they run trembling fingers along the blade. The handle is hand-carved and shellacked.

Yogi goes, "I should go psycho, right?" to which Skipper coolly replies, "You were born psycho."

Yogi wheels on Skipper, her knees bent in a crouch. "You real funny, Skip," she waves the knife in his face. My sister can use either hand to do anything. That's how Dad trained us, but Yogi's the only one who took to it.

"Right there," she moves in closer, tracing a triangle with the knife, "both eyes, then your tongue. Feed 'em to stray dogs."

Still Skipper won't flinch. "Like the weapon?" he asks.

"You know I do," Yogi retorts quickly, as if she's anticipating what he's thinking. She's totally into her butch mode. Tomcat. "Wanna tell me what I won't do with this here knife?" She can't help but challenge him in the only way she knows how. It's been brewing all evening, that Yogi don't much care for Skipper Douglass. "Go on, gimme a bet."

"Won't change anything," Skipper says, looking at Terrell. It's a signal, and Terrell promptly parks herself once more in his lap, sidesaddle this time. The two of them look at Yolanda, their eyes flat and unfriendly.

"Not this again," Naldo heaves a handful of coins out into the darkness. He turns to me as if we're the only two with any sense. Me not being here wouldn't change anything though. This is probably the way it happens between them. It isn't friendship. Not anymore. I wonder if they realize it yet. Did it frighten them when they found out?

The thought rocks me a little, the clearness of Skipper's lenses, the smell of Sambuca licorice, "wild horses in a nighted graveyard," Terrell had whispered to me earlier.

Terrell likes to whisper. And she's a better poet than Yogi. And she's given me three sips of the Sambuca while Yogi wasn't looking. At first there was the burn in my throat, but it won't drop to my stomach. Instead it has risen to my head, behind my eyes, rose-colored blossoms.

"Choices are questions and answers are rewards," Skipper informs Yolanda, then sighs as if he's tired of trying to teach everyone else what only he can understand. I watch him. I haven't got a clue what he's talking about. But Yogi does. She's hypnotized by what he has said, or what he's about to say. She can't wait to hear more.

"A yard of silk or a patch of wool." His words come slowly, his mouth a cross between a sneer and a smile. I guess he's a poet too.

Naldo taps me on the shoulder and points at Terrell as an explanation. He doesn't have to say anything more. I already know Terrell. It's Skipper I can't take my eyes from. He's wearing starched cords and fag-yellow sneakers with eggshell-blue laces tied in neat floppy bows. Everything about him is pressed and manicured, his hair neatly trimmed with a pencil-thin part just off center, maybe an inch and a half long.

"It's like this, Yolanda." He's very tolerant. "Whatever it is in life that you'll ever want, I'll already have. And you hate that, wanting what I have and having to ask me for it." He strokes Terrell's neck. "Take your time then, Princess Yolanda, because any choice you'll ever make in life, it gets made right now."

This little speech trips all the alarms. Yogi is hysterical.

"Tell him he's a bitch! Tell him, Terrell! Tell that candyass mothafucka he's a bitch!"

"Let's break camp ya'll," Naldo says. "Drop all the dumb shit. Mike, get yo ass up 'fore we leave you out here."

"Naw," Yolanda holds him off, "we ain't goin nowhere till Terrell says it. Say he's a bitch, Terrell!"

Yogi's almost crying and I know I'm not supposed to see this. She's forgotten I'm here. "Say it!" she waves the knife at them; threats and tears 'cause she knows she can't use it.

Terrell Daniels considers my sister with cold eyes, looking her up and down. She's in no rush. This is right where she wants to be, reclining in somebody's arms with people standing around watching her.

Terrell goes, "You see what she wants, Skip. I told you. It's what she always wants."

"Am I supposed to tell her what she wants," Skipper laughs, and before I can stop it, the warm dripping noise begins to pulse at my temples. I can't hold it back. "Gimme six months and I'm gonna—," but Yogi won't let me finish.

"Shut up, boy," she gives me a forearm swat. She hates anyone defending her, and anyway, it's her beef. Skipper doesn't even bother to look at me.

"Am I supposed to make Yogi's selections for her," he says. He's king of the graveyard. "Am I to be Yogi's imagination."

Terrell thinks this is funny and Skipper gives her the chance to laugh that laugh of hers, like she can't really enjoy a joke unless it's meant to hurt someone. She's right in the middle of Yogi's emotions, jumping up and down. The whole thing is just so hilarious.

Skipper waits for her to finish. We're all waiting. Even Mike's awake now. And he's seen this before. He's got his chin propped in his hand, sleepy-eyed, waiting to see who's turn it is.

Skipper. "You've got to choose, Yogi dear," he says, "silk or wool?" and in perfect time, like they've rehearsed it, Terrell echoes, "Cock or cunt."

I know these words. I know when they're meant to be dirty. I've seen the magazines the eighth-grade boys look at behind the gym—swollen flesh bruised to the point of bleeding, shaven crotches and rings through nipples. Nothing like the diagrams in the health textbook. I know which way Terrell means it, like in *Hustler*, cock or cunt.

"Ya'll need to stop," Naldo tries to break it up, but Skipper's know-it-all smile says he's already won something. I move closer to Yogi to let her know I'm there. It seems strange to see Terrell taking sides against her. And Skipper. He isn't just smart, he's mean too. The two of them smile up into my sister's face, Skipper stroking the other girl's throat.

"A kitten," he says, certain that he's trumped us all without even caring. "The bet is that you won't use that knife on a kitten."

The skin on Yogi's face is pulled tight. "Think I won't?" she says quickly. Hesitating would mean she's afraid.

Terrell's eyes light up. "Not a cat. A kitten," she explains, host for a perverted game show. Host and the grand prize, all wrapped up in one.

"Check out big sis." Skipper finally sees me through his crystal clear lenses.

"A kitten?" I turn to Yogi. "What kinda crazy bet is that?"

"Shut up. I told you you didn't wanna come along."

"Yeah, but what does it prove?"

Yogi doesn't reply. She's locked in some death stare with Terrell. " 'Maturity is the place of the dispossessed,' " I quote her journal.

"What do you know about it?" she snaps, then before I can answer, "Just make sure you keep your mouth shut or I'll substitute you for the kitten."

"I'll give style points for that," Skipper cracks.

"Six months . . ." I take a step toward him, but Yogi gives me another whack, four knuckles in the mouth, and I'm reeling to the ground.

"Shut up, boy."

Naldo helps me up and starts to dust me off, but I push him aside. He grabs me tighter (a reminder that I'm just a kid) so I don't go after Skipper.

Terrell says, "So is it a bet? You're actually gonna do it? You're gonna slit a kitten's throat, Yogi?"

"Come Monday we'll see what's what. Then it'll be my turn, ain't that so, Skipper?"

"Whatever you say, Princess."

c h a p t e r
11

Back when I was very small and thought my family would never lie to me, when I didn't know lies at all, my mom would bathe me late in the evening and tell me about Dad.

I'd ask her, "Ma, where's Daddy?" and she'd smile 'cause that meant I knew what time it was.

"He's out helping people, Randall," she'd say while her hands were sudsing me clean behind my ears and around my face and body. She used one of those soft soaps that bubbled up perfectly white and didn't sting your eyes. When we were finished she'd make me stand, and she'd rinse me with cool water to close my pores.

"Daddy's at the hospital?" I would ask. I already knew he healed people, but most times Ma would call it helping.

"And if Daddy ever needs help," I'd ask the third question, "where will he go?" They were always the same questions; our little secrets since I was like Dad in a way that Son and Yogi couldn't be.

"If your Daddy ever needs help, Randall, that's what you're for."

September 30—weekend—backyard

Sunday afternoon. He strides out to the center of his back lawn, ax in hand, and unrolls the canvas covering he has used to wrap the four ten-foot logs of healthy barked timber. Along with being a frustrated athlete, chef, fisherman, painter, and mechanic, our victim is a frustrated lumberjack as well. For a man so comfortably set up in life, he is constantly identifying his shortcomings with the intention of lengthening them.

He kneels on the grass to cut the rope, allowing the logs to roll free side by side. Across the fence his neighbor, Ike Gary, stands over a steaming barbecue grill, flipping burgers with one hand and nursing a highball in the other.

"What'chya got there, Frankie boy?" Ike drives eighteen wheels cross-country for a living. Keeps his rig around on the side, always shined up like new. To hear him tell, he's the best damn driver ever was.

"Looks like punishment." The neighbor gives him a chipped-tooth grin and waggles his spatula. "You musta been a real naughty boy."

The victim smiles, wraps a wet bandanna around his forehead, and starts in on the timber, turning the log slightly with his foot to make sure the cut is even around the entire circle.

It comes to him simply: if a jack changes the tempo of his swinging, he'll miss the solid mark in the wood. If he misses the solid mark consecutively, there isn't progress.

After the first log, he moves the smaller pieces aside and sits on the ground. He's wearing long johns under his pants and a rubber corset. For the sweat. He loves the sweat. He pulls the business end of the ax between his knees and runs a file over the blade. On the second log the blade starts sharp and clean, making the thwacking sound into the wood.

Jacks were like ear, nose, and throat doctors whose work was right in front of them to touch. Whatever they did could be left behind until they touched it again. It was never that way for the victim. He'd found that out from the beginning.

There was a woman he'd counseled some years before who owned an eternal claim to his company. She slashed her wrist one evening after a late session at his office; took a suite at the Sheraton three blocks over, ran a tub of warm water, and did herself. Just like that. No dialing 911 for this lady, no edging out onto a ledge overlooking a busy street, waiting for a crowd to gather.

He'd seen that stunt often enough, the desperate cry for help. It was an inside joke with his colleagues, the "heads" over at the Sanitarium, how they got paid for being an audience. "Theatre" they called it, and had the nerve to critique performance. Donald Manes, the dirty politician out of Queens, was their consensus hero. They'd even got up a pool to see who could pick the right date. "It's a beautiful day for a suicide," they sang it like the theme song from Mr. Rogers' neighborhood. You had to have a sense of humor about it; it came with the territory.

After Manes failed the first time (the night he sliced himself to ribbons and drove up and down the Van Wyck), any doctor worth his signature knew sooner or later he'd finish the job. March 18, 1986—in his kitchen—a butcher knife to the heart. Impressed all hell out of the psych crowd. None of them wrote about it in their pretentious little journals, but over drinks at Houlihan's the victim could see the admiration in his peers' faces. Nobody had ever heard of anything so bold, so sincere. In history books you read about Romans falling on their swords, yet to initiate the incision without the aid of gravity, to continue the inward thrust even after the skin was broken, well now that took some doing. There wasn't the suddenness of a gunshot or the drowsy seduction of a fistful of pills.

They'd put up a shrine to Manes in the doctors' lounge, partly as a joke and partly in tribute. Had to be he was strung out to where anybody who knew anything about it, insanity, you had to figure he'd crossed over onto virgin soil. No way he was coming back.

For all the same reasons, the victim respected this lady who'd finished herself at the Sheraton, her singleness of purpose. He'd seen her body at the morgue, the wrists all dug out, her left hand almost severed free. Whatever demon she was possessed by had overmatched his skill as a doctor by a long shot. Technically, it wasn't his fault though. He had pulled out all the stops. Even tried emulating Christ.

John, chapter 4, Jesus and the woman at the well.

And Jesus saith, "If thou knewest the gift of God, and who it is that saith to thee, Give me to drink; thou wouldest have asked of him, and he would have given thee living water."

The woman replied: "Sir, thou has nothing to draw with and the well is deep: from whence then hast thou that living water?"

And Jesus answered, "Whosoever drinketh of this water shall thirst again: But whosoever drinketh of the water that I shall give him shall never thirst; but the water that I shall give him shall be in him a well of water springing up into everlasting life."

More than the words, the victim can see Jesus' style, his presence. A walking staff at his side perhaps, his face the dark red of sunset. He was a big guy, maybe 6'4", a carpenter. Had himself propped up along the rim of the well, watching the woman carefully, no hurry, no rush. Maybe he lets his sandals drop off, a healthy musk odor on his skin, the sweat of his travel. A man acquainted with sorrow. He knew who he was. A carpenter. A god.

The timber is breaking up cleanly. The victim's ax has force behind it, the wood parting beneath his effort.

Salvation was what his modern-day woman at the well was after. That was what they were all after, but she'd had the guts to demand it by name. The last time he saw her, she pinned him down to let him know exactly what she expected.

It was an eerie night. He had turned off the lights in his office, she insisted on it. There was snow on the ground and out his office window the Hudson was a cold dirty gray. He was trying to tell her how life was a sacred gift from God, the same way Jesus had done. His delivery must've been lacking though, because she'd laid into him before he could get to the good part.

"If life is a gift," she'd taunted him, her words echoing a familiar uncertainty embedded deep in his own mind, "how come I need to be saved from it?"

"To have it 'more abundantly' is the way Jesus phrased it."

This line had gone over like gangbusters in the New Testament, but not that night. She was leaning toward him, trying to corner him even as she moved farther away, floating from the chair, her image thinning into an apparition right before his eyes—her soul, her will to live.

"More abundantly?" She was almost laughing. "Come now, doctor, you can do better than that." There hadn't been any desperation in her voice. If anything, he was the one racing against the clock. Not that it would do any good, yet still he tried. It was what he got paid for.

"Life on earth is temporary and therefore restricted," he had explained. "The gift of salvation offers it eternally and at a higher quality."

"That's too easy. There's more. The money you charge, you damn well better have more."

"I only have hope," he had said gently, wondering what her method would be. For all his words were worth, he could have been in the room alone. "I only have hope that love will prevail," he told himself.

He'd lost a little of his own soul that night. That's what happened when your limits were exposed, you got hooked on the idea that it happened, sometimes you lost, and it would happen again. He'd spend the rest of his life waiting to witness the horror of a fleeing spirit, like touching a sore to feel the pain.

From the upstairs bathroom I can almost reach down and touch the ax as Dad brings it up and over and down into the wood. His grunts are words. Lamentations. He's directly beneath me, within four arm's length, and what is taking place, the firewood, Ike Gary's barbecue, the ax, it is all written in his journal as prophecy.

"Don't betray me."

These are his words, scrawled in large print across the top of each page. He has doubts about me, and he should. I don't know that I can do this.

—the pale face bobbing just above the surface of the bath water, her hair soaked crimson, his modern-day woman at the well of water turned to wine.

The victim looks across the fence at Ike Gary swinging heavily in his hammock, balancing the highball on his bare belly. The trucker seems amused by something. He smiles and waves.

"Doin real fine, Frankie boy. Musta been one helluva crime to make you go at it that hard."

The victim spits into his palms for grip and goes once more after the wood with a vengeance. His T-shirt is heavy now, clinging to his shoulders with sweat.

Again it comes to him simply: success for a jack was immediate and audible, and once the wood was split, it stayed split. Wood wasn't fickle. It had no expectations. It was unencumbered by life.

A trickle has begun inside his nose and the victim sees it fall red on the canvas covering. Punishment. "There is no remission of sin except for the shedding of blood." He tosses the ax aside and falls wearily into one of the lawn chairs. It is what he has been working up to, his own personal Golgotha—a nosebleed.

Next door, Ike the trucker is burning the barbecue and throwing ice cubes at the dog to keep him away from the meat. They're nice sounds. Weekend sounds. Trivial. Restful. Forgettable. A dog yapping and a man bellowing at him to shut up. The victim feels his body loosen, his mind ease and settle itself. The cushioned chair gives way comfortably under his weight. In the cool of the evening, he imagines . . . and closes his eyes to sleep.

* * *

Out in the lawn chair he's still sleeping. I've buried his journal back in his desk drawer. I've got the kitten, Yogi's new
pet.

"Lookit." I kneel next to the lawn chair, but Dad doesn't
stir. He's barely breathing.

I lift his hand and place the kitten beneath it. "See." I kiss
him lightly on the cheek. There's stubble and the smell of
liquor. That's what he's been doing when he plays hooky
from work. Ma don't know yet.

"Here—now," he comes out of the sleep with a start,
something he's overheard.

"Lookit, Dad."

He nods his head, his eyes registering on me as if I'm far
away, coming closer. For a moment he seems afraid of me
until he sees the kitten.

"You didn't steal this, did you, Randall?"

" 'Course not."

"Steal means borrow too," he smiles and gently tugs my
ear.

"Nuhuh. I didn't do that neither," I say, waiting for him
to appear normal. He wipes at his eyes with his free hand.

"Then who's the owner?"

"Yogi."

"Where'd she steal it?" Dad's always prepared for the
worst.

"In the alley behind Pathmark. Stray cats hang out there."

"And what was Yogi doing in an alley behind Pathmark?"

"You mad?" I ask him, even though I can see he isn't. He
never worries about Yogi. Ma does. But not Dad. Sometimes
I think it bothers Yogi that he doesn't.

"I'm not mad," he changes his position in the lawn chair,
wincing from the ache he gets in his back sometimes. The
calm in his voice pulls me closer. I've got my hand on his
shoulder while he inspects the cat. His touch is always the

same, firm and gentle. The kitten likes Dad touching it. Everyone does.

"The fur is like new." His voice is hushed, but the eyes don't go with the voice. They're Yogi's eyes. Except Dad doesn't act out his thoughts the way Yogi does. Not yet he hasn't.

I look at him for a long while, seeing my sister. Maybe he never worries about any of us. Maybe he thinks nothing can ever happen to any of us. Maybe he's going to see to that.

"Yogi can take care of herself," he enters me briefly, then jokes, "it's the kitten I'm worried about."

"You like it?"

"It's so small." He sits it up in his hand. "Has Yogi fed it yet?"

"I did. I fed it some tea."

"Randall, kittens drink milk."

"Not this one. Anyway, wanna see something?" I move his hand to the pulse on the kitten's neck. Yogi had shown it to me and Terrell the night before. She said that was where she was gonna slit it, but I don't mention this to Dad. The pulse is beating like a drum roll.

Dad gives me a weak smile. He's tired, the same drag that's been pulling him for the last few months. "Go on back in the house, son."

I get up and begin to back away, trying to make a picture of him lying on the lawn chair, the ax at his side. My dad. A big guy. A lumberjack. A god.

"Dad?" I call, but he won't turn to look at me. Like always, he knows what I'm about to say. "I don't wanna play no more," I tell him. "It doesn't make sense. It isn't funny."

"In due time," he says, "in due time."

c h a p t e r

12

"I heard you, Dad. All right! I heard you!"

A few weeks later we're out in the front yard raking leaves. It's Columbus Day, a Sunday, the day Dad got stroked. He planned the sickness, or scheduled it. At the very least he expected the damn thing, he welcomed it. He even described it to me, and it wasn't like I was all that curious. I coulda done without seeing my old man down on all fours, his eyes gone white.

The leaves. We've got 'em mostly bagged. It's a big yard with an elm to the left of the front walk. Dad planted it when we bought the property, and on evenings like this one, the branches do spider-leg shadows across the top of the house.

"You heard me?" he asks for the fourth time.

The lawn has started to brown now that the autumn chill has threatened. Set back on this lawn, our house is strong and square. A place to be protected, trapped.

"All day, Randall. You're making me ask again and again." He's smiling. "Why, Randall?"

So I tell him something he'll like, something he'd say. "I just wanna be sure you're sure."

I grab another Baggies and make the opening yawn. He begins to fill it. He's got on two sweatshirts with a corset, the sweat pouring off him in steady streams. I can smell his huskiness. His breathing is heavy and infrequent, a tired smile in his eyes.

Ma and Yogi are off to the City to help Son and Gil decorate their apartment, then they're supposed to go to a show. Dad bought the tickets. They thought it was his way of making amends for behaving so badly about Son and the toehead getting married, but not really. He just wanted the chance to show me something new—clawing stuffing out of the couch, his eyelids aflutter.

The day is all but gone, a soft sunset, and far off there are the sounds of holiday traffic, soft sounds that barely reach my hearing. My head feels puffy as I remember the night before, up in the library with Dad, following the stars through his telescope during the lunar cycles EST, whatever that means.

"It isn't random," he had said, "the way the stars run. They rotate, but their paths are never broken in relation to each other. And each, in its time, will rule the heavens."

"That in the Bible?"

"And when He spake, it was so."

I lift my head a little to hear the distant holiday traffic better, but it can't seem to come any closer. Dad keeps asking me questions that I won't answer. He doesn't need an OK from me. Many things I can give him, but a green light, no. He will do as he pleases. He will have his way.

I strain desperately to hear the faraway car noises until finally a late-model Peugeot takes a right at the corner and moves toward our house. It's our godfather, Dr. Mitchell Benjamin. Son and Yogi call him Uncle Benji.

Dad ties the mouth of the garbage bag and walks toward the car, his hands shoved down in the pockets of his overalls.

"Like the eighteenth hole at Saratoga." Dr. Benjamin climbs from the car, his gaze crossing the lawn. He's Dad's age, but still he never wears socks with his deck shoes. It's fashion when he does it; when I do it Ma calls me a hobo.

There's a lady on the passenger side listening to a CD and drinking Mistic water, her hairdo piled clear through the sunroof. I bend my face inside the window to get a good look. She's closer to my age than Dr. Benjamin's.

"A lawn this nice," Dr. B laughs, "and I'm ready to start a family and settle down." He's not gonna introduce his date. He never does. He's wearing designer jeans and an olive green pullover that smells like English Leather.

Dad keeps quiet, his arms folded across his chest, a carpenter. They're about the same height. They shake hands.

"Is it sod you've come to talk about, Mitch?"

"Since when did a friend need an invitation to speak his mind."

"Hasn't it been spoken and heard yet?"

"Evidently not."

This Q and A happens in a split second, an unfinished argument.

"I'll put the yard tools away," I speak up, giving Dad the chance to tell Uncle Benji to get lost. Dad's been that way for the last few weeks, setting a private little stage for himself with me as an audience, always making sure he's got my full attention up in the library, or after dinner we go down to the game room to work the jigsaw. It's his reward for goading Ma into all those arguments she knew she could never win. It's a settlement she's granted him, an understanding, a separation.

"Family bonds are the paths between stars," he had told me the night before. "They can never be weakened, only rearranged as was also the body of Christ."

I stack the yard tools in the back of the garage. Dad's funny sometimes, the things he says. Other times he's scary. From a distance he's a joke, but I can't help but draw nearer. Back out in front of the house I lean against Uncle Benji's car and watch while Dad makes promises to his friend, lies.

"First thing tomorrow morning," Dad says. He's trying to escort Dr. Benjamin back to his car, but the good doctor doesn't seem to want to leave.

"I've earned the right, Frank," he says, taking off his aviator sunglasses.

I lean my head into the Peugeot again, "Your Mitch has gotta be kidding," I tell the Mistic date, who tilts her head at me as if she's being emotionally challenged by the situation.

Dad's got a grip on the other guy's shoulder. "Tomorrow, Mitch," he says firmly, "you've got my word. You can give me a full checkup, run a damn MRI if you want."

"It's gone on long enough, man, whatever this is." He pulls Dad into a clinch. "I'm tired of lying to Georgia. She's very concerned." He glances at me as if I should know better.

I move in on him. "Can't you take a hint?" I ask, causing Dr. Benjamin to take a step back. He looks to Dad as if he were expecting me to get yelled at for speaking out of turn. Dad opens the car door for him.

"See you later, Mitch," he says and shuts the door. We stand together and watch the Peugeot drive off.

"Think he's mad?"

Dad smiles and shrugs. "Put the leaves out by the mailbox. I'll go make some tea."

He's possessed. That's how I find him when I return from setting out the leaves. On my way up the front walk I hear the fall, a crash, furniture turning over, glass breaking. The possession comes from outside of him, just out of his reach, "a great falling of heaven," the journal would later explain, "stars suspended by string, held aloft just beyond touching." That's what he sees as he rears up like a spooked horse, his arms outstretched; then suddenly he's prostrate. I edge closer, fearful; I think he's gone blind and his limbs are quivering, his arms lengthening, the middle of his body crumpling.

"Wandl," my name is slobbered on his lips as he reaches toward me. There's the thing about swallowing your tongue. I'm not supposed to stick my fingers in his mouth. He isn't panicked. My heart is thumping fast.

"You can't do this to me!" I scream.

Destruction doesn't unfold in an orderly fashion. It sneaks up on you, but not so quietly so that you don't know it's there. Destruction wants you to know it's close, if only to frighten you into becoming its ally. In the end, destruction comes from one's own hands. To give in to fear, to befriend it, that's what I learned at my father's feet. Once you've tapped into fear, nothing is sure except fear. That's when you can stop running.

From down the hall Ma comes streaming out the elevator, herringbone blazer and snakeskin pumps. She's all jazzed up on account of the theater tickets she's obviously decided to ignore. It doesn't figure. I mean, how did she know the old man took a fall? How did she know to come to the hospital?

Her face is severe and I shrink in my chair as she brushes past. The hospital people haven't let me in to see Dad, but when Ma shows, I know she won't be asking permission. I fall in step right behind her, through the double doors and down the corridor where the sick people live.

He's hooked to a machine. Tubes are running from both nostrils and one in his arm. They've got him drugged but he's fighting it, tiny twitchings around his eyes. Dr. Benjamin is here too and the moment he sees Ma, he's in her arms. I tap him on the shoulder.

"What happened?"

He won't look at me. He's looking so deep in Ma's eyes that he's damn near cross-eyed. It comes to me that I've never liked him for just that reason, the way he looks at Ma, the way he's always making snide remarks about other women just to see her laugh.

"It was a stroke," he tells her finally, dramatically. Moments like this are probably what drew him to medicine, not the chance to help, but the suspense.

"Dammit, Mitch, spit it out already. How bad is it?"

"The right side of his body has shut down. His organs seem to be working fine. We should have the results of the CAT scan soon."

"When is he gonna wake up?" I ask.

"Maybe once or twice during the night," Dr. Benjamin tells Ma. "But he won't be conversational for a few days. Why don't you take the boy down to get something to eat. I'll be down in a few minutes."

c h a p t e r

13

Once when we were kids, I tried to tell Yolanda some stuff. Because I could imagine it, that made it so. But she ignored me. That's when I decided it was best to keep a private sanctuary.

"Lay not up for yourselves treasures upon earth, where moth and rust doth corrupt . . . ," so I set it foursquare, with attachments to lengthen and deepen it, and divided it into sections that sometimes borrow from one another. The largest section consists of colors. Then there's sound and intent, gurgling bubbles beneath the deepest blue that announce the dominion of water from the tips of feet and fingers all the way to the heart afloat. Or gouged eye sockets filled with sparkling powdered glass, the features stolid, lifeless clay, the cheeks streaked red. Shapes are in another section, shadows long and tall at forward angles. And the silhouettes which are truer figures, sometimes a face or the side of a building, skylines carved from night's lighted sky.

Then still farther, slats and rope bridge unsteady steps across a great divide into a larger darkness where the unshared fears of the small and frightened take root. Vanity. Insecurity. Where the worst is shaped by fearful hands, and confronted and overcome.

Sometimes I'll see things from the window of a moving bus and it'll remind me of my possessions by sight. We all need the reinforcement. Seeing it once is never enough.

Most of the things spirited away into this holy place aren't so nice, 'cause the stuff that's worth the most, it usually ain't so nice. Most of what was in my family's world after Dad went nuts was evil and provoked entrance. Even before the stroke, I sensed the evil. In due time I learned about wickedness and I learned about evil. I learned that wickedness is only evil made visible for the fascination of mankind. Wickedness can be blatantly vulgar, which makes for slick pictures, garish and mean. But evil is elusive. Whenever evil is the theme of a sketch, I'm sure to be frustrated by it. I've tried everything, but nothing can show it like I want, not even dipped in the blood of my father can I picture it properly.

Perhaps it's 'cause evil doesn't need to be glorified, only acknowledged as forceful and sincere. There are no holidays set aside to celebrate evil, for it is as consistent and inevitable as nightfall, as resilient as the weeds of the field, as determined as the ocean's tide, as volatile as a cornered beast. It is a function that begins within the seed of our existence, a reality woven into the fabric of a society that believes itself civilized; it is the mother of every government and religion, an appeal that cannot be denied or ignored.

The mistake is thinking love can conquer evil, which is what this story is all about, if I can find a way to finish it with the ending already blotted and framed.

Those last few months before the shooting, evil took on a personality for me, and I could see that it was jealous because people preferred love. Love is like dope and all the dopey musicians are always singing about having their heart broken. Love is what everybody wants, they wanna get disappointed and cry. What's wild about the whole thing is people dig evil, they're just scared to say it, which is fine with me. I don't like sharing much anyway.

Most times people don't realize they dig it. Evil's got this invisible lure that can pull you against your will. When I figured that out, I hardened myself not to be afraid or pull away, but to flow with its force and harness the power until the alliance drew itself in a sketch: boy charms snake.

How could I change that, even if I wanted to, and I don't. Why should I? It was gonna happen anyway. Besides, this birthright of knowledge I received from my father transcends art unto prophecy and reveals the beauty of a family—and a world—fallen short of its purpose and potential. This birthright is worth more than anything, including salvation to a higher place. It is my evolution to a higher being.

c h a p t e r
14

How did Ma know he had fallen?

I'd rather she come straight out with it, but she wants the details, she wants me to tell her about my father's pain. My story goes something like, "We were out on the patio, see, drinking sassafras tea and telling riddles. So Dad just starts to nod off, like it's a joke. But then he rolls out his chair. He wouldn't move. That's when I dragged him back in the—"

Ma takes one of those monumental deep breaths that make her temples throb. She never believes me. "We'll discuss it later," she says.

It's about 9 P.M. and we're in the hospital cafeteria on the ground floor. Ma isn't hungry and her eyesight has shortened. Cigarettes do that to her, making her appear careless and impatient. "Grieving is for the dead," she's been telling Dad's colleagues. They keep dropping by our table in tidy little groups of three. They are shocked and concerned about the stroke; Ma is rude.

"I never knew my husband was this popular," she'll say, then sit there and blow cigarette smoke all over the place. There's a giant NO SMOKING sign posted on the wall but nobody wants to point that out to her.

My mother would rather be alone, that's obvious. But where am I supposed to go? Every once in a while she'll look at me, but not for too long. She can't quite consider me right now. So I keep my mouth shut, keep it simple for the both of us. Besides, being seen but not heard is easy, though that is not the prize I covet.

The weather has turned chilly, and out along the garden walk a young couple is sitting at one of the picnic tables. The lady's got on a nurse's uniform, a white cape wrapped around her shoulders. They're too far away for me to eavesdrop. I watch for a few minutes until finally the man sees that it's no use—whatever he's trying to make her believe, she ain't going for it. She's getting an attitude about the whole thing, but she's just like me, she's got no place else to go.

I turn to Ma. "Where's Yogi?" I'm not expecting much of an answer.

"With Son and Gil." She stubs out a cigarette and lights another. She never smokes unless it's to chain-smoke: a heavy filterless brand that leaves mushroom clouds thick enough to write your name in.

"They know about what happened to Dad?" I ask.

She shakes her head no and looks at me.

"We gonna call them tonight?"

"Only something bad could come of that."

"Oh," I nod, scooping through my pie à la mode. I repeat it. "Only something bad." Dad was always weak, that's what we're both thinking. It's the reason we're both here.

She moves her chair closer. Her hand is soft and warm

against the side of my face. It always surprises me how soft she is since her touch is so rare. She could go a year and never come near me, wouldn't matter to her one bit. For example, this here tenderness she's showing me, she's only doing what she thinks I expect. That's what pisses me off.

"You don't have to," I tell her, my teeth clenched, my shoulders tightening. It's what she's been trying to forget about: what Mommy is supposed do at a time like this.

"It's OK if you want to cry," she offers.

"I already did," I lie, hoping she'll know that I'm lying. "In the ambulance on the way over I cried and cried and—"

"That's enough, Randall. Everything isn't about you all the time. How you react has nothing to do with your father's health."

"Yeah, well, I was the only one there when it happened, so—" I stop short when I get a look at Dr. Benjamin striding over to the table with two Styrofoam cups.

Swear to God, one time I saw him get his nasal hairs clipped. It was at this barbershop Dad used to hang around in Freeport called Barney's. Every Saturday Uncle Benji had to get the full treatment, a hot towel around his face to tighten his skin and some guy sticking tweezers up his nose.

"Hi, Dr. Benjamin," I grin at him.

He gives me a wary look. For as long as I've known this guy he's been dropping gifts on me and I don't think we've ever had conversation.

"Is that tea?" I ask.

"No, it's coffee and it's for your mother."

He peels the lid and hands Ma the cup of coffee. "Light and sweet," he says. Nobody's offered him a seat so he stands there like a jerk.

Ma sighs and pulls off her earrings. "How's Frank?" she asks.

"Critical but stable."

"What's that mean?" I pipe in.

"You just mind your food," Ma snaps, "I'll ask the questions."

"It means we've got every chance to make sure his recovery is complete." Dr. Benjamin eases into a seat and gently takes Ma's hand. Several lines crease his forehead, but not many. His face is more youthful than Dad's. The creases aren't as deep, there isn't the fatigue and stress. I glance at Ma to see if she sees Dr. Benjamin that way, but all she's got is contempt.

"There could be a rehab period of six to eight months," the doctor says patiently. "That's the best-case scenario. But his life is not in danger."

"You guarantee me that?"

"I'm as concerned about this as you are. But after monitoring him, I'm relieved. He's going to be fine."

"That's not what I want to hear, Mitchell." Her voice isn't shrill, yet there's a blare to it that says her terms aren't negotiable. "Goddammit, Mitchell, you say it for me."

"I guarantee you, all right, Georgia? But some of it has to do with Frank. If he doesn't want the same life he had before, he won't."

"You let me worry about that. As long as you tell me straight. You don't tell me straight, Mitchell, then you don't tell me at all."

"I guarantee you."

For a second Ma still isn't satisfied, but then it all seems to hit her again, that Dad's sick in a way that's out of her hands. She relaxes back in her chair, pulling another cigarette out. Dr. Feelgood is right on time with a light.

"Thanks for calling earlier," Ma exhales a cloud of smoke just over his shoulder. "But I thought you were off this weekend. How did you know?"

"One of the nurses beeped me over at the country club when they brought him in."

It registers slowly at first, how Ma knew Dad got stroked. Dr. Benjamin told her. More than that, she had to have told him she'd be in Park Slope at Son and Gil's apartment, she gave him the damn number even. Why? Had they been discussing Dad? Obviously. And there he was earlier in the evening feeding Dad the old "I'm tired of lying to Georgia" routine, when all the time he was lying to Dad.

I close my mind. They don't deserve a chance to understand me. I don't understand them. They don't love him like I do. I picture Dad alone and unconscious, vulnerable. "I gotta go to the rest room," I get up to leave.

Ma grabs my arm. "Randall, don't go wandering off to places you're not supposed to be," she says. She's one step ahead of me but it doesn't matter anyhow. She can sit here with her pal, Uncle Benji. He's got as much attention for her as she could ever want.

I leave the cafeteria and head down the hall to take the staircase up to the second floor where I can catch the elevator. I know Ma and she knows me. That's the way it should be, except the things we know about each other are the things we're careful of. As I leave the caf, I can feel her eyes on me, constantly judging my actions. The trust between us is in short supply.

Up on the fifth floor there's little activity in ICU. The nurses' station is vacant. I can't resist going behind the counter. They got schedules, patient's charts, prescriptions, syringes, and, check this out, a package of disposable rubber gloves. It can't be much of a life, not from what I can tell. I swipe four bottles of pills, a stick of Wrigley's Juicy Fruit, and walk back through the double doors, farther into where I don't belong. I might be invisible but there's no one around to prove it.

The lighting down the hallway is dimmed for the dying. In a room to the right a doctor and nurse stand over a patient. They are not moving to assist. This moment they share has deranged them, cuffed their hands and gagged their mouths while they wait, eager to get a glimpse of how it happens.

"Sometimes we can make death not hurt," Dad told me once when I asked him what he liked about being a doctor. "We can turn death into sleep," he had explained with tears in his eyes.

I ease past the door without the doctor or nurse seeing me. All the way down the end of the hall is where they've put Dad. There are two other sick guys in the room with him. I step to his side and put my hand to his face. Checking for a temperature is the only helpful thing I know how to do.

"Dad?"

There isn't any movement or sound save for his ragged breathing, a reminder of the afternoon chopping wood, his words echoing as prophecy. I pull up a chair next to the bed and take his hand. After a few minutes he shifts his weight in the bed. His eyelids begin to flutter, he's pressing forward to reach out to me.

"Dad?"

I'm urgent. Before long Ma will come along to break up the party. She knows I'm here. "Dad," I squeeze his hand and lean close to his face.

"Randall."

I feel my heart swell. Ma should hear this too. I can imagine it: she comes to be by his side and it is my name he speaks to her.

I press my face against the stubble on his jaw. "Speak Lord, for thy servant heareth."

chapter
15

For the next ten days our house seems empty. Every evening when I get home I half expect a For Sale sign to be staked out front. Late at night I can hear Ma and Yogi going through their paces, first mother then daughter, prowling the house, looking for the other two, trying to remember what it was like last year at this time. They're both expecting things to get worse. So am I.

It has occurred to me that I could live without any of them.

Sonny and Gil came out to the Island for a visit a few days ago. I think they had dropped by the hospital first, but the subject of Dad never came up. There was nothing to discuss. He hasn't been cordial to visitors, that's what Yogi told me, that he wouldn't even look at her. He just lies there. He might as well be unconscious, even if his eyes are open, staring out the window. When next I see him, that's not something I'm looking forward to. He has his little ways, his little attitudes, our father the nut, lying perfectly still in his hospital bed.

"It's the initial stage of recovery," Dr. Benjamin had explained, "the body's reaction to trauma. It'll take some time for him to regain his strength."

It sounded reasonable enough, except I think Dad's got plenty of strength after what he went through. I saw what happened, the good doctor didn't.

"His life isn't in danger," we've been assured. There's a host of doctors involved, even though they insist the stroke is minor. Doctors are like cops: they look out for their own.

Mind you, Ma hasn't asked for any second opinions. But these doctors, every chance they get they're leaving messages on our phone. "He's going to be just fine," they'll say in closing, "thank God for that."

They just don't get it. He's remade, born-again in the body of his burial. These doctors don't recognize the domination. It didn't show up on their CAT scan. If they ever did know him, which I doubt, they don't anymore. They do not see where he's headed.

Ma has an idea, so does Son. Yogi doesn't want to imagine it. Son almost seemed frightened when she and Gil stopped by the house. There was suspicion in her face when she came through the front door. I could almost hear the gasp get caught in her throat. She was actually surprised to see us in the house, as if it came tumbling down like a ton of bricks that more had changed than just her last name. She was with Gil now and we mattered a little bit less than we used to. Gil mattered more to her and it scared her. Quite naturally Gil looked scared by reflex. If Sonny's scared, Gil's scared.

They only stayed an awkward fifteen minutes, then when they were about to leave, Sonny starts with the apologizing. She said it had been eating away at her, the sequence of events, her marriage then the stroke. Wasn't any secret he'd been letting himself go.

"I was selfish."

She'd made the confession bluntly without mentioning the toehead by name. "We could've waited," she'd said and shook her head while Gil slunk out the door to go warm up the car. Nobody stopped Sonny from taking the blame either.

I had followed the in-law out to the car. I wanted to see if things had begun to gnaw at him.

It's still early in the season, November, but frozen rain was pelting down like crazy. Gil was wiping at the windshield with a scraper. Most anything you could think of, Gillis Turner will be prepared for. He was wearing one of those coats that has a hood zippered to the collar, plus he had on an Elmer Fudd-looking hat with the straps that buckle under your chin.

"Gillis, how come you got a hood and a hat?" I asked him. I like Gil. He can multiply or divide any equation in a matter of seconds.

"Hoods aren't very snug," he said over the sound of the engine.

"Snug." I nodded. I'd had the word "snug" on a spelling test once—s-n-u-g—one of them words only good for rhyming, or if you have to give an antonym or synonym. "Snug." I scratched my arm and frowned.

"Hoods don't keep your ears warm the way a hat will." He lifted one of the flaps. "See, it's trimmed in fur."

I kept scratching and looking at him. I coulda asked him, "Why are you such an asshole, Gil?" and he'd probably have an answer for that too, 'cause he really wasn't an asshole. If somebody took it for granted that he was though, I don't think it would bother him. He'd just give 'em a chance to see that they were an asshole for thinking he was one.

"You think it's a cool hat, Gil?"

"No. Warm," he corrected me and smiled.

"You smart, Gil?"

He shook his head and waited for another question. First

time Son brought him home to meet the family, I asked him questions back to back to back till he got winded.

"You dumb, Gil?" I tried him again.

He shook his head.

"Weak?" I asked, knowing for the first time that he wasn't.

"What do you think?" he said quickly, but not as though he was trying to one-up me. He started back to scraping the windshield while I watched him.

"Boy, I swear, if you come down with the flu, Randall . . ."

Wouldn't you know Ma had to come stick her head out the front door to add her two cents. I was in my sock feet with no coat, standing in front of Gil, trying to see into his eyes but his glasses had started to fog up.

Just then Sonny came up the walk toward the car. She seemed in a rush to leave, her head down, like she was being careful not to make the same mistake Lot's wife had made. Nothing about our house was the same and there wasn't a damn thing any of us could do about it.

"Did you see him?" I asked, but she wanted no part of me or my questions.

"Go on back inside, honey. You'll catch cold."

It's evening, the following Thursday, downstairs in the game room watching TV with Yogi and Ma. Ma ordered out again but I'm the only one eating. After a while I summon the nerve to start up with her.

"I wanna see him tomorrow."

"No," she says, and flips the channel.

We've been going up and down the stations. First I wanted A&E's "Search for Mandrake's Hidden Treasure" featuring Liza Minnelli in a frog suit, then Yogi starts flipping between *Liquid TV* and Dan Rather, and now Ma's turned to a buck-toothed British fag on PBS who's got baking soda crusted in his eyebrow. He's standing over a stove with a chef's hat tilted on his head, sipping broth from a pot while his chicken liver sortees in the skillet.

"How come I can't visit Dad tomorrow," I ask. We're on the couch with Yogi in the middle. She's staring at the screen, holding the little kitten she's supposed to slit. She's postponed the bet with Skipper, or maybe she hasn't seen him. Our daily schedules remain the same (wake up, go to school, come home, and eat), but it's all become a circle, a ritual that's supposed to mean progress.

"Huh, Ma?" I persist. "How come. If there's a reason, how come you can't say it?" I've already made my plans for tomorrow. Smart money says Mommy dear knows that.

"No," she says.

"But—"

"Randall. I said no!"

The doorbell rings upstairs. "I'll get it," I volunteer for no reason. These two, they'd just leave it ringing. Nobody's been answering the doorbell or the phone. Even when Sonny came by, she wouldn't have gotten in if she didn't still have her key.

I peek through the drapes to see the Peugeot, Uncle Benji. He's just about moved in, he's been here so much. Next thing you know he'll be using Dad's shaving kit. At least he hasn't brought any of them little debutantes with him, and don't I know why.

I greet him at the door with a big grin.

"Randall," he grits his teeth. His smile is tight beneath a trimmed salt-and-pepper moustache. He looks past me, his eyes shifting nervously, an unspoken plea ready to come out of his mouth. "I'm doing the best I can," is what he wants everybody to believe, when deep down in his heart he knows it's not true. A guy like him, insecure, it just doesn't figure.

He stands there in the doorway, a Totes cap mushed down on his head.

"What can I do for you, Mitch?" I ask. I'm not supposed to call him that but he never bothers with scolding.

"Where's your mother, Randall?" he sighs, like I'm a burr permanently embedded in the left cheek of his ass.

"Hey, Mmmmaaaa!" I yell. "Guess who!"

Ma comes trudging up the stairs, a bit too weary to get pissed. She shoots me a dead-cold stare.

Dr. Benjamin says, "Thought I'd bring the equipment by tonight if you don't mind."

She just nods.

It takes three trips for me and Uncle Benji to lug all the Nautilus equipment down to the game room.

"What's he need all this for if you say the stroke was minor?" Yogi asks when we're finished. Her voice almost startles me, it's been so long.

"Sixty percent of all stroke cases leave the victim sedentary for life. And atrophy is not a pretty sight, young lady. Luckily, your father was in good health when this—"

"Blah blah blah," Yogi blows him off. "But who's gonna see to it that he uses this stuff?"

"I'm sure he understands the importance of consistent rehab."

Yogi looks at me. "The only exercise this equipment is going to see is the work it takes to put it together."

"And guess who's going to do that?"

"Aw, Ma," Yolanda groans, "I got school tomorrow. I'm an intellectual. I need my rest."

"Come on, Yogi," I take the instruction manual from Uncle Benji. "It'll only take a half hour. Besides, Dr. Benjamin and Ma gotta go upstairs to draw up Dad's will."

"Randall, you are pressing it, boy. You hear me?" Ma takes two giant steps and is standing directly in front of me. She stoops a little—gives me that close-up of hers.

"I got him," Yogi says and snatches me by the ear. "Never know when to call it enough, do you? Always gotta push it to the limit, Mr. Wiseass."

Ma and Dr. B head off upstairs.

"How come he's always here?" I say. I'm putting the metal together while Yogi hands me the pieces in the right order.

"Randall, don't start. I ain't up for your nonsense."

"But he's always buggin Ma."

"What else is new? Just pretend it's a brother-sister thing, same as you're always buggin me. That's what Ma does."

"Yeah?"

"Of course. He's going through the midlife thing, just like Dad, except Uncle Benji's been going through it since he was thirty. That's what Sonny said. You know he hit on her once?"

"No foolin?"

"Yeah. Long time ago. Sonny was only fifteen."

"How come nobody ever told me."

"If you'd have known and I didn't, would you have told me?"

"You know I would."

"No way, Randall. Even now you're keeping secrets, you and Dad. Think I don't know?"

"Swear it, Yogi. I told you everything about the journal. I don't even read it anymore. But fifteen, how could he do it?"

"Men. They're all crazy. See, you're just a boy, which makes you stupid. When you get to be a man, you'll be crazy instead of stupid. That's what you got to look forward to."

I stare at her a second. She's dead serious. She says, "You think a woman could've pulled a Hitler, and what about—"

"But Dad. What he do when he found out about Uncle Benji molestin Son?"

"To this day Dad doesn't know. Son only told Ma. Ma never called Uncle Benji on it either. She waited for him to show some guts for a change by bringing it up on his own.

So everything went along for about a year like nobody was the wiser till one day he calls Ma up crying, begging like a dog."

"How come Ma didn't tell Dad?"

Yogi shrugs. We've finished off the shoulder pull, a sort of tripod deal with elastic pulleys and a stool. Next is a bench press, then the leg press attachments.

"How'd it happen?"

"We'd gone to Coney Island and Uncle Benji took me and Son off Ma's hands 'cause you were still in a stroller, actin up the way you used to always do in public."

"Where was Dad?"

"Who knows? Off at the library or at the hospital. Anyhow, Uncle B takes us off to do a ride where you hop in a canoe and you go through a cave. Son was in a canoe with him and he groped her in the dark. Even tried to kiss her."

"She screamed?"

"Nuhuh. She just wouldn't let him."

"Where were you?"

"In the backseat, but I was too young to figure anything was wrong. You know how Son is. She's used to guys trying to do stuff to her, even way back then."

"So now 'cause Sonny wouldn't, Uncle Benji's settling for Ma?"

"You could say that. But I'd bet he started with Ma first, then tried Son, now he's back on Ma. If he ever tries me, I'll kick him in the nuts."

"That's why he's always running errands for Ma?"

"Probably."

"Think Ma would kick him in the nuts if he tries to grope her?"

Yogi mulls the question over. "Naa. She'd probably slap him if worse came to worse. Anyway, he already tried last summer. 'Member when he took us out on Long Island Sound in his forty-footer? Well, when he let you steer, and Sonny was water-skiing off the back, I saw him put his hands at Ma's waist while he showed her the view of the sunset on the water."

"That ain't so bad, is it?"

"One hand on her waist would've been cool, but he was behind her with both his hands at her waist, tryna cop a feel, the dog. She gave him a chance to take his hands away, then she did it for him, and led him around to stand at her side instead of whispering at the back of her neck."

"This guy, man. Unreal. Put him in a boat and he turns into a rapist."

"He's a sick fuck. And him and Dad are supposed to be best friends, from kindergarten straight through med school. What the hell, he can't help it nohow."

c h a p t e r
16

Come Friday I'm through dealing with the whole classroom scene. Fed up.

So I take it on the lam, the most serious offense I can think
of, a ruthless truant. Screw 'em. I'm in the wind, long gone
and hard to find. Who of them can stop me if I choose to
take the rest of the day off? They'll laugh to spite me, and
the older ones, my teachers, the ones who're supposed to
be genuinely concerned, they can tell me I'm naughty. My
teachers jump at the opportunity to say this word,
"naughty." They say it as if they're proud to recognize it.
"That Randall Roberts," they'll whisper to each other and
shake their heads.

So what? They've found me out. I'm naughty.

My classmates? Well, let's just say I'm on the outs with
the in crowd. Fifth grade no less, and these kids think
they're altogether hip. Even if they wanted me to be a part
of whatever they call themselves, I wouldn't be interested.

This time it was Shelly Tyson, who happens to wear braces that look like a face mask. Every year she wins the spelling bee so she figures that gives her the right to get snotty with me. There I was, minding my own business when she decides I'm in her way.

"Would you move, Randall Roberts. I'd like to sharpen my pencil."

Now figure this: she's standing there holding an ink pen, but that wasn't even the point. It was all about manners. A simple "excuse me" and I'm out of her way in a flash. But she gotta get aloof, and on top of that she gotta say my whole name 'cause they think it sounds goofy to have your first and last name start with the same letter.

She goes, "I said move, Randall Roberts!" and like usual the whole class was tuned in to our petty little spat. Ms. McElroy had stepped out into the hallway to gossip with another teacher. Call me paranoid, but I think it was a conspiracy hatched between Ms. McElroy and the rest of the class. It's probably something they can all agree on, sort of like a class project: bustin Randall's chops.

"How come you're always in the way, Randall Roberts," Shelly Tyson whined. The other kids looked on indignantly.

What do I do? I ignore them. I take my sweet precious time, twirling the sharpener slowly, then checking the lead and blowing the wood shavings off the tip. I could hear the natives whispering, taking sides against me. They always pretend that I'm annoying them, but it's what they want anyway.

"Listen here, Randall Roberts," Shelly was about to start again, but her friend Kathy Mason wants to jump in instead—a couple of future airline stewardesses giving me grief about my seatbelt.

"There's other people who wanna use the pencil sharpener, Randall Roberts," Kathy chimed in, eager to be a pain in the neck.

I turned around, "What's that to—," and before I could

get it out of my mouth, Kathy Mason slugged me, POW, right in the mouth.

First off, don't think I'm afraid of Kathy Mason. Don't think that because she can beat most of the eighth-grade guys in a foot race that I'm scared. If she's the best soccer goalie in school, big deal, that don't bother me none. It's more a matter of being a gentleman, and anyway, it's useless to reason with some people. They wanna start an argument, then they wanna belt me, and if I choose to tell the teacher it'll still be my fault since I'm "naughty."

For me there is only Ma to fear, and lately she's been in retreat. It's what my father has given me, a power over Ma that he's never used. He's been saving it up for me to use. It's simple. Everything is as simple now as it will ever be. No one has to explain.

He loves me too much and she not enough.

See me? I've just entered Massapequa, ten blocks up Sunrise Highway, I'm crossing the street back and forth against the lights, pleased by the imaginary danger that will lose its power if I attach a name to it. We'll just say I've infiltrated enemy territory—I'm undercover. A double agent.

It's a bright cold day with moderate traffic. At the Schwinn shop I stop off to look at a ten-speed with skinny wheels and an air pump notched along the center strip, then farther along I stop to watch three guys up on a scaffold, piecing together an advertisement out front of an auto repair shop.

It's a cool three miles from the elementary school to Pinelawn High. That's where I'm headed. I've got a date with Terrell Daniels, who she's supposed to take me to the hospital to pick up a tape from my old man. She agreed to give me the ride after I told her about the collection of pills I stole from ICU a couple weeks ago. She got dizzy when I described them, every color in the rainbow, a thousand ups and downs, a seesaw out of control.

When I swiped them, I had no idea how useful they'd be. It's what Dad's always talking about, resourcefulness and vision. Every once in a while his little lessons come in handy, though I've noticed resourcefulness is sometimes the same as cold-blooded thievery. Life's a mixed bag, that's the way I choose to figure it.

Did I mention that my Dad the fruitcake is taping his journal now, and boy am I thankful. Penmanship's never been a strong point with Dad. They'll tell you it's an occupational-whatever with doctors, but I think things just rush to my Dad's head too quick and he can't write them down fast enough.

After a few more blocks I'm finally off the main road, just over the Copiague town line. I take a left and circle around through a residential neighborhood, cross over through a few backyards, hop a fence, and end up out on Juniper Ave. Pinelawn High is right next to the firehouse. The double doors around back that lead into the gym is the safest place for entrance. I know this from experience, though I really don't have to be that careful. By sight, no one is frightened by a boy. Still, I crouch low as I come into the school's parking lot, stopping behind each fender, marking the distance between me and the gym door. The last fifty yards I take as a sprint and slip through the doors into the empty gymnasium.

It's dark and quiet here, the halogen lights turned down to half power. A check of the schedule posted on the door tells me all the gym classes have been completed for the day. It's afternoon, about 2:30. All the way to the rear is the equipment closet and the gym teacher's office where that Eric Hazzard guy hangs out. Yeah, of course, that's another reason why I'm here. My father has brought me; it's his will I'm following. He's leading me farther into his journal so that the puzzle is becoming more than words on a page. There are pieces to be fit together, and E. Hazzard is one of the bigger pieces, even if he doesn't have a clue that he has been chosen for something. Puzzles are surprises. They will all be surprised when everything falls into place.

The gym teacher's office is small and windowless, but he keeps it reasonably neat, which probably means he don't do much of anything. What is there for a gym teacher to do anyway except blow his whistle and make people run laps? I start to go through his drawers when I hear the sound of footsteps echoing off the hardwood gym floor. A giddy rush of panic washes over me. Quickly I scamper into the equipment closet.

The footsteps come closer and I squat down to peek through the keyhole as two people come into the office, E. Hazzard and the Spanish teacher, Stacy Rodriguez.

Hazzard is tall and light-brown skinned. He's got reddish hair and freckles. Pepperdine is where he's from, a California boy. Terrell and Yogi have already snooped through Ma's files to see what was on his résumé: he graduated last spring without any of the lauding that colleges do over their best students. He majored in phys ed. and minored in philosophy—played basketball, swam, and ran track.

What Hazzard's résumé didn't mention is how sure he is of himself. You can see it in the way he walks, the way he's moving on Stacy Rodriguez without any hesitation. Not ten seconds after they enter the office and he's all over her, kicking the office door shut and backing her against the wall. He's palming her ass with both hands while she sucks on his chin.

Now look very closely and I'll tell you what you see: that I want to give something to Eric Hazzard, to force it on him. I want him to have something he won't want to forget, he cannot forget. I want to whisper in his ear using his voice.

I like this guy. He's nobody's gym teacher.

My body starts to rock. I can hear his heart beat, like a clock ticktocking. Here, right here in this office, this is where

Yogi and me will have him. He's so right it's scary. He's so right for my father's use, and for my mother's as well. Do they understand? Dad does, but does Ma see it the same way, how right he is? He's so right it excites me and I want to lay hands on him now, to know him the way my father knows me.

Yogi and Terrell have talked about burglarizing his place. He's got a trailer house along Route 110 and sometimes they'll drive by the lot. There's about twenty trailers and his is the last on the left in the back row. From the street you can barely see it, it's tucked so far back.

Terrell says Eric is scared of Yogi. I told her lots of people are.

A few weeks ago on a Monday night, before Dad had the stroke, they let me come along while they staked out the trailer. Terrell borrowed some guy's truck, a mini-halfton with five-on-the-floor and brand-new radial tires. Yogi did the driving and damn near tore the clutch out. She's too impatient for standard transmission. She was popping the gears from one to three to five, making the truck do those little hiccups and laying down burned rubber after every red light.

We parked about twenty yards up the street from the trailer homes. I'm not exactly sure what we were waiting for, but my sister and her dippy friend are specialists at surveillance.

"Hazzard's dyslexic," Yogi said to me and waited. They were drinking Robitussin.

"Me too."

"No you ain't. You just stupid."

"No, Terrell, really. They sent me away once, to a horrible house. I could only read from right to left, which that's pretty cool if you're Arab or Chinee, but I ain't neither of those."

"He for real, Yogi?"

"It's true. They sent my brother to the Danbury Release Program."

"Get out," Terrell said. She was impressed. I leaned forward against the bucket seats.

"They never beat me, though."

"You sound disappointed."

"In a roundabout way, I am. I guess it depends on how you look at it."

"And he's dyslexic," Yogi said, "just like the big E."

"I'll bet it means Hazzard don't feel pain quick. His brain and his heart are too far apart."

"What's that got to do with pain?" I asked, but they ignored me.

Terrell said, "How'd you get out of the Danbury?"

"He was faking," Yogi answered, "just to get out of homework and Ma called his bluff. Sent him up to the big-house. Makes you wonder, don't it?"

"Your mom ain't no joke."

"Tell me about it."

"How long was he there?" Terrell asked Yogi. I leaned back in my seat. They never let me talk unless I could think of something clever. "Hey," I broke into the conversation, "maybe we should get a better look at Eric's trailer, maybe shine a flashlight in the window."

"No way."

"Then you stay out here, Terrell."

"What do I do if he drives up?"

"Just cool out. We'll be right back." Yogi got a flashlight from the glove compartment. She took lipstick from Terrell's purse. "Maybe I'll leave a poem for loverboy. Blow his mind."

"You're breaking in?" Terrell said. "You gonna boost?"

"Just sit tight."

Yogi tucked a pinch of chewing tobacco in her bottom lip and hopped down from the truck. She was wearing cheap plastic shades, a black bomber, and suede boots. We walked up toward the lot. The super's trailer was clear down the other end and we casually slipped down the first alley we got to. The rows were four deep.

Yogi said, "If he's got a padlock we're sunk."

"Can you open a slide bolt?"

"Sure thing. What is it?"

Most of the lights were off in the other trailers. There was some noise in two of them, people drinking and watching TV. All the cars out front were used and dented, dropouts and factory workers living on somebody else's property.

We circled around to the rear of Eric's trailer. Just behind it was a line of trees. On the other side of the fence was Safeway's discount store.

Yogi handed me the flashlight and took a butter knife from out of her boot. She felt along the side of the door and slipped the knife just under the jamb, then jimmied it a little, working the blade and pushing forward against the door with her knee.

I grabbed her arm. "Maybe he's inside," I whispered.

"Then where's his Jeep?"

"He coulda loaned it out."

She shrugged me off and gave it one more shove with her shoulder, popping the door clean open.

"He's going to know you did that."

"Good. I want him to know. He's lucky I don't torch the place."

The kitchen was very close, the walls. There were bread crumbs on the counter and crushed soda cans in the sink, but no dirty dishes. Yogi looked in the fridge. There was a box of baking soda and a deck of cards. She pocketed the cards and turned on the lights. "It'll look less suspicious this way."

From the kitchen you could see straight back to the end

of the trailer. It was very narrow. A few steps out of the kitchen there was a doorless bathroom to the left, about the size of a closet. The rest of the place, I guess you could call it the bedroom. There was a mattress on the floor with a blanket and two pillows. The sheet and pillowcases had blue sailboats on them. It made me crazy with insomnia just looking at them. I can only sleep on basic colors.

i checked the medicine cabinet. Yogi rummaged through his trunk. Nothing.

"How much rent you think he pays?"

"Too much."

Yogi went to the dresser and opened a bottle of cologne. She dabbed some behind her ears while looking over his CD collection, all rap. "He got the dumb South Central bullshit," she said. "Buncha wifebeaters."

"Doesn't look like he spends much time here."

"Who can blame him."

There were pictures of girls lining the mirror, maybe fifteen in all. They seemed to range in age, from grade school through college. Stacy Rodriguez wasn't one of them. Inside a duffel bag in the corner, I found letters, an old yearbook, and a Dodgers' baseball cap. The cap was sky blue and I put it on, turning it around backwards so the bill wouldn't flop down over my eyes.

"Here, lemme see," Yogi pushed me aside and took the letters. I sat on the bed with the yearbook. Eric's picture was near the back. He had a Jheri-Kurl-ed afro. I tore the page out, folded it, and put it in my pocket. I put the yearbook back in the bag.

"Who the letters from?" I asked.

Yogi looked at me as though she'd been reminded of something. She was suddenly sober and a little bit frightened. She looked around the room, then down at her hands. Jail had always scared Yogi, like she already knew she'd spend time there. Ma said so often enough.

"His old man's in the joint," she said and showed me the return address.

"I wonder what for?"

She stuffed the letters in the manilla envelope and put it back in the duffel bag. "Don't mention that to Terrell," she said. "Come on, let's get outta here."

c h a p t e r
17

That was maybe a month ago that we did the gym teacher's trailer. Since then he's been popping up all over the place. Twice we've seen him at the mall and another time he called Ma at the house about his lesson plans. She reamed him out pretty good 'cause she don't like it, having teachers call her at home. She told him to see Stacy about his problem.

Ma knows they're dating, but I wonder what she'd say about these two slobbering all over each other. I about gotta shit my pants watching this crap, they've been at it so long. Tarzan gets bored first and sits at his desk with a magazine. Stacy sits on the corner of the desk and strokes the side of his face. He's reading while she talks. He wants her to get lost. Talk isn't why he hangs around with her, but that's not really her fault. I know cause I saw her naked once. It was during the summer she stayed in the guest room at our house. Swear to God, it was a coincidence.

One evening, see, everybody's out the house and I'm sitting in the doorway of my room, the way I do sometimes 'cause I got no hobbies other than drawing and getting twisted off my old man's journal.

Anyhow, this Spanish teacher, Stacy, comes sauntering out of the bathroom still a little wet, drying her hair with a towel. It was nothing obvious, but she's gotta know I'm there. And I sure as hell wasn't gonna turn my head. Lookit, she's the visitor. She strolls down the hallway naked as a jaybird, I gotta take that as rent, am I right?

I'd never seen the real thing before but I didn't need to be persuaded. She makes Yogi look like the Tarmac at JFK; better even than Terrell 'cause the tips on Stacy's point in different directions yet still they're identical, which struck me as pretty amazing. Then, like outta the blue, she up and disappears into the guest room. I called after her but not loud enough for her to hear 'cause I really didn't have a hell of a lot to say, I just wanted to see her naked again, and I don't mean that in a bad way, wanting to see her naked.

I was just curious. Is that a crime?

Odd situations mean you resort to what you know best. That way if you're making a fool of yourself, at least it don't look like you're doing it by mistake. That notion brought me to the idea of TEA, and zap, before I could decide, I was making the suggestion in a loud voice that I didn't recognize. Now get this, I'm still sitting in the doorway, which that made it plenty dumb, making this blind request to a naked Puerto Rican about drinking tea and tracing the stars. All I could see was an empty hallway. Dumb but cool, right?

At first she said, "Tea? Stars?" like she was surprised, 'cause probably she really hadn't seen me when she got out the shower. Or if she did, she didn't care. She must've been sitting in front of the mirror in the guest room. There wasn't any hurried sounds coming from her room, no scurrying after a robe or anything.

"Bagged?" I asked into the empty hallway. "Or maybe

root? We got fresh leaves too. Broken. Whole. Shredded."

I think she laughed then, but them babes from the Bronx won't let nobody know when they're laughing on account of growing up around purse snatchers or whatever.

"You're making that up," she said. "There's no such thing as shredded tea."

"Is too. I shred 'em myself, even though I prefer root in summer. It's not as heavy."

"Randall," she said in a chiding voice. People love saying my name. They love to draw it out (it's the two *l*s at the end), or they'll say it three times.

"Randall, Randall, Randall," the naked Puerto Rican from the Bronx said. She goes, "I thought only little girls drank tea with their make-believe friends, Randall."

That last bit was a joke between us from when she caught me talking to myself. Big deal. Ain't no secret anyway.

I said, "Now you know different. I'm nobody's little girl. So root or shredded or whole or bagged."

"I'll let you choose."

I scooted down the stairs and shoved a pot on boil, one of the bigger ones so I'd have time to figure out what exactly I was planning to do, and enough tea to give me time to do what I planned.

I kept it simple. "Can I touch them?" I asked after I'd had my second cup. I didn't want the tea to get too cold.

We were out on the patio. A gentle breeze was blowing over us from the south. She was wearing a white terry cloth robe. I took it for granted wasn't nothin underneath.

"Can you touch what?" She stirred her cup. She wasn't drinking and I don't believe she was all that pleased to be out on the patio.

I furrowed up then, started worrying that I had planned poorly. At this point I'm seriously considering a major tea spill. You know, cut my losses and get the hell out. Nothing clears a table quicker than a big spill.

"Randall," she wouldn't let the damn thing alone, "what is it you want to touch?"

I furrowed my brow a little more, real sophisticated and gentlemanly-like, and nodded. It was all lost on Stacy, though she seemed to realize my gestures were for her benefit. She wiped at her shiny black hair with the towel around her neck.

"Why don't you give me a clue, Randall," she said flatly, without an ounce of pleasantness.

I was halfway out my chair before I even realized that I didn't have anywhere to go. "Never mind," I said and grabbed a napkin to wipe up an imaginary spill.

"This you should know, little boy. When you talk like an adult, that's the way you'll be treated. Understand?"

"You gonna get me in trouble, is that it?"

"Do you want to be a man yet?"

"Naw, Ms. Rodriguez. I can wait. We gonna leave this a lesson learned, or are you gonna tell my ma?"

"Not this time," she said.

We sat quiet for a few minutes while I tried to muster up a tear. It was useless. Mostly I was happy she was gonna forget the whole incident. Before we went back inside, she'd taken my hand and held it against the side of her face. Must've been she figured I didn't know any better but to think it was the same thing.

After school I'm out in the parking lot with that bitch, Terrell Daniels. Her stepdad must be out of town on "business" 'cause she's driving his hog today, the Deuce-and-a-Quarter that Buick doesn't make anymore (and is probably embarrassed to admit it ever made).

My opinion can't be worth much when it comes to cars since I don't drive, but your Electra 225 strikes me as the sort of thing a Polish czar might be buried in. It's a LOAD, solid cast iron, a goddamn battleship. Even so, it's got that hint of elegance, and it mystifies the hell out of me, how Buick managed to make such a crate that still has enough style to suit a pimp, while at the same time it could survive an afternoon of riots and earthquakes in L.A. And Mr. Daniels has his hooked up with all the trimmings—diamond in the back, eight-track tape deck, shag carpeting, car phone, convertible top . . . the whole nine.

I hop in on the passenger side and settle back into the rich Corinthian leather. It makes me feel like that Hispanic guy who kicked Captain Kirk's ass on *Star Trek* one time. Ricardo Montalban. But I think the car commercials he does are for Chrysler Cordoba, which happens to be another American-made heap that ought to get discontinued.

Anyway, I'm in this Buick hog with my slutty neighbor, Terrell Daniels. We're pulling out of the parking lot on our way to see my old man, and wouldn't you know it, it's the middle of November but Terrell's got the goddam convertible look in effect. 'Course, she's all dolled up in a floor-length mink and a matching hat, nice and warm, and it occurs to me that her intention is for me to freeze my ass off. Her happiness is based on my personal discomfort.

"I hope you brought money to fill the gas tank, Randall," she says, admiring herself in the rearview.

I try to explain it, "I'm eleven, Terrell. It ain't like I walk around with wads of money in my pocket."

"Yeah, well, this shit is going on your bill. Now let's have a look-see at the merchandise."

"Why can't you wait till we get to the hospital?"

"Don't dick me around, Randall."

"Terrell, you start talking sex and money and I'm lost, OK? I'm an innocent child."

"My ass."

"Let's not bring that into it."

"Lookit boy, I'll swing this car around right this second if you don't make good on your promise. Four bottles of pills, lemme see 'em."

As it is, Terrell Daniels operates the gas and brake with both feet, steers with one finger (her pinkie), and rarely looks at where she's pointing the car. Like right now, we're straddling between two lanes and she's looking at me while I stare in wild-eyed terror at the road. Yeah, sure, we're going in a straight line but we're driving dead up the ass of an eighteen-wheeler and the guy behind us is riding his horn, tryna tell us to make a choice between which lane we want.

I ease the bottles out of my jacket pocket. "How come you gotta check out the pills and drive the damn car at the same time?" I ask, knowing it's a stupid question. Everything's gotta be an adventure with this air-headed broad.

"Shut up and take the wheel," she says and pops open each bottle while I steer the car.

We're on the Meadowbrook Parkway doing an eighty-five mile per hour clip with the top down when Terrell lets go a piercing scream that quickly gets lost behind us, her dreads flying wildly about her face. I ease the hog into the third lane but I can barely see the lip of the road. One wrong move and we'll be scraping up against the guard rail.

"What gives?" I ask. She's dumped the pills into her lap and counting them by color, the solid blues on her left leg and the pinks on her right. The two-toned gelcaps she puts in the valley between her knees.

"Stairway to Heaven and Hell."

"You gonna do all those by yourself?"

"Hell no." She's careful to put all the pills back in the correct bottle. "I got this action lined up for some rock'n'-rollers in Wantagh. Two bills."

"Congratulations. Now you wanna take the wheel?"

"Ya done good, Randall," she says and takes control of the car, sort of.

"Just get us there safe, OK, Terrell. Me getting to the hospital isn't an emergency unless you make it one."

"Anything you say, sweetie." She eyes me for a second

and I can just about see her warped little mind working. "So what's doin around you guys house? Usually you're the first family on the street to go up with the seasonal decorations, Thanksgiving and all that shit."

"We'll get around to it."

"Well, it's understandable, this thing with your dad and whatnot. What was it exactly, this shit that happened?"

"A stroke."

"Yeah, so is he gonna, you know, will he be OK? I mean is he gonna be a cripple or somethin?"

I shrug.

"I don't mean to be nosy, Randall—"

"Oh sure, Terrell. You'd never pry."

"Hey, you don't have to get sarcastic with me. You don't have to pull any punches, either. I'm like family, right?"

"Sure, Terrell. Family."

"Anyway," she sighs, "Yogi's problems are my problems, and to be honest, I'm all shook up about it. She's stone-cold trippin. It's not like I'm gonna trash her for actin out the way she been doing, but how is anybody suppose to deal with her. One second everything's straight, next second she buggin. Take today for instance, she slapped the shit outta this little ninth grader in the girls' room for no reason at all."

"So what you want me to do about it?"

"I'm just telling you that she's wearing on my nerves. Skipper and Naldo feel the same way. And Mike? Forget about it. You know he likes her, right?"

"This stuff means nothing to me."

"You don't care about your sister's emotional health?"

"I don't care about what you have to say about it."

"Then excuse me, Randall. I'm just trying to be helpful."

I nod and watch the scenery go whizzing by.

It isn't something I want to think about, but I can't help it. Truth is, he could be discharged from the hospital today, but we are in worse condition than he is. Even before the stroke there was this tension in the house, like we were all sharing each other's thoughts; like our thoughts were being scribbled in the sand, lurid sins for everyone to read.

"Who's going to follow Son's lead?" our collective mind might've been saying. "Who wants out?"

Me, I got no choice except to stay, but Yogi's got options. Last I looked at her journal, she can't wait to skip town after graduation. The other day she got mail from UCLA. She wants to get as far away from this house as possible, and who can blame her? Last night was so typical, the same fuckin routine with Ma at everybody's throat.

I was like, "Hey, Ma, since when did you care so much about the stereo?" That was the beef, the goddamn stereo. Absolutely nobody even uses that damn thing anymore; still she wants a piece of Yogi 'cause the turntable was left uncovered. And you know Yogi, she can't take but so much yelling till she's gonna start yelling back and I got a full-scale riot on my hands.

So I jump in, "Yeah, I confess, Ma. OK? So go ahead and punish me so we can drop it."

That got Ma completely royal. "Fine," she snapped, her voice cracking a little. She knew she was in the wrong but she wasn't gonna admit nothin, her head held upright, devout, and me thinking ten thousand spankings would be easier than to hear her mouth for the next half hour.

She was like, "Your father was right about there not being enough love in this house," then she started accusing me of not caring what happens to him. First she was mumblin like she was going nuts, so I said, 'What'd you say, Ma?', and she started screaming about us leaving the top up on the stereo, which I don't remember there ever being any rule about not letting dust get on the turntable.

The whole flap was slightly ridiculous. Then she goes on rambling about us not pulling our share to make things work. She's like making this speech about teamwork isn't teamwork unless we act as a team. I mean the woman was totally unhinged, her spool is unwinding, she's losing it little by little. Then it looked like she was about to cry, and that totally blew everybody's mind, including hers.

I've never seen my moms cry, but the night it happened, when the old man got stroked, I caught her crying in the shower. The water wasn't even running and the lights were out. It scared all hell outta me. I walk into the bathroom and hear these sobs coming from the shower. Unbelievable. Then when I turned on the light, she yelled at me to turn it off and get out. It was real fucked up.

chapter
18

November 12—Intensive Care Unit

A third shoe drops and cowardly demons skulk impatiently in the half-light. The victim is prepared to sign off on their sniveling claim. Always it has been just a matter of time, and too, it is their right. But they're so damned tedious, these demons, whining and whimpering and insisting on payment due. They're scared he might call the whole thing off, as though that were ever an option.

The darkness has come a few minutes early this evening and our victim is dozing, set adrift on a variety of sedatives. He has been vaguely comforted by the first true sign of fear: the demonic pacing, their worrisome hands fidgeting at chapped lips in anticipation.

"A girl's gotta make a living," they'll tell you. They imagine themselves to be maidens with that unfuckable quality that can make a girl a star. And if you accuse them of lying, well then of course it is in a demon's nature to lie, isn't it? "Ex-cherubs Who

Couldn't Cut It in Prime Time," that's what the headlines will read. *"B-girls unwilling to take a waitressing job at the Fat-Burgers joint down the block from the subway."*

I mean, get real, they're demons for Christ's sake. Only a fool would believe they're virgins. Check the facts, but not too closely. Our simpleminded victim has them employed, hired out a half dozen, plus the three or four consultants who specialize in deviant thought processes.

"And His name shall be call-ed," the dirty half dozen murmur their blasphemous refrain.

Tonight they're reluctant pallbearers, sagging beneath the weight of the victim's prone body, ushering him forward through a dense morphine sleep toward a whirling reality that will bring him sharp pain.

"Much more then," the ritual chorus drones on, *"being now justified by His blood, we shall be saved from wrath through Him."*

"Cheaters!"

The victim suddenly lurches toward consciousness, slightly incoherent. He suspects that his evil minions aren't really putting out. They've begun the dirge in the middle, skipped portions of the eulogy even.

"Scalawags! Carpetbaggers! Bodysnatchers!" he yells with disgust and sits upright to eye them sternly.

The satanic underlings have no recourse but to take flight, scattering to the four corners of the earth, leaving the victim to make his own way through the lonely night.

"Worthy is the Lamb that was slain," he ponders his future while counting his fingers and toes to be sure that his body, if not his mind, is still functioning properly. The range of motion in his joints has been shortened by the stroke, but at least his orifices are clear.

Demons prefer mortal panic. They are amused by mass hysteria, the scrambling of languages at the Tower of Babel. Their idea of hijinks is filling Santino Cardosa's nose with cement and taping his mouth shut. Poor fucker's eyeballs popped out of his head from the built-up pressure, or that's the story the lead demon, Manto the Beloved, always told.

"Everybody knows Cardosa threw races at Belmont in the '60s," Manto reasoned. "Who's gonna miss him anyway."

Satisfied that he won't suffer a similar fate, the victim concentrates on the results of his stroke, his blessing; a progression that has brought him within spitting distance of Death itself. He can see Death marshaling its forces for a charge. It will come at him low and hard, but at the moment of truth, the victim is determined to stand tall. He will mock the beast in the midnight hour.

At a glance he surveys his surroundings. His hospital room is large and white with two other patients a lot worse off. The victim makes a snap diagnosis of the patient nearest him. Failed organ —renal complications—in need of a replacement—prospects for transplant are slim. The donor reserve is nearly empty, and kidneys in particular are in scarce supply. He'd read about the kidney shortage just recently, a small story in the Post that alleged a fledgling terrorist group had body-jacked internal organs from major hospitals all over the world as well as from mobile surgical units in the Occupied Territories and the Gaza Strip.

This group of young terrorists, who denied any affiliation with the Muslim or Shiite chapters, said their goal was to have a monopoly on internal body parts. They'd already warehoused the lion's share of available anal sphincters in numbers as high as twenty-five thousand. Now they'd made inroads on the kidney market, which had the largest demand outside of lungs and livers.

Intelligence officials were also looking into how the brazen desperados were able to drop brochures from a helicopter onto World Health Organization headquarters in Geneva two weeks ago: "Two kidneys for a grand," the advertisement read, "and a bucket of piss to go."

It was sad. Tragic. Obviously these hooligans had been lead astray; they were possessed. Hubcaps were one thing, but kidneys? The victim recognizes the procedure, the telltale signs. If a demon couldn't have your soul, he'd gladly settle for an anal sphincter. "Grab 'em by the ass," the saying went, "and their hearts and minds will follow."

He turns his eyes on the second patient. He can't refuse himself the feel of another man's injuries. This patient is wrapped in bandages from his head to his waist. He is younger, early twenties, perhaps a participant in a car accident at high speed. Cracked ribs, burns across his scalp and the side of his face. From the way his left leg is positioned, the ligament damage is extensive, the anterior cruciate. The right leg is in a cast too. Walking will be an altogether different proposition once he's back on his feet. A DWI maybe, or on the receiving end. Both patients are in plain sight but he can't move to help them. Really, it has always been that way. He never was quite able to help at all.

A fly comes thumping into the room, easily seen against the whiteness—big, buzzing, and black. It checks the far reaches of all four walls and the ceiling, realizing its limits, challenging its boundaries. It takes him five minutes to be sure of the large white box and ten minutes later he is a dot on the wall. The room hast that effect, bringing all living things to rest, to death.

Thank God he will not have to die here. The Lord will provide, just as he has awarded him this unique illness.

Yes, this sickness is his, not as for another. That had occurred to him before, how every sickness is different because every individual reacts to it differently. His will take him to a higher place, or lower. Whatever, the view will be the same. And without legs, he cannot run from it any longer.

As he settles back in his bed, the incantation of Revelation's four and twenty elders rings out loud and clear: "Thou art worthy, O Lord, to receive glory and honour and power: for Thou hast created all things, and for Thy pleasure they are and were created."

A strong wind comes blowing in from the north to combine with the persistently triumphant music of strings and horns and cymbals. And all things begin to pass before the victim, that which *was made by God and reshaped by man—their symbols seen darkly through a thick glass. And the things he sees are not loyal to a chronological history of the earth's events, but the trends of confusion are consistent with the purpose of Creation. That is the revelation he is being granted. Earth's purpose is made clear through repetitions and cycles, and the suffering of the people is secondary to the pleasure of God.*

There is rope and cattle and barbed wire and laws used in substitution for justice, and dreams and bright stones and the scarred feet of the elderly, and flexible codes of morality and debates over whether to execute unborns or criminals, and children playing in fields mined by the violence of their forefathers and praise for enslavement and the annihilation of races and the smell of singed flesh and clear water that runs murky with pollution that falls from the sky to make heaps of dung that multiply on landscapes once green.

And there is phallic dominance and artforms displaced by vulgarity and the combining of cultures into a global market that stifles diversification while "learned" men shape clever inventions for the sake of modernity, moving society from civilization to barbarism, and depraved celebrations for self-destruction and greater budgets for guns than for the care of those in need because the ability to take life is viewed as more important than its quality.

And families beget groups which beget communities which beget states which beget nations of different tongues and colors and masses of people surge through the streets to fall in line behind the flawed ideologies proposed by arrogant men wearing plastered smiles, and creases in the earth spread apart to shake the inhabitants and metal and plastic and neon.

And there also comes the spectacle of slim-waisted round-bottomed male harlots, adorned in feathers and red silk who rule for a time until children with painted faces move forth defiantly to "wild" upon the effeminate and all who stand in the way of their demented lust, swinging chains round their shaven heads with great strength to rip open the bellies of the pregnant so that no more will be born after them while piercing screams tear through the night for joy and pain for there are acts and occurrences that warrant both.

And there are wars and rumors of wars and the wounds of war that are healed and from which grow flowers of hatred that bloom beautifully into death in the changing of the seasons as might conquers intellect and tears flow like mighty rivers for the dying and laughter and merrymaking for the giving of birth that is followed by further crying and parades for the dead who have lived valiantly and monuments to peace and purity because neither exists in people.

And among these things the victim sees himself pass quickly. He is small in size and importance as in relation to the rest of creation and he belongs to these things as do these things also belong to him. All the things that pass before him are as one and are his possession by the sight within him.

Then, as quickly as he had ascended, mortality takes hold of his consciousness and lowers him in the blink of an eye, his body being jolted on impact of his mind's return to earth.

chapter
19

Dad is partially paralyzed on his right side. The right leg can barely bend and he keeps it on an even plane while sitting stiffly near the edge of his wheelchair. One corner of his mouth is twisted. His shoulders seem uneven and he has to use his left hand to eat. He also uses it to drink. He drinks red wine.

Our Thanksgiving dinner has come a day late and there isn't any heat in the house. Nobody turned it on.

"Is it a little chilly in here?" Gil asks after we've recited the holiday grace. He nervously glances around the table as though he's suddenly realized he's dining with an exhibit in the wax museum. For a long moment every one is as still as a photo.

"Randall, turn up the heat for your brother," Ma says finally, her lips barely moving.

I scratch my head in wonder. "Who?"

Ma's hospitality is forced and the turkey is cold and dry,

a slick pale yellow. It's been carved very neatly but nobody wants to go first, so it just sits there like a bomb. Even Gil won't give it a whiff. Out in the hallway the thermostat is down to a chilly fifty-five degrees. I turn it all the way off and stand at the entrance of the dining room, waiting for somebody to say something, but after a while it occurs to me that they hear me listening.

"How long does it take to turn up the thermostat?" Ma asks when I come back to the table.

"Yes ma'am."

"That isn't an answer."

"OK." I poke at the mound of stuffing on my plate. For a second I think she might send me to bed with no dinner, but we have all done him dirty. Sitting through an awkward dinner is punishment enough, that and the food.

"My God, what do we have to be thankful for! That he isn't dead!"

That had been Sonny's contribution to the little meeting we had the Wednesday night before Dad came home from the hospital. We were in the den downstairs, picking over week-old mushroom pizza. November had been a pissy month for eating but I couldn't find the right moment to ask Ma if the stove was busted.

We were meeting to resolve the problem about Dad; it's that simple. Wasn't like we didn't want him around, it was more that none of us wanted to be around each other. Oh yeah, Gil was at the meeting too, staring at the rug like a dumbbell.

"Then what lie do we feed him?" I had asked.

"Why it gotta be a lie?" Yogi mumbled.

"Then who's gonna tell him that he isn't welcome in his own house?"

"Don't put it that way."

"Why not?" I said. "I'll tell him."

That's when Ma went upstairs and made the call. Later

on I found out she gave it to him straight: "We'd rather not have you home for the holiday," she'd said. Dad responded by calling her a bitch, or at least he says he did, though I wouldn't bet on it. And anyway, calling somebody a bitch doesn't count unless it's face-to-face. Wasn't like Ma meant to do him wrong, but it was definitely intentional. Whatever she could've done, somebody's feelings were going to get hurt.

So he has a free ride over our Friday dinner, drinking that heavy La Bou Jolet that comes in a jug. I think it's made on the outskirts of a French hamlet where they got peasants to stomp the grapes. You can tell it's the cheap shit by the way it's staining Dad's teeth. Between the wine and the unlit stogie he's been chomping on, he looks hard and grizzled with stubble on his chin. The veins in his neck are bulging from all the weight he's lost. He smells a little too. Not the pungent kinda of odor like urine or your basic shit-on-the-underwear. It's more of a rusty bedpan scent that ten minutes outdoors in the fresh air might cure.

La Bou Jolet is his dessert while we have banana cake with broken pecans in lemon frosting. All through dinner he's been buggin. Like right now he's eyeing Ma with this amused sneer that doesn't unsettle her, but she's very much aware of it. Every once in a while she'll give him a flat hard stare just to let him know he can't rattle her cage.

'Course, Dad is all too anxious to make her react. For spite he starts sloshing his cigar around in his wine glass, splashing some onto the tablecloth with a playful "whoops."

Ma looks at the stain, then at Dad, as though she's keeping score.

She says, "Let's keep the nonsense to a minimum, OK, Frank. We all know how difficult the last few weeks have been for you, but we can stretch sympathy but so far."

"Listen to Mrs. Sensitivity. Hey, Georgia, don't pull any punches. Come right out and tell us exactly what's on your mind."

"I just did," Ma monotones.

I have to pretend I'm holding down a belch in order to keep from laughing.

"Yeah? Well, who's looking for sympathy, anyway," Dad shoots back, a little bit ticked that she's getting the better of him, which shouldn't come as any surprise.

"Just try acting your age, Frank. It might matter to your children if you conducted yourself like an adult."

Dad turns to me to try 'n save face, "Guess there's a kill-joy in every family," he chuckles, to which I joke, "You married her, Dad."

"If you don't watch your mouth . . . ," Ma lashes out abruptly but leaves the rest to my imagination. I lower my head and she backs off.

None of it is gonna happen too fast. She glares at me from across the table like a hawk, blinking only when I blink.

"What I wouldn't do to hang out with just the guys," Dad starts up again, making Ma switch her attention back to him. Between the two of us we've been working her over pretty good.

He says, "Take old Fred Sanford. I'll bet he never had a wife trying to undermine him, telling him what to talk about over dinner. Nope, all he got is Rob and Chip and Ernie. That's what I should've had, all boys."

"Like *Bonanza*?" I ask.

"The Cartwrights were horse thieves and bushwhackers," Dad proclaims.

"Naw, that was the Barkleys."

"You mean Matt Dillon and his posse?" Dad says, somewhat taken aback.

"No way. He was a sheriff."

"A man's man," Dad concludes and makes a toast.

"Yeah, but I think he spent quite a bit of time with Kitty over at the saloon."

"Tramp," Dad says indignantly.

"Yeah, but with a heart of gold. Then there was Festus."

"The uncle?"

"No, the deputy."

"Like Barney was to Andy?"

"Yeah, but Festus was tougher. He never bathed."

"Is that a fact?" Dad digs at his armpit then runs his fingers beneath his nose.

"Franklin, please," Ma sighs.

"Mmmmm." He's thoughtful for a second, then waves her off. "Look into that for me," he says urgently and with great agitation. "This thing with Dillon and Kitty and Festus, it doesn't strike me as quite right. And the Barkleys too, don't forget those redneck hooligans."

"You got it, Dad," I pour him up more of the wine. It's so thick that there are dregs at the bottom of the jug. "But how am I supposed to find out? They're on TV."

"By God, find a way, son. By persistence and resilience."

"Resourcefulness and vision?" I suggest.

"Not any more. They're wise to that tack. We'll find out by the spoken word, though I prefer printed. That way, it'll be permissible in a court of law. Isn't that so, Georgia?"

She ignores him, so he turns to me. "Are you getting this, Randall?"

"You bet. One if by land, two if by sea."

"Exactly." He takes in a mouthful of thick wine and gargles it before swallowing. He's peering down the table at Gil Turner, who returns a look of baffled reverence. Gil's dressed in a shirt and tie and suspenders.

"It's Thanksgiving, Gil," Dad announces joyfully, "and like Job, I feel fortunate." He reaches for Ma's hand but she moves it away. "Nope, I certainly have no complaints. A man, his family, a turkey, and an in-law. Who could ask for more than that?"

"It's certainly plenty," Gil nods.

"In all honesty," Dad points the soggy stogie in the toehead's direction, "I didn't ask for any of this."

"Like you said, sir, you're quite fortunate."

"And if I considered myself unfortunate, if I decided that I had made a mistake, what could I do about it?"

"I wouldn't know, sir."

"Is that why you're here, then, to be informed?"

"It ain't for the food," I quip, but Dad isn't amused. He's about to spin one of his cockeyed riddles. He says, "Then why is Gillis Turner here? And how did Gillis Turner get here?"

"Daddy," Sonny pleads, "there's no point in being rude."

"Now, now, Son," Dad chides her, "you've made your choice, and that means you no longer count in the grand scheme of things. Your future has been predestined, my child. Barefoot and pregnant, that's your lot in life. And if you want to use the bathroom, you'll have to ask permission. That'll be one finger for a tinkle and two for a dump. Now then go ahead, Randall, tell us why Gil is here, and how he got here."

"Love?"

"Wrong!" Dad pounds the table with his crippled fist. "He's a taker. He just walked in and took a seat. He saw something he liked, namely my daughter, so he took it."

Gil looks at Sonny. She shrugs.

"What's that?" Dad's face has hardened and it appears that all the flesh has been drawn from it. During his stay at the hospital, they fed him through an IV 'cause he wouldn't eat. The doctors were still insisting that the stroke was minor but they couldn't explain the "premature atrophy."

The muscles in his arms are sagging and the tips of his shoulders are bony and pointed. His jaws are sunken. The bones surrounding his eyes have become more prominent, creating dark rings around his eyes with bags underneath from lack of sleep. The lines of his face are lean and sharp. His body might be weaker, yet it makes him appear more spirited, as though his advantage is being prepared to endure any discomfort.

"Secrets in my home?" Without cause he explodes with anger. He is trembling. His face appears hard and desperate and I frame all of it—the six of us sitting in the largest room in the house, the brightness of the chandelier reflecting off the shiny hardwood floor. It will be his last supper with us and he is fighting the wine to witness it.

"You'd better learn to open up your heart, Gil, because there are some things you cannot take. You've got to sit back, fold your hands, and wait for it to be given to you. To accept pain, patiently and willingly, it is the same as to give it. Do you understand that?"

"Yessir."

"Like hell you do. You don't understand 'cause you're a taker, always the aggressor, a sucker to be distracted by anything that smells of money. Takers don't have ears to hear, just hands to take. They never hear the still small voice, too busy looting and chasing every bright stone that passes. You're just one big id, same as my wife."

Ma shifts in her chair to look at him now. Her head has been frozen solid all day, and still she remains calm, but as she turns I catch the rapid eye movement beginning to tremor. If Dad has much more to say, he's going to have to save it for another occasion. Yolanda is crying softly in the chair next to me.

"Ids grab," Dad yells, allowing himself a side glance at Ma to see how close she was to running out of patience. The wine is nearly finished and so is he. "Ids see and grab," he keeps on, his eyes rolling, trying to focus. He turns on her suddenly and almost loses his balance. He's never been much good at bullying.

I try to prop him up in his chair but he shoves me away.

"Did you hear that, Georgia," he screams. "You know what it's short for, Mrs. Id? Do you know? Idiot! Isn't that right, Georgia?"

"Sure, Frank," she bristles, her eyes aquiver. "Whatever

you say. It's your party, so whatever you say is law. The whole world is callous and you're the only one who's sensitive, the only one who cares."

"That's not what I said."

"Oh, well pardon me. I meant to say the whole world is sober and you're cross-eyed drunk. It's your party, Frank, so go right ahead and make a fool of yourself."

"I'm drunk, is what you're saying?"

"Yes, and it didn't take very long, did it? It never does. I hope this serves as a lesson you won't ever forget. There are some things in this world you cannot handle."

"Should I include you among those things, my dearest wife?" he asks needlessly, his head dangling heavily to one side.

She isn't going to answer him so I speak up, "Yeah, Dad," I say, and watch him fall face first into the table, bloodying his nose.

c h a p t e r
20

An hour after dinner he is still in his chair, his head on the tablecloth, a smear of wine and blood on his face. His eyes are closed.

In the kitchen Ma is washing the dishes. Her movements bring a familiar calm to the house. Yogi, Son, and Gil are down in the game room watching TV. I stand quietly in the shadows next to the staircase, listening to Ma in the kitchen. It is the sound of things being taken care of, of things being handled with a determined strength.

She comes back out to the table to clean the blood and wine from Dad's face. It seems she may have come from a far distance to do him this one last favor. I feel uncomfortable seeing it, but I watch and let it hurt me until I feel it like hot coal in my belly.

When the truth comes rushing from the back of your head and presents itself, you can't ignore it anymore. Ma is stronger than Dad. She is going to outlive him. It could've been the thing that first attracted her to him. She's the type who can't appreciate happiness until it's replaced by something bitter. In ten years her memory of what our family had been will be flawless.

For Son and Yogi, Dad's performance over dinner was a shock. After he passed out, they were glassy-eyed, their faces wet with tears. Gil had to lead them by the hand away from the table. They wanted to take Dad in their arms and revive him, to love him, to make him love them. But it wouldn't do any good. Gil understands. He has put himself between them and the sight of our drunken father.

"He'll be able to talk sensibly in the morning," Gil insists. "It'll all be better by then."

Those are the right words to say, though he probably doesn't believe them himself. Me being the youngest, I half expected him to lead me away from the mess as well. But I don't think it ever occurs to him that I might be in shock too. Come to think of it, he made a point of not looking at me at all.

Anyway, the girls need him 'cause Ma has always avoided drying people's tears, and I sure as hell wasn't going to. What for? They're gonna keep crying anyway. Somebody's gotta cry when fucked-up stuff happens. It is only proper.

All the dramatics haven't fazed Ma one bit though. She has gone about clearing the table of dishes without giving any of her feelings away. But she was stunned, she had to be. Say maybe she knew he was weak and she'd outlive him—and say maybe the sickness was something she could deal with—still, she has to be surprised at how he's using the stroke to tear our love to shreds. She has to be asking herself why, just like Son and Yogi are. Just like I am.

Upstairs in my room, I begin crossing a new pair of laces into my sneakers. A knock comes at the door.

"Yes, Ma?"

She comes in and sits down in the chair next to the closet.

When I look into her face, it's almost as if she has become a different person. At dinner, Son and Yogi looked different too. Obviously the old man was different, and that's what has changed them. I am changed too. The evil is within me and I feel myself drifting farther away from these people, my family.

A few moments pass and I can feel her watching me intently. When she speaks, she chooses her words carefully, as if everything matters ten times more than it has ever mattered before.

"Just now, when I knocked at the door, how did you know it was me?"

I wait the question out to pull her closer.

"Huh, baby?" She is concerned, her eyes narrowing. "How did you know?"

"Yogi never comes to my room," I say, crossing the laces of my sneakers. "She only comes when I'm not here, then she raids my jar of quarters."

"Does she?" Ma strokes my leg hesitantly and looks into my face.

I can see it start to work on her, the doubt. Ma's not one to tolerate doubt. She won't allow it to settle on her. She will never put off making up her mind so that her acts are always deliberate and aggressive. Her thoughts are probably aggressive too, and the decision she's making now is evident on her face, a look of surprise spreading over her features.

I have nothing to hide. I lift my face and smile to let her know her decision about me is correct, then start back with my lacing.

"What was that?" she asks quickly, as if she's caught me in a lie. "That silly little smile."

"What do you mean, Ma?"

"You're acting strange, Randall. Tonight over dinner you were very rude. I hope you didn't think you could take advantage of an awkward situation by misbehaving."

"Of course not."

It seems like a silly thing for her to say, like I'm gonna actually say, "Yeah, I was trying to take advantage."

I shove a three-piece wad of bubble gum in my mouth and wait for her some more. She doesn't like this, my waiting and blowing bubbles in her face. A balance between us has begun to shift, the same as it had shifted over dinner with her and Dad. She can't rule over things that she wants no part of. That's the decision she is trying to deny or ignore; that she doesn't understand us, and more than that, she doesn't really want any part of us. She doesn't need the headache.

She says, "I've told you once before how you're supposed to act when someone has too much wine over dinner. That includes your father as well."

"He was bombed," I agree.

"Is that supposed to be funny?"

"No ma'am."

"You're acting very strange and I don't like it."

"You always say that. Anything I do you say it's rude or strange or wrong."

"Is that why you keep doing those things, to hear me scold you?"

I shrug. We both knew it was true anyhow.

"Whatever the reason, I don't have time for it, Randall, not now. Your father needs my attention more than you do."

"So what else is new?"

"What's that supposed to mean?"

"Dad needs you, that's the way you want it anyway. Besides, he met you before I did. That makes him always first." I say this to confuse her, but it starts to make sense so I add more. "You chose him. You didn't choose me. You couldn't have said you didn't want me once you had me, could you?"

"I—," she starts, stops. She gives my question some

thought, as if she's trying to put the words in the correct order 'cause I'm not capable of doing it. Then, like clock-work, she gets pissed off. You know, like all a sudden, the way mothers do when they're confused but don't want you to know it. She isn't pissed off as in angry, it's more like she's pissed off as in pleading for me to do right for a change.

"You're just trying to make me forget that you misbe-haved, but I'm not, Randall Roberts. You know better and I know you do because I've taught you better. Just this once, try to make my life easier, son. Instead of pretending you're a victim all the time, try taking responsibility. Before you speak out of turn, before you do something wrong, try using your head first. Can you do that for your mother?"

Her voice wavered in the air and I let it die without an-swering her. I can't tell whether I've said something that makes her feel guilty. I look her in the face.

I can almost see her struggling to hold her composure, the firmness returning to her voice. "I asked you a ques-tion," she says.

"Yeah, I guess. But what you want me to do?"

"It's what I want you not to do." And then she starts listing all my favorite sins. "No more digging up road signs or climbing onto the roof late at night. No more wandering off down the highway by yourself. No more walking the neighbor's dog without their permission. No more talking back to your teachers at school, no more fighting with your classmates, no more of any of it. Understand?"

"OK," I say cheerfully and go back to lacing my sneakers as if the conversation is over.

Ma snatches the sneaker from my hand to get my full attention. She wants to look me square in the face for the absolute proof of what she does not want to believe.

"Has any of what's happened registered with you, young man? Any of it?"

"Aw, Ma, come on. I'm just a kid."

"Don't hand me that. You can pass that bit off on your father, but don't think I believe for one second you don't understand that your actions are of concern to others."

I turn my face away and try to make my top lip quiver.

"Now the tears. Not the tears, Randall."

"Geeeooorrrgggiiiaaa," a bellowing comes from downstairs.

"I think that's Dad," I say and snatch my sneaker back. She doesn't notice though. She seems to be weighing the importance of me and him, or maybe the annoyance of both of us put together. Probably it's occurring to her that we had planned to ruin her evening. But that's not the case at all. We're doing it by coincidence actually. At least I am. Hell, I've been ruining her evenings by coincidence for as long as I can remember. Not to be malicious, it just comes naturally, her being my mom and whatnot.

She turns to give me one last warning on her way out the door. "I won't stand for any more nonsense, do you hear?"

Naw, I'm deaf. That's what I want to say. "Yes, ma'am," I reply instead, then wait ten seconds before following her downstairs.

I stand at the foot of the stairs and peek down the hallway to see Ma go into the master bedroom. For a moment I consider myself and wonder what my sisters would make of all the things I've learned from eavesdropping. It's a bad thing, snooping, yet it isn't bad to know what other people aren't going to come right out and tell me. I reason it all out in my head and try to picture myself the way my sisters would. It isn't very pretty, me looking like a sneak and an all around bad seed.

I can hear Dad yelling in the bedroom, something about needing a screwdriver. His voice is muffled and I figure he might be in the bathroom adjoining the master bedroom. "Get me a screwdriver from the toolbox downstairs," he keeps saying.

On a normal night it would've been a strange request, except our family is fresh out of normal nights.

Ma: "What on earth are you doing?"

"Just get it!" Dad barks.

I hide in the hall closet as Ma passes on her way downstairs, then slip around to the locked bathroom door.

"It's Randall," I whisper.

He peeps out and scratches his chin. He's bleary-eyed, confused, so I rush him. "Hurry up," I push at the door, "before she gets back."

He lets me in and the two of us crouch next to the door, waiting for Ma to return.

"Frank, you have to unlock the door if you want the screwdriver."

When Dad cracks the door open to snatch the tool, I catch a glimpse of Ma in the bathroom mirror but I don't think she sees me. Even if she does, there isn't much she can do about it. From where she's standing we must look pretty ridiculous. She's probably thinking we deserve each other.

"Do you need help with something?" she asks wearily after Dad has locked us in.

"No. Stop nagging me and go to bed."

He moves his walker aside and manages to prop one hip up on the Formica next to the sink.

"Can I help?" I whisper.

He points me into the corner and starts unscrewing the hinges on the mirror. When the bolt is almost out, he begins on the lower one. He isn't used to using his left hand and the job takes some time. The head of the driver keeps slipping out of the groove. I watch as the ache in his arm begins to awaken him from the wine.

"Your mother hates me," he says while working steadily at the hinge.

"Naw, I don't think so."

"I didn't ask you, I'm telling you. The others, your sisters, they fear what I've become. Your mother too. Only difference is that for your mom, fear translates into hate."

"Oh."

I start to ask him if that's what he wants, but realize I didn't really want to know yet. A little at a time I can take. Not too much though.

He keeps after the bolt until the mirror is unhinged, then slips down off the Formica and sits on the lidded toilet. He places the mirror between his feet to look down at his face.

"Dad?" I call, but he doesn't hear me. He appears to be fascinated and horrified at the same time. I huddle more tightly into the corner.

His face is wretched and he is barely able to look at himself. He turns to each profile, then looks at the reflection straight on. Sweat begins to roll into the stubble on his chin. His body rocks back and forth on the toilet, his fist in his mouth, the tears and sweat mixing together on his face.

I reach out to him and feel the narrowness of his back. He flinches and groans a little. I don't think he realizes I'm here.

We stayed there in the bathroom without talking for most of the night. At around dawn, I slip back out, kiss Ma's sleeping face good-night, then tiptoe off to bed.

chapter
21

Heaven came down and glory filled my soul. The snow came stuffed within a host of angry seraphim, purple cumulus that hovered menacingly like puffy stains against the black backdrop of sky. At a little past midnight I witnessed the first snow of winter, a magnificent falling that nobody could have planned or prevented.

The moment I stepped outside, the snow all belonged to me. The pureness was beneath my feet and swirling about my head and above the trees and houses. It was pure and white and I trudged a virgin path down the middle of the street. The world was asleep. I held my head back and caught the wet coldness of several flakes on my tongue. The snow was falling so heavy and thick that I could feel it brush my eyelashes, the soft landing of a million flakes in soundless unison.

I chose one to track its fall, straining to distinguish it from all the others, to follow it as the steady wind brought it toward me. Snowflakes were all supposed to be different, just like people were all supposed to be different, but seen together, all going in the same direction and traveling at the same speed, they were all the same.

I lost track of my flake and continued down the street, around a bend, stepping high to make sure my feet left neat prints in the snow. This was the time for which I had been claimed, and not by coincidence it was the time I met my father as no one else ever would. Before, it was always me waiting for him to get home from the hospital; now he waited for me. The others weren't so lucky. They'd lost him, and now they were losing each other.

Late at night when I bring him his dinner in the library, he'll want to know exactly where the others are.

"Yolanda?"

"In her room."

"And your mother?"

"In your room." I wait to see whether this means anything to him. It doesn't appear to, so why is he asking? He's sitting in the wheelchair with his eyes closed.

On his last day at the hospital, he forced one of the nurses to shave his head. At first she said no, so he took his IV out and busted the bottle. Kept doing it each time she replaced the IV till she finally gave in to him (or ran out of bottles). I can just about picture it—all the nurses huddled around outside his door—concerned whisperings about how he used to be such a refined gentleman.

Aw, the beast within.

He'd wanted a mohawk but they were able to talk him into a more traditional onyx. In the end, he charmed those nurses though. Made out like it was a big joke and had his picture taken with them. When we picked him up that Friday, they were all in his room, having a little party, a bunch of giggling nurses and Dad's head shiny and bald. None of them wanted to think Dr. Roberts had gone koo koo.

"It was just the stress," that was their explanation to Ma,

who nodded and bit her tongue. I'd wanted to ask where Dr. Benjamin was to let something so silly happen. Then again, what difference would Dr. Benjamin have made.

His hair? Well it's just about grown back in, full and fuzzy, whiter than before.

"Are you sure your mother came home tonight?" he asks. He could look out the window and see the damn car himself, but that would be too simple.

"Where else would she go, Dad. Huh? Isn't she supposed to come home, or don't you want her here anymore?"

Instead of answering, he starts humming some tune, swinging his arm back and forth like he's conductor for the Lunatic Philharmonic.

"Hey," I yell, "maybe it's not Ma who hates you, maybe it's you who hates her. You're the one who treats her like dirt. You're the one making her feel unwelcome."

"I'm not the one who abandoned her Thanksgiving day."

"That wasn't her decision."

"Aw, then the truth comes out."

"Yeah, the truth. Knowing the truth when you hear is no big deal," I repeat one of his favorite sayings. "Why don't you try speaking it instead of handing me these goofy riddles. Do you want Ma around, yes or no?"

He angrily rolls toward me, making me back off. The white part of his eyes are the color of unflushed toilet water, yet the pupils are on a clear sharp line into my eyes.

"Thirty years I've had her around," he snaps. "Time comes when I don't, you won't have to ask me about it. Time comes . . ."

He allows these words to lodge in my head, then says, "Your mother and my wife, she's the first constant between us. I can never be alone with you because her spirit is in touch with my heart, and by extension, yours as well. She doesn't force herself between us. We need her there."

"Fascinating." I yawn and move a little to the left of the wheelchair. He follows me with his discolored eyes. His

stare is persistent and so is mine. His eyes can make of me
what they will. He's the one who has changed, not me. Well,
maybe I've changed a little, though the change in me is not
nearly as complete as his appears to be. Finally I feel my
eyes start to tear. I hold my gaze steady.

"There is no point in speaking the obvious," Dad says.
"Neither of us has any use for that."

"OK," I tell him. When he says things out of the blue, I
can only allow space for them in my mind and hope their
value increases in the future. Hopefully I'll know what the
fuck he's talking about by then.

"I don't have to make sense for you," he sneers. He's
gauging my facial expression to read my thoughts. He
knows me better than I know myself. For all it matters, he's
known me longer.

He says, "It's you who has to adjust to me. You've got to
keep fighting to understand me, otherwise it's no good. You
have to want it bad enough to kill for it."

"OK. Then I want it real bad," I say coolly, "I gotta have
it. Now why don't you come out with it, whatever 'it' is."

"Apparently you lack the passion, that's why. Besides
that, you couldn't keep up anyway. What I need is for you
to tell me you'll keep fighting to understand."

"I'll fight if I feel like it."

"And do you feel like it?"

"I do," I say simply.

He laughs. "Sounds like a wedding vow."

"I do," I say firmly and pass my hand over his hair and
down his neck. It's the only gesture of affection I've ever
learned from my mother.

Again Dad comes from out of left field, "People should
be known by their perspective, not by their names."

I resist the urge to tell him the remark went straight over
my head. Sometimes he speaks to remind himself as much
as to tell me.

"Do I need to say it again?" he asks.

"Doesn't matter."

"Good. I owe you an explanation for that. I owe you, and you need me."

"What else do you owe me?"

"The whys and whens, the point and the purpose. The means—"

"The means," I jump on the word before he can go on. It startles him and I quickly try to make the most of it, putting him on the defensive. I make a small movement of nodding my head, signaling him as if to keep our secret safe from Ma.

He returns my little nod. He knows I want him to build on it. I need something I can sink my teeth into. I want to be jarred suddenly, to be frightened in some subtle way or shaken by some unnatural act. The stroke was incredible for both of us, though at the time it scared me half to death. I wasn't able to appreciate it until later that night.

"Getting stroked isn't enough, Dad," I tell him bluntly. "It's all got to be spelled out for me."

"You're speaking out of turn, Randall. Be patient, son. All good things to those who wait."

I shrug.

It might be jokes tonight. If he wants to tell any, I'll laugh when they're funny, and they usually are. The important stuff though, he's in no rush to share it. He'll go at his own speed, perhaps 'cause he's feeling his way through the dark as well.

"In the fullness of time," he keeps reminding me. "The time comes—it is the method of time that it should always come," he says. "We must wait for it."

My father is remade and now he is remaking me. Not in image, but in mind. To be honest, it scares the shit outta me, considering what kind of mind my old man is equipped with. And now he wants to tamper with mine. Just my luck.

"Love and faith are the same," he's reassured me.

"Fine, Dad. Whatever you say," I've told him, and I mean

it. I'm down to go as far as he wants, in any given direction. I don't think he realizes how much pressure that will put on him in the coming weeks.

I uncover his tray of food and spread a napkin across his lap. He frowns and jabs at the dinner with a knife. "Let's see what you've forgotten tonight," he says.

He thinks I've forgotten his seasoning again. He's probably hoping I have so he can throw another tantrum. He's up to about five tantrums a day. Until two weeks ago he didn't even use seasoning, but now that he's got people telling him what he can't have, suddenly he's addicted to paprika. What a pain. I'm ready to crown him King of the Motherfuckers.

I take the shaker from my pocket and put it on his tray.

"The day I stop seasoning my food," he says proudly, "is the day I sell my scrotum to a neutered Shetland."

I give him a fake chuckle and pull up a chair. It's not one of his better lines.

"Dietary restraint," he says with a huff and starts dumping paprika on his food, not that he's gonna actually eat it. "I'll tell you a little something about hospital prescriptions," he says. "They're defined by the patient's preference, and if there's something that you don't like, you're sure to get a healthy dose of it."

"But Dad, doing stuff you don't like builds character. That's what my teachers have been saying since kindergarten."

"Dovenuts!" He flings his silverware against the wall in a brief rage.

"Want 'em back?" I ask.

He shrugs and stares out the window. I'll be with him for the rest of the night. We've got so much time and I don't mind it, regardless of his constant cursing, words he isn't too good at using. He even makes up his own curses when he really gets wound up into a frenzy, like whenever the subject of the hospital comes up. They're the only employer he's ever had.

He says, "You could go to that hospital with a broken leg and those dickswingers would blame it on salt intake."

"How come?"

"Incompetence. They have no use for medicinal knowledge, only money. It's simple. Elbows are nickels," he whispers this bit confidentially, "and knees are quarters. It's all relative to money, don't you see it, sweet Mother of Peter, Paul, and Mary. Blood, Sweat, and Tears, that's what they'll tell you, those bloodletters standing so high above moral reproach. Rubber-gloved masterbastards, every single one of 'em."

c h a p t e r
22

That was a week ago Wednesday when he talked to me that way. Wednesday night is his gin night. Every other night it's vodka. When he wants a full night's rest, he does whiskey, then pukes and falls into a peaceful sleep. In the corner there's a line of mason jars that he pisses in. Each jar has the number of deposits along with the times and dates. Don't ask me what the point is 'cause I haven't asked him. And I don't plan to either.

He snaps at me more than he used to. I think I'm gonna snap back at him next time he does it. He's got me doing all his little chores: transcribing his taped entries into his journal. It's for my benefit, he says, as if I'm supposed to understand all his mumble-jumbles. Sometimes he just grunts and coughs into the recorder and he'll get upset when he checks my transcription and sees that I've written "grumble" or "mumble" or "he's raving and ranting again."

He hit the ceiling when I wrote "the fuck if I know" to describe one of his more spirited eruptions. It was during one of his talks on peace and joy and contentment. Lovely stuff, let me tell you. Theology and philosophy make for a hearty turd stew if you ask me, but he hasn't asked yet. He keeps saying it's all for my benefit whether I like it or not.

Every now and then he's in a good humor though, but first thing in the morning he can be a real son of a bitch. You can't fluff his pillow or make him tea or get him a cigar or anything. Nothing is good enough.

Ma hasn't said too much about Dad depending on me for everything. She's been busy like you wouldn't believe. She can make herself get that way, drown herself with work. She's got this project where she figured out the average GPA for sophomores, juniors, and seniors for each of the last fifteen years. Then she did a year-by-year comparison of the curriculum in place for the four major subjects—English, math, history, and science—to see which served best.

Guarantee you this little project is gonna cost some poor teacher their job.

She had me do some of the averaging, just so I wouldn't be spending so much time with Dad. She would never guess it but I was glad to help her. Usually my moms won't let you do anything for her, which was something she and Dad used to argue about. Now they don't speak at all. Sometimes she'll peek her head in the library just to look at him while he's sleeping in his chair, and one night she came all the way in the room.

It was around three in the morning and only the desk light was on. I was in the corner. She never saw me. She stood in front of his chair and watched him for about ten minutes, her arms folded. The form of her body was rigid as she leaned a little toward him, almost as though she were losing her balance in slow motion or fighting against the pull of some great magnet. For a second I thought she might fall on top of him, but she never even touched him. She brought her hand close to his face, then put her hand to her mouth. It could've meant anything. My mother is capable of mixing her emotions, and still, underneath all of it, there is the smallest trace of love.

The fall of snow has thickened and I'm having trouble seeing where I'm going. I'm not worried though. I feel very alone, and that makes me feel very safe. My mother, my sisters, they might feel alone also. Too bad they don't know how to attach the two, loneliness and safety.

When we were small and our parents took us on trips, Yogi always had to sit in the middle. She needs the contact, the company of Naldo, Skipper, Mike, and Terrell. They remind her that she's funny sometimes, and acceptable.

It's 'cause she knows she'll never be as pretty as Son. I've always thought Yolanda was pretty enough, but no one in the world is as pretty as Sonny, except maybe Ma. They both have a fullness around their mouth that sets them apart. I discovered it from drawing them and figured Yogi realized she didn't have it and that people wouldn't be as attracted to her like they were to Sonny.

When Yogi was young she always had Sonny, but after Sonny went away to college, Yogi turned to Terrell, and now that the family has been split by the stroke, and Sonny is married, Yogi's gonna turn to Terrell even more. Even so, Terrell still isn't enough. There will never be enough love in this world for Yolanda. More than all of us put together, Yolanda has bought into the notion of love. It's why she is the most alone, now in the time of our family's end.

Being alone doesn't come naturally to Son either, but for a different reason. She's smart and pretty and other people have always draped themselves on her, never letting her alone long enough to learn how to be alone and enjoy it. She's never been given the space to dare herself to change the whole world for her eyes only while everyone else sees just the lies.

Once I explained to Son one of the ways I can make myself disappear. At first she didn't know what I meant, then I explained that I didn't really make myself disappear, I just kept quiet and that kept people from being able to see me. If I didn't say anything, I was disconnected and they didn't know what I was thinking, and after a while they'd ignore me and it was the same as disappearing, except I saw them 'cause I heard them and knew what they were thinking. When a person doesn't say anything, they're protected. When I make myself disconnect, Yogi calls me a mongoloid. I told it privately to Sonny though, and she understands.

Being disconnected brings a frightening yet tranquil feeling to you. It brings you fear and protection from that fear. Isolation serves as the protection and can set you apart to witness the things that harm other people without being threatened by those things yourself. More so, it can distance you and dissolve your sympathy for those being harmed.

Disconnection can open the door to a small room with a big window. The room is small so you don't have to share, and the window is big so you can see as much as you can handle. During this holy time for which I was claimed, I witnessed through this window the sacred cow called LOVE being placed upon an altar to be butchered instead of worshipped. Through this window I saw the blood of my father streaming through my fingers. Through this window I saw my family as bugs caught in a jar with no holes punched in the lid, suffocating. They had overestimated love, and now it had forsaken them.

See it?

It isn't love's fault, it's ours. We think love has powers it doesn't really have. Yeah, love can be beautiful. But strong? No. It is neither strong nor resilient nor everlasting. Not against opposition from evil, an aggressive command fallen down from the foot of the throne of Almighty God.

I begin back up toward the house. The snow is still falling in thick waves.

c h a p t e r
23

Back indoors the dark warm stillness of our house sends a
jolt of excitement through me. Somebody has turned the
heat on. I stand at the door for a moment to let it all wash
back over me. The images are simple and clear: the barbecue
. . . an ice cream moon . . . skipping coins off tombstones
. . . Uncle Benji's Peugeot . . . the leaves . . . the stroke.

Upstairs in my room I sit at my desk with my coat still
on and the light off. Time passes and I can't move. When I
shake myself free, I strip naked and leave my clothes in a
heap in the middle of the floor, then head down to my parents' bedroom, Ma's nightstand. The bed is still made. She
is sleeping over at the school again.

I take her journal from the nightstand and climb into their
bed. There is a clean stiffness between the sheets and it
makes goose bumps rise on my skin. I've never been in their
bed before. My legs feel very cool against the firm, flat mattress. I pull the covers up to my waist and turn on the lamp

on the nightstand. The light is dim and casts shadows around the room.

I sit up and face the mirror and my reflection. There are my teeth and my eyebrow, that's all I see. A wild animal won't respond to "please don't."

Ma's journal isn't locked and I take this as an invitation. Everybody needs to share their problems with somebody else. So why not with flesh and blood? You don't have to be too brilliant to see she's in trouble; just from her handwriting I can tell. She's taken to print instead of script, and yes, she's started using a pencil. Admitting her own uncertainty is a good step. She's allowing herself the chance to erase. If she could, she would erase it all. I picture her writing the entries, holding the pencil tightly, pressing down so hard until the lead snaps.

Her office at the high school is small and crowdedly neat with dark-paneled walls and an adjoining file room and fax machine to the right. The curtains are drawn, and though the afternoon sun radiates brightly against the newly fallen snow, inside the office is dark and she is reading only by the two small lamps on either side of her desk.

Pinelawn High has never been shut down because of snow since Ma's been principal, and she's been principal from day one. When she dies they'll probably name the place after her. There's probably alumni who can't wait to name the damn thing after the bitch.

It's Friday, almost an hour after school was dismissed. I'm anxious to get home to see Dad, but I'm stuck here in Ma's office, sitting in the cushy chair in the corner, watching and waiting for her to finish up so we can leave. My school got the day off on account of the snow, but Ma wouldn't let me stay home. She's getting paranoid about me and the old man hanging out so much, especially with him being drunk all the time. Probably she thinks we're conspiring against her. I don't think we are, but sometimes I wonder.

I get up to shut the window behind her. She's probably got it open to keep herself awake. She looks like shit, and it's little wonder after spending the last few weeks sleeping over at her office on the couch. It's not even a couch that converts into a bed. I think she gets off on torturing herself, or maybe she's filled with guilt. There's stuff between her and Dad that I'm sure I'll never know, except it's there, clouding the air between them, making them overreact. A burst of anger, a clap of thunder, and the two of them striking out at each other and nobody knows how the yelling started. Marriage—who needs it?

Just look at her. She's frazzled and harried and all it would take is a decent meal and a full night's sleep. She don't even notice me closing the window behind her.

"I've had about as much of this as I'm going to stand for," she mumbles, flipping through her Rolodex.

"Henry," she rails into the phone intercom after dialing a number. She never talks into the receiver.

"Georgia, Georgia," the voice comes back over the line with dutiful cheeriness. "How can I help?"

"Don't give me any of that Georgia, Georgia crap. I didn't call for one of your Ray Charles impersonations."

"A little Stevie Wonder perhaps?" the man chuckles.

Henry MacInnis is the superintendent down at the Board of Education. I met him at one of Ma's parties. He's a pale little pigeon-toed man with tiny yellow teeth.

"Henry, if you could see my face right now, you would notice that I'm not laughing. No, Henry, I'm not even smiling. As a matter of fact, I'm slightly teed off. Suffice it to say, I didn't call for an earful of Irish humor."

"To what, then, do I owe the pleasure?"

"Another software requisition has been lost in that pit you're running over there. I sent through paperwork at the end of August and was told three to six weeks before we get the shipment. It's been three and a half months, Henry.

Three and a half months. Do I need to count that up for you?"

"Requisitions would be handled in Purchasing. Hold on and I'll transfer—"

"You'll do no such thing. What's going on over there? I thought you could handle the job—run a tight ship. Maybe I was wrong."

"Did you talk to Bea?"

"Bea Turnbull!" Ma's offended by the very mention of the name. "If she's your top buyer in Purchasing, then you've got real problems. Hear this! I've spoken to her already about my requisition, and your Bea Turnbull told me her hands were tied, Henry. I asked her who tied them. Know what she said, Henry? Would you like to hear what the very clever Bea Turnbull said?"

"Why don't I call the manufacturer?"

"An idea?! An idea has occurred to you? I certainly hope so. Come now, let me hear your idea."

"I'll look into it for you. I'll get in touch with the order fulfillment people and get some action. But you have to understand, this kind of thing happens all the time."

"No, I don't have to understand a damn thing. All I understand is that I don't have the merchandise in-house yet. By God how can we expect kids to be punctual and efficient if we can't even get their materials here on time. That's priceless. You should frame it: Kids in School, Materials en Route."

"It'll be handled, Georgia, I guarantee you. I'll get on it right away."

"Evaluations are coming up real soon, MacInnis. You'll do well to keep that in mind."

"Happy holidays to you too, Georgia."

She flips off the speakerphone. A knock comes at the door. It's Yogi. She timidly pokes her head in. "Should I get a ride home with Terrell?"

For a second Ma doesn't respond. She leans to the side of the desk to get her briefcase, then looks at Yogi still standing outside the door.

"Well, come on in."

Yolanda gives an awed look around the office as though it's been years since she's visited. Could be it's the most dreaded room in the building.

Fifteen minutes later we're on our way home, breezing out along the Parkway in the Lincoln, the vents in the car feeding us a steady dose of sleepy warm air. And we are silent.

I want to hear them speak so I can compare it to the words Dad and I exchange. I want to own my mother's thoughts and my sister's fears. My shoes are off and I'm curled up on the soft velour of the backseat. I can feel the four-door luxury car glide swiftly and evenly over the bumps in the road, my face turned in toward the seat and my back to Ma and Yogi in front.

"The college you attend is your choice," Ma picks up a line of conversation that will certainly lead to trouble. They've got two standing beefs: Yogi's friends and Yogi's choice for college.

When Yolanda takes too long to reply, I turn over so I can see them. She's nervously tugging at her seatbelt. She knows Ma never talks while she's driving unless it's to haul a little ass.

"I know," she says finally. She tries to leave it at that, but Ma's anxious for a fight. I can hear it in her voice.

She's like, "And you're considering places other than Columbia?"

"Me and Terrell talk about it sometimes. We're gonna room together whatever college we choose."

"Well, Yolanda, I'm all too aware that you and Terrell Daniels have formed some kind of union between yourselves, but you should know that sooner or later you're going to outgrow her friendship."

"I don't think I will, Ma. And I hate it when you say stuff like that about my friends."

"I only say it about Terrell."

"Yeah, and she's my best friend. It's not fair."

"Fair is coincidental, my dear. This is real life—"

"Aw, Christ!" Yogi exclaims. "That is so tired. Any time I talk honest with you, you hand me some canned line."

I lay motionless in the backseat, listening with my eyes closed. Ma's words are spoken slowly. Yogi sounds unsure of whether to retreat, defend, or attack. She'll choose to attack though. Aggression is always safer. She learned that from Ma, though Ma would never admit it. Either way, there won't be any winners. There never is when these two bicker.

Yogi's so easy to bait into an argument that I almost want to speak up and tell her there's no use. But she wants it. They both do. So do I, even though I've heard it all before.

When Dad and Ma argue it's different. It's still ugly, but with Yogi and Ma it's worse 'cause Yogi's really pleading for Ma to respect her the same as she respects Son. But that'll never happen. The degree of love and respect, as well as the amount of attention that Ma gives, changes depending on who she's directing it toward. And that's logical, isn't it? But Yogi just doesn't get it. Sometimes I wish I didn't either, but I do and now I have to accept it, the way Ma acts toward me, the things she expects.

"Why you always have to rate people, Ma? Huh?" Yolanda has turned in her seat to assure that there will be a confrontation. "What gives you the right to rate people with rules only you understand?"

"Everyone knows Terrell's father is a drunk and a sleep-around."

"Big deal. He's only her stepdad."

"It isn't heredity I'm talking about, it's environment. You aren't better because of genes, you're better because we brought you up in surroundings conducive to training children to be responsible adults."

"That's not real life, Ma. It's a cop-out parents use to pick their kids' friends. All that heredity-environment stuff is schoolbook talk."

"What do you think schoolbooks are based on, dear heart?"

"How should I know, dear heart," Yolanda returns smugly, her sarcasm snapping Ma's head from the road like a right hook to the chin.

I prop myself up on my elbow to get a better view. There were things that all of us wanted to say to Ma's face, but didn't have the nerve. One time Yogi said it out loud to me and Son: "You know, sometimes Ma acts like a snotty bitch." Sonny had responded by slapping Yogi's face, as if she had blasphemed or something. It was unreal. It was true too, and that's why Yogi didn't bother kicking Sonny's ass, even though we all knew Yogi could have.

But now, since the stroke, our relationships are shifting and there's the uneasiness of change in the air. Nobody knows what is appropriate to say anymore. Naw, it wouldn't be a nice thing to say it to Ma's face, that she's a snotty bitch. Naw, of course you couldn't say that, not unless everything had changed and there wasn't anyone cooking and cleaning and curfew was suspended cause there wasn't anyone around to enforce it. If there wasn't any heat in the damn house and nobody cared, if nobody lifted a finger to shovel the walk or water the plants, then, well, maybe . . . yeah, hell yeah, you could say whatever the fuck you wanted. If the boat was gonna sink anyhow, rocking it a little really didn't fucking matter anymore.

To hell with it. To hell with giving love and respect and while you were at it, to hell with expecting love and respect in return.

Ma's still steering the car without looking at the road because none of it fucking matters, whether or not we tear through the divider and end up wrapping the car around the trunk of a tree, who gives a shit.

"Why you always gotta rate people, huh? Why do you have to put me against Terrell? To put our family against everyone else? You do it at school, with the neighbors. Always. You always gotta compare."

"How are you going to make choices if you don't compare?" Ma says, and for a brief instant I'm amazed at how quickly our mother has regained her composure. She hasn't exactly sidestepped the question, yet she's answering it on her terms.

And then an example is sure to follow from Mother Clarity.

"You see what's happened to your sister," she continues smoothly, casually turning her attention back to the road. "Sonny made an important decision about getting married instead of going to med school, and she still doesn't know all the ramifications. It should be a lesson—"

"Oh, let's skip the ramifications," Yogi butts in, determined. She's annoyed at not being able to match Ma's self-confidence but she can't give in. She knows giving in would disappoint Ma, and Yogi couldn't bear that.

She says, "You always make out like I'm better 'cause our family's better, but I'm not all of us. Sonny is Sonny and I'm me, no worse no better. Her grades are her grades and mine are mine."

"What's that supposed to mean?"

"It means that just 'cause you and Dad built a house in the suburbs doesn't mean I have to. I might not even want to."

"You'd rather live in the projects?"

"Maybe. But sometimes I feel like if I don't do what you did, then you won't love me. If I'm not a professional, you won't visit me."

"No one's setting goals for you, Yolanda. But you have to recognize the assets you've been given and take advantage of them."

"Which means you'll tell me who I'm supposed to be by the way you're bringing me up."

"Is something wrong with that?"

"That means you're choosing who I'm gonna be instead of me choosing."

"And if you choose, you'll follow after Terrell Daniels?"

"I'm not going to follow anyone; that's the whole point. But why can't I be influenced by people outside of our family? It's not like Terrell is a criminal."

"I didn't say she was. All I'm saying is that her background is displayed in the way she carries herself. And whether you know it or not, you're acting more like her every day. Understand, I'm not blaming Terrell; it's her mother that's—"

"Well, just go ahead and say it then! You think you're better than Mrs. Daniels 'cause she lives off men."

"Listen, the fact of the matter is her first three marriages ended in divorce, and I wouldn't bet against this one ending the same way. What I'm trying to tell you, if you'll put away this childish loyalty, is that children from broken homes tend to lack respect for the correct values. There are things about that family you don't know."

"Maybe," Yolanda says, her eyes so spaced out that I'm certain she's about to go for the throat, "but there are things about our family that aren't so great either. We've got our own drunk waiting for us at home."

I sit all the way up now, waiting for the explosion, but nothing happens. I move to the far corner of the seat to get a look at the side of Ma's face and to my surprise I see hurt instead of anger. It is a distinct kind of hurt, like a physical pain is rippling through her face. I've never seen anyone look this way before. Maybe in a fuzzy dream that I could back out of, but this is all real, like an airbrushed photo under a magnifying glass. It is graphic and unforgettable.

It seems like every day something new is happening that isn't just tearing us apart, but tearing us apart for good. There isn't gonna be any rebuilding either. The scars will run too deep, and anyway, he'll still be a cripple.

That's what Ma's thinking. She's hemmed in with no way out. The look on her face is more than hurt. It might even be fear. She knows Yogi is telling her that it's as good as lost, what she had imagined our family to be. Really, Yogi doesn't have to tell her that at all. Ma recognizes where we're going. But the realization that Yogi has gotten a glimpse of our future means the end is even closer than she thought.

That's what the look on Ma's face says. It's a look that borders on surrender. Carefully I store it in my sanctuary and listen while Yogi hopelessly tries to lessen the pain.

"I'm sorry, Ma. I didn't mean it. But who are we kidding? You know that lately every one of us hates setting foot in that house."

Ma comes back at her quickly, trying to muster some of her typical stubborn arrogance. "I don't see anyone fighting to leave *that* house either."

"Give it a break, will you, Ma? You know what's going on. I know where you've been sleeping lately."

Again Ma is rocked. From behind, her head appears grimly still. She's latched on to the steering wheel with both hands, holding her breath, trying to swallow the sobs of grief. The grief has come to life within her, and along with the fear, she is being beaten into submission.

"Sonny knows it too," Yolanda says quietly. "Dad is—"

"That—is—e—nough." Ma's words are garbled. She's trying to fight off the facts. If nothing else, she's game. "Seems to me you owe us something for the love we've surrounded you with."

"Is this what it boils down to?" Yolanda asks. "Does love really have a price tag?" She's looking out the window, crying. I start to reach for her, but catch myself and search out Ma's attention in the rearview mirror. When she looks at me, she seems surprised I'm even there, as if I'm intruding on something not meant for my ears. She's still watching me, totally ignoring the road. When I begin to mouth the word "Mother," she turns away.

She can't bear to see that the same forces that are destroying her are within me as well. Only difference is, I've embraced the grief and pain and fear. They are my pets. As our family weakens, I will grow stronger.

"Mother," I lean close to her ear, "behold thy son."

c h a p t e r
24

On weekdays Dad has an aide, Mrs. Harewood, a short old lady with leathery skin. Her mouth is pinched and drawn like a lizard's but she lets me follow her around, and oddly enough, she isn't half as smart as she looks.

Weekday mornings she gets to our house about fifteen minutes before we leave for school. That's when I watch her go through Dad's mess. Dad's tough on the aide and usually trails behind her to mess up whatever she cleans up. It's their private little game and the aide never seems to mind. One morning Dad passionately announced that he loved his aide and she cried like a schoolgirl.

Dad can make people get emotional. I think it's 'cause he doesn't give a shit and that probably struck an old bird like Mrs. Harewood as being cavalier. Me, I wasn't too impressed with his dying obsession. "I prefer action," I told him. "If you need any help . . ."

I made the offer over and over and he just laughed 'cause he didn't think I was ready to handle the assignment.

Oh sure, I know what he wants; he doesn't have to say a word. Neither of us has any use for the obvious and we often talk openly about dying and killing in front of Mrs. Harewood. When we do, she hunches her shoulders, pretends not to hear us. Other times she ruefully shakes the dust off her sandals and cross herself when she leaves the library.

Mrs. Harewood is a fascinating lady despite resembling a reptile. In the morning, without fail, she smells of witch hazel, a sanitary aroma that she bears with potent consistency. She claims to be an expert gardener and I've taken her word for it. She said she has most of her success with gardenias and tulips.

Dad loves Mrs. Harewood dearly but says her feet have giant corns on them. He noticed them one afternoon when she was soaking her feet while reading to him from *Foxes' Book of Martyrs*. Dad called it a hideous experience but I kind of envied him, spending his leisure time with such a fine woman.

"Him not so bad today," the aide begins her daily report before Ma can ask. We've just returned home and Mrs. Harewood is waiting for Ma in the living room. Her bags are packed. She doesn't appreciate Ma expecting her to make a difference in our suburban asylum.

"No, no, of course not," Ma says with a pleasant smile. "My husband is never much trouble."

Ma tucks herself neatly into a corner of the couch and eyes Mrs. Harewood as if the woman were a savage. They share a feminine dislike that I can't quite follow except I imagine the aide blames Ma for whatever has sent Dad over the deep end. I sit on the edge of the piano bench to listen to Mrs. Harewood talk. She's from St. Kitts and her singsong accent gives me the peculiar feeling that she's chiding Ma about things neither of them can change.

"Did he eat all his food?"

"All him didn't trow gainst dee wall, him ate."

"His exercises?" Ma asks doubtfully.

The aide shakes her head. Her eyes are sad. They are sadder than the day before.

"He was in the study all day?"

The aide smiles apologetically and nods.

"Did he—"

"Ya mon," she breaks in. "Drinkin 'fore noon. Half dee bottle. Tuesday, me try hidin it but him turned sore bit-ta. Cussin. Yellin like a baby for its meeilk."

Ma rises from her chair, unaware of herself. Her knees buckle as she looks around the living room. She could be considering whether it's still worth anything. She starts up the stairs at a weary angle, her hands thrust down in her coat pockets like stones.

At the time I held a faint hope that seeing her like this would be the worst of it, and I could consider myself lucky, 'cause seeing her pain wasn't exactly ripping me up inside. I'd taken it for granted that she would adjust to whatever happened.

"She's OK," I say.

Ma turns around and sways unsteadily. My voice must sound far away. She appears confused by where it's coming from.

"Is the heat on?" she asks Mrs. Harewood, who has moved to the foot of the stairs to assist Ma in case she misses a step.

"She's OK," I repeat.

In the blink of an eye my mother is blind to the world, her sight glossing over with tears that won't fall. She continues up the stairs and I follow. Without looking back or hearing me, she knows I'm there. I put my hand gently in the small of her back, prodding her on but not rushing her. She wanders down the hall to Yolanda's room and stands frozen for a long moment, unable to knock.

I could be wrong, but I think she's mumbling, "If I don't let go, I can't lose it," and still she won't let the teardrops fall.

"Yogi already left," I say. "I think she went to Terrell's house."

Ma's body sags against the closed door. I move closer. "Yogi's gone."

"Sonny too," she says and looks at me to see if we're both coming to the same conclusion. Her eyes are out of focus. "You see what he's doing, don't you?" she asks.

"Who?" I whisper and widen my eyes.

"Knock it off," she hisses. "You know who. Your father."

"He's probably asleep."

"Is that what he told you to say?"

"You're angry?"

"Should I be?"

"He thinks you're going to have him committed."

"The thought has crossed my mind," she says. "But that isn't something for me to discuss with you."

"Why not? It would matter to me more than it would to Dr. Benjamin. He'd jump at the chance to have Dad committed."

I say these words quickly because she's right, Dad has told me to say them. He's one step ahead of her.

She touches the skin beneath her eyes, over the bridge of her nose. She keeps watching me, trying to decide on what she should accuse me of. There is so much, maybe she can't choose.

"He won't be committed," I tell her. "I won't allow it."

She makes a sound that comes up from the pit of her stomach. I step closer, insistent. "He is God." She shudders and draws away from me.

"He's got a hold over you, doesn't he? He's brainwashing you."

"He's trying to stay out of the nuthouse, Ma. Is something wrong with that? Besides, what'll the neighbors say?"

She doesn't think this is funny. She turns her face. Her forehead is resting against the wall and all her weight is leaning forward. It looks extremely uncomfortable. When I try to step still closer, she stops me.

"Then go to him. Go give praise to your God."

"I will. But he said first I should watch you weep."

Later that night I sit with Dad in the library. He's in a good mood until Ma comes knocking at the door. At first we ignore her like usual, but then Dad says to let her in.

She enters the room with quick, confident steps. Her head is held high and she brushes past me as if I'm not there.

"Leave us," she says. She's standing in front of Dad but she's talking to me. "I want to speak in private with your God."

"No, Georgia," his voice is cold. "If anyone is leaving, it's you."

"I'm not asking him, Your Holiness," she says with contempt. "I'm telling him."

I try to console her by stroking her hair but she slaps my hand away. "You're always telling me how you're only eleven," she turns on me with a burst of anger, "that you're only a child. I suggest you start acting like it before I get my strap and give you a reminder."

"Beating the boy isn't going to solve anything. It's me you want to beat, isn't that so?"

"And you deserve it, though I doubt it would do any good."

Dad motions to me. "Get the camcorder. She's in rare form tonight."

For the last few days he's had me filming him while he gives lectures to an empty room. He's been reciting poetry too, stuff he very well might have made up himself for all the sense it makes. I told him that he was getting overly vain, but he blamed it on the wheelchair. He said being an invalid makes you more self-centered.

I position myself to the left of my parents and gauge the light in the room. Ma has washed her face and her skin looks tight and fresh. She hasn't changed since leaving school and wears a light gray suit jacket and trousers a darker shade of gray. Underneath she has on a black turtleneck. She looks very handsome and I try telling her that but she tells me to shut up.

"What do you want?" Dad cues her and rolls his chair over to the window so she'll follow him. He beckons me over too and shows me just where to stand so I get his good side.

c h a p t e r
25

"You're an ass."

"You didn't come in here to say that, did you?"

"Hey, Dad, I think she's saying it for the record." I have the audio on to go along with the film. "This is gonna make a poignant home movie. Ma, what does poignant mean?"

"Shut up," Ma tells me for the third time.

I zoom in for a close-up.

"Now, what else do you want?" Dad asks.

"The part of you that was promised to me at our wedding."

"Yeah? Well, here it is." He tries to flash her but can't get his pajama bottoms down.

Ma ignores him. "You're taking everything from me, Frank. You're taking things I've earned with my time and energy."

"Like what?"

"Like respect. It isn't right. I'm trying to understand, but

I don't. I know you've spent your career in the field of detecting and treating mental illness—substance abuse, and . . ." She waves her hand to fill in the blanks. "You know the stuff people need help with. If you're researching questions you have, fine. I can live with that."

He laughs.

"Then what's this thing all about? You staying up here, misleading this child. He's my son too and I won't stand for you poisoning his mind against me."

"What me and the boy talk about is none of your business."

"Do you want a divorce?" she asks.

"I don't have time for it. As long we both know our situation, there's no reason for one."

"The absence of mutual love and respect isn't a reason for divorce?"

Dad mugs a silly face to frustrate her. Sometimes his clowning is accompanied by a rendition of "The Battle Hymn of the Republic" or a passage from "The Dark Rivers of Georgia."

"Is that the only reason you don't want a divorce?" she snaps. "Because you don't have time?"

"You didn't think that was a funny face?"

"No, Frank. Why do you insist on hurting me this way?"

Dad winks at the camera. "The little Missus is full of questions tonight, isn't she?"

"Dammit, you answer me." She whirls his chair around to face her.

"If you're hurt, Georgia, why don't you prove it? Why don't you grovel and beg?"

"If you could avoid hurting me," she presses him, "would you? Or is hurting me the whole point of why you've been acting this way?"

"I'm sure this will come as a shock, dearest, but you've become a coincidence. I don't give a damn whether I'm hurting you or not. Now show me a tit, then get the fuck out."

Ma looks at the ceiling and exhales. She rephrases the request slowly and quietly. "If I told you how to make things bearable for me, would you at least try and be helpful?"

"Yeah, yeah! Get to your demands, Counselor!"

"Mitchell says you shouldn't be so thin."

"What does he care?"

"He's your friend."

"Bullshit. He knows I can make or break him, especially since I'm on the way out. Boy, those hospital politicians don't miss a trick."

"What kind of craziness is that?"

"They'll probably have a lottery to see who does my autopsy."

"Frank, that's sick."

"No, I'm sick and my colleagues are the parasites. They'll wanna patronize me as a reminder of who my real friends are. They're just trying to make sure that whatever reorganization takes place favors them. It's the nature of the business."

"I don't believe you."

He laughs. "You think I care what you believe? Now what's your stupid prescription?"

I begin circling them, trying to find a different angle. Dad appreciates this technique while Ma is oblivious to my filming, which makes me feel pointless and small. She's good at doing that.

"How about more eating and less drinking. Maybe that'll curb some of your cynicism."

"Look who's talking. Attila the Hun turned Florence Nightingale."

"And you should use your cane more. Maybe go outdoors every afternoon to get some fresh air. The doctor says you should be getting some flexibility back if you'll work at it."

"Second-rate physicians always put the burden of recovery on the patient so they won't feel guilty if the rehab goes sour."

"But you haven't even tried the rehab. Mrs. Harewood says you never do your exercises, you ignore your diet . . ."

"Mrs. Harewood." Dad gives me a prim smile and sighs dreamily. "I think I'll pick her a passel of poseys. You know we're going steady, Mrs. Harewood and I."

". . . you don't take your medication," Ma keeps after him. "It would mean so much to me if I saw progress."

"Why?"

"Because you could be functional, maybe even resume your practice."

He reaches for the bottle, but she beats him to it. "No! You owe me," she says. "At the very least, you owe me an explanation. I made an investment in you, Frank Roberts. The past three decades of my life I invested."

"It's out of our hands, Georgia. It's over. I'm trying to break this to you as easy as I can, but you've got to look at it with your head and not your heart."

"Believe me, buster, I passed that stage long ago. You've already broken my heart."

"Very nice," Dad applauds and motions for me to stand on top of the desk so I could do the skycam routine. He clears his voice and takes Ma's hand.

"Don't you see," he's speaking gently. "You're upholding this moral code that people imagine they live by. You'd like to believe that the vows we made are more than they are. But they're just words. Situations cancel out words."

"Frank, please don't get philosophical."

"No, no. I've given this serious thought. You mentioned love and respect earlier. Those are just buzzwords. You say "love" or "respect" and more authority is implied than actually exists. The theory is that if mutual love and respect are present, then peace and satisfaction will come as a reward. However good that might sound, it's a lie. Love and respect are useful only when people are joined in an effort to reach social and economic goals."

He hesitates, uncertain. He isn't bullshitting anymore. This is what he traded his soul and his marriage for: a wild notion that his death will be worth more than his life. "Where was that," he mumbles distractedly, pulling at a piece of paper on the desk. "You're standing on it, Randall." He pounds down on my big toe. I kick the sheet from under my sneaker. The two words are scrawled in giant letters.

LOVE. RESPECT.

There's an involuntary twitch in Dad's eye. He's holding the pencil awkwardly in his left hand between his third and fourth fingers. I site Ma in the lens. There's pity in her eyes and I almost make the joke about what they do with lame horses, but I don't think she'd appreciate the humor right about now.

"There," he points at it several times. "That's where we are." He underlines. "There!"

He looks up at her, but she only sighs. "I'm losing patience with this, Frank. You go around showing this chicken scratch to people, and they'll send you off to the funny farm. And I'm not so sure it isn't what you need."

"You're not giving me a chance." Now he's the one pleading. "Listen. Love and respect are spiritual in nature, just like peace and satisfaction. And I defy you to show me an instance where people have attained spiritual contentment by using something else that's spiritual. That's why religion is so popular. It's a placebo. People think they can attain spiritual contentment when all they're getting is hope. I'll grant you that sometimes people can take a tangible attribute like physical strength or beauty and find a spiritual asset like pride. But that's a lie too because physical strength and beauty fade. A tangible asset like physical strength or beauty can also lead to material acquisitions like finances, but again, that acquisition is fleeting. But to start with a spiritual quality and expect to attain anything other than material goals, or perhaps social status, is crazy. Spiritual fulfillment can only be gained through situations. Situations, like the one we're facing now, you don't have to reach for those. They aren't dependent on anything else and they come to you whether you want them to or not. That's because they come from God. It's His way of communing with His select children. Don't you see, we've been selected."

He looks at her hopefully but sees she doesn't get it. I've stopped trying myself. Some of the things he says, you'd need to share space with him in his own little world in order to understand. Just when I think he's about to make sense, he turns the screw and gets more obscure. That's how he leads me. But Ma, she's about done with him.

"Look at the Bible," Dad says. "Look at the torturous crucible Job had to endure before he found true happiness. The Old Testament is full of prophets who were introverts and outcasts, sleeping out in the wilderness, eating locusts and honey. You see, they had to fall on the rock and be broken, just as I have. They had to be confronted by situations that appeared insurmountable."

He lets go of her hand. His face is uplifted, his eyes blank and unseeing. He seems raptly attentive to what he's saying.

"Situations have weight," he says gravely, "and sometimes they are beyond our control. 'Thou art worthy, O Lord, to receive glory and honor and power: for Thou has created all things, and for Thy pleasure they are and were created.' You see?"

"No. No, Frank, the only thing I see is that it's hopeless and I'm not going to patronize you any further. This is absolute stupidity and you are a fool. I don't care how you try and make it sound like a reasonable conclusion, it's stupid. This isn't the wilderness, Frank, it's our library. And you aren't a prophet, you're my husband. You're up here thinking of ways to make a joke of our marriage, and all the way home I'm defending you to Yolanda. Remember her? One of the children you want to abandon, one of the daughters you wish you never had."

She puts her hands on the armrest of either side of his chair and rolls him backward until he hits the wall. I follow them, hovering just over Ma's left shoulder.

"You have insulted me," she explodes, "in front of the son I bore for you. You want to all but leave me," she lists by holding up a finger. "You want to insult me," she holds up another. "You want to talk to me any kind of way when and if you bother talking to me at all. You want to be foul-mouthed and inconsiderate."

She stomps her foot. "Whether you like it or not, I made a deal with you. You can't back out of it just like that. You can't hand me some half-baked tale about spirituality and situations and quote the Bible with your breath reeking of liquor and expect me to listen and be satisfied."

She mimicks a sweet voice to ridicule him. "Oh, sure, Frank, I get it. You found out you're not Jesus Christ so you're settling for plain old masochistic. Sure, that's it. We're mortal so we're not going to live forever so it's just fine if you want to become a drunk and bathe once a week and frighten and embarrass the whole family. After all these years," she booms, "you must know me a little better than that."

He tries to say something now, to make a concession per-haps, but she hushes him with a clap of her hand. "I didn't need you thirty-one years ago. I didn't need a husband to be a success. You told me you needed me. And nothing's changed, sweetheart, you still need me. You don't want sympathy? Fine. I won't give you any. You don't deserve it. And furthermore, you don't deserve me. You never did. Only God knows what my options would have been by now if I'd never seen your face."

"Well now, baby, don't you waste any more time on me,"

Dad says nastily. "Why don't you try running for fucking mayor?"

"Maybe I will," she snaps back at him. "But whatever I do won't be any of your business."

"Are you done?"

She stands for a moment to speculate, her hands on her hips. "Yeah Frank, I think that just about covers it."

He nods and smiles and quotes the self-righteous accusation of betrayal. "What you do," he says innocently, "do quickly."

"Enough said." She pauses a moment, her feet spaced for balance, and slaps his face as hard as she can. Twice she slaps him, with the front of her hand and the back, then turns and leaves the room.

chapter
26

Give it some thought, that's what I did. I listened to the tape of my parents' argument three times early the next morning and came to the conclusion that I was adopted. It could be worse. I coulda been abandoned, left in the wilds of New Delhi to suckle an orangutan during the monsoon season. But I was fortunate. I couldn't complain too much. Even a charmed life had its drawbacks, and I certainly experienced a few.

I didn't understand what happened that night in the library. It was funny while it was going on, but afterward the whole episode gave me a headache. My parents made a pact right in front of my face, discussed the terms, stated their grievances, and none of it added up.

Don't get me wrong. It was their choice. Dad might've forced her hand, but not much. She didn't hesitate when it came time to questioning his backbone. By my scorecard, I'd say she won the fight on points.

Still, there was a lot they were forgetting about.

There was this time, back when I was maybe seven and Dad had decided to take us on this trip cross-country to see a miniature village built with pebbles out in the Arizona desert. Damn near three days we were on the road 'cause Dad was driving at like forty-five miles per hour, and me, being an insomniac, I couldn't sleep during the whole trip. But he and Ma were having a grand time while me, Son, and Yogi got saddle sores from sitting so long. We didn't stop at a hotel either, just straight road with a few stops for gas and to use the can or eat. It was unbelievable, seeing my parents snuggled up in the front seat, singing along with the songs on the radio.

I didn't dream that up. It happened. So now, these four years later, I ask the bastard point-blank: "Who was kidding who?"

It's the weekend, Saturday afternoon, and Dad's a quarter of the way into a liter of Jack.

"People make mistakes, Randall."

"A mistake is when you do someting wrong."

"No. A mistake is when you aren't true to yourself. I thought it would mean a lot to her. She thought it would mean a lot to me. Each of us was doing it for the other's benefit. It was insincere, self-serving, and presumptuous."

"So were you lying to her all those years? She's my ma; I got a right to know."

"Don't tell me about your rights."

"You ever read her diary?" I ask.

"No. You?"

"Yeah." I hand it to him. "I want you to read something. I want you to read what she wrote about you last night after she gangster-slapped you. She wrote it as if you were already dead."

December 7

He waved bye-bye. What was I supposed to do? Nothing. There was nothing for me to do but cut my losses and get out. Already it's sunk in. Good. The quicker I let go of it, the better.

The small silly things I will miss the most, and didn't that man have plenty of those? Eccentricities you could call them, but they were more like phobias and neuroses. He was far too logical and organized, so he always had to have an outlet, someplace to misplace his passion, a place in his head where nothing had to make sense.

He liked all vegetables but not when they were mixed. The same was true with fruits and ice cream, they had to be kept separate. He didn't want chunks of anything foreign in his ice cream, and only cereal, either Corn or Wheat Chex, in his morning milk. I bought him a silk shirt once that broke him out in hives. My mink coat made him sneeze. In summer he slept with one arm hanging off the side of the bed. In winter he slept on his stomach with both arms tucked awkwardly beneath him. He was a poor yet enthusiastic fisherman and could never be convinced that his robust enthusiasm was what scared the fish away. Frank fished for bass in a canoe on a stocked pond as if he were on a forty-foot boat in the middle of the ocean reeling in a great white.

He hated television movies. He didn't like movies you paid to go see either. He only tolerated performed drama when it was onstage and one of his children was participating and he could take a million photos of them in costume. The only thing he watched on television was the news, although he preferred radio to television and print to radio. He seldom read books for entertainment, only information. He had dressed in the same style for the three decades I'd known him, a preference for the conservative. He liked grays with burgundy and was square-shoulderedly handsome in pinstripes. He looked at ease in whatever he wore and his clothes weren't the first thing anyone would notice about him. He liked soft cotton to lounge around the house in, and pullover sweaters. On workdays he tied a bulky, unattractive necktie that he kept loosened. His children bought him Bermuda shorts one year that he never wore because he thought his legs were too skinny.

Along with his parents, I was the only person to ever see his legs. When the family went to the beach, he would embarrass the kids by wearing sweatpants. He could not swim. He was perpetually obsessed with the size of his stomach and did a nightly set of one hundred sit-ups. He signed up for a karate course once but never found the time to attend. He tried learning yoga from a book but decided he meditated best while smoking a cigar and looking out the window.

He had a wonderful and timely sense of humor. I always envied his ability to make people happy and he seemed ever alert for the right moment to make a fool of himself for the benefit of someone who needed a reason to smile. He was insightful and bright, and frank when he needed to be. His anger was as bold as it was infrequent, though he never stayed angry long. He was an accomplished storyteller and could hold the children's attention even when they were too young to understand what he was saying.

When we first married, I hoarded him shamelessly. That was why we waited so long before having kids. For six years I had him all to myself. After both our careers blossomed and hosting or attending dinner parties was an unavoidable social function, we would often play games that the other people present were aware of but couldn't make sense of. It was a rude thing to do, but I always initiated the games because I wanted everyone to know that a portion of him was exclusively mine. We knew each other's body language so well that we rarely lost at bridge.

His religion was a private source of strength to him. Every night after the sit-ups, he went to the library to pray. His work was also private. There was a connection between the two and he humbly awarded his successes to God. Twice I shared failure with him, the woman who committed suicide and a premature baby he had delivered and helped hold on to life for three months before it died. He clearly saw his mission as upgrading the quality of life for the distressed and protecting the sick from death. For the sake of all his patients, he had fought death.

Dad finished the entry. He looked at me. No remorse. I took the journal and poured him up another glass of Jack.

c h a p t e r
27

We had company today, E. Hazzard. Dad would tell you the invitation was my idea but it wasn't. I just egged him on, which might not have been such a smart thing to do, seeing how his brain's been skipping beats. He wanted to start the invitation with "Dear Homewrecker."

"Hey, Dad—"

"You just write it."

"Sure," I tell him and tone it down a little.

Earlier today Ma almost belted him again. I called her off, sort of. She was telling him he couldn't have company cause he smelled and Dad resented it.

"We'll just air the place out a little." I wrapped him in a blanket. "I can take you for a spin."

"I can't be seen in broad daylight," he balked.

"Why not?"

"Your father is vain, Randall. About what, no one knows."

At one-thirty that Sunday afternoon the gym teacher shows up and we've got him right where we want him, up in the library. We've got the NFL on CBS, Summerall and Madden, and Dad's wearing a smoking jacket. Something he had me pull out of the garage. Took me half the night to find it, digging through his collection. He's been nuts for longer than I thought.

"Don't let the doorknob . . ." Dad says to Ma. She's standing at the door, pretending to be interested in watching the Jets blow another one.

". . . a double for me," he says to Eric, "and a cup of tea for Randall."

"He the houseboy, Dad?"

"Certainly is. You're out of a job."

"But can you trust him with the important stuff?"

Dad looks at Hazzard, who is being safe, acting as though it's a gag. It would take this guy a millennium to get tense. When Dad asked him had he ever been scared, Eric mentioned tearing up both knees playing Pop Warner. Dad called him a puppy and the three of us smiled about that too.

"Had you seen my father before he went lame," I ask.

"No," Dad says, luring the teacher.

"Sure I did, Dr. Roberts. At a barbecue."

"And the azure sky," I put in.

Eric looks at me and he isn't smiling anymore. I'm wearing shoe-black today, horizontal streaks under my eyes.

"Does Stacy only suck chin," I ask.

Hazzard does a doubletake at me, then stares with astonishment at Dad.

"Be nice, Randall." Dad smiles at me, gently patting my head, but I know better. "It so seldom we have guests anymore," my father says.

"Hey, Mr. Hazzard, my Dad thinks he's a hoot. Check out the jacket."

"If you don't mind my saying," this is Eric giving me a

lecture, "it isn't nice, the way you're talking to your father. A young man like you—"

"Skip it," Dad gets angry, quickly. We're facing the TV console, the three of us sitting across in a row with Dad in the middle. I've never been happier.

"I'll father my own boy," Dad says. "Can you?"

Ma silently slips out the door, but not too far away.

"Then tell me this," Dad says to Hazzard, "your résumé, I've seen it. Makes me wonder how you got here."

I ignore the cue and let it simmer. Guys like Hazzard, knowledge will show on their face, like a kid at a magic show. He's like, "Maybe I should—"

"Oh, no. You just sit there."

"No, no, of course not," I pipe in and hand him another beer, that dark shit that looks like diarrhea. "I wish you were my brother, don't you, Dad? Don't you wish that Eric was your boy too?"

"You know, son, I do." He takes Eric's hand. "Georgia miscarried once—"

"He's lying," I whisper to Eric, but Dad lifts his hand for silence. There's disgust in the gym teacher's shrinking smile. Dad's maybe a little bit stupid today. He says, "Being a doctor, I can't afford to be squeamish, but you can see the worst shit in OR."

"I can imagine."

"And why are you here then? Would you like to see it, blood on the floor of an operating room."

"Not really—"

"Not really," I jump at the guest with my voice. I've put on a Dodger's cap, the one I took from his trailer. Four even lines crease his forehead.

"Well, at least that's a start." Dad winks at me.

"Pardon?"

"My father asks, 'Then why are you here?' and I'm supposed to say, 'love.' "

"I don't get it," Eric shrugs and checks his watch. He's been losing interest since Ma left the room.

"Want me to go get her?" I kneel at Dad's feet. "Huh, Eric. Want me to?"

"Get who," Eric asks.

"My Mom."

His neck perks up as though he just spotted trouble. His shoulders spread wider. He's sitting upright in his chair, waiting to see if Dad even hears me. The three of us wait until Eric sees we'll wait all day.

"No," he answers finally. "What for?"

I shrug.

I wouldn't be surprised if she's already put the seed in his head. I could just see it, Ma telling him that he'll get some if he'll just humor Dad about it. Lately she hasn't been saying much, but anything she says has got a needle. She's been calling Eric "Harold," even though Dad and I have corrected her a half-dozen times.

"Randall said love brought you here."

"I love a good time," Eric tries.

"And are we having that yet, a good time?"

Eric makes a face. He looks at me, still down at Dad's feet.

"But Eric wants more fun," I grin. "Don't you, Eric?"

He doesn't even attempt an answer. He knows I'm not drunk. I was probably the kinda of kid he slapped around when he was eleven. "You'll have your chance," I tell him. He remains motionless, his eyes putting me together as a piece of my family.

"I don't get scared either," I keep after him. "But you, I could scare you, same as Yogi scares you. I think she's got something for you, Yogi does."

"Now wait a second, Doctor. I think you need to rein your son in. My old man hits the bottle too," he stands to leave, "but he'd bust me when I needed it."

"What did you say?"

"I'll get your coat," I offer and circle behind the teacher. Dad has rolled himself backward, all the way to the wall, getting himself revved up to make a charge at the gym teacher. He does it to Mrs. Harewood all the time, chases her around the room until she climbs up on a chair. Eric isn't going to run though. He's never learned to run away, and it will cost him, sooner or later. Just as I dip behind his knees to clip him, Ma's gotta barge in to ruin the prank.

"This will not do!"

"Then take him," Dad waves her off. "We're finished. You just see to it that he understands this is a cash sell. No checks or credit cards."

"What's the price, Dad?"

"I'll let you decide."

After they leave the room, Dad unlatches the window and throws the oval glass open. A gust of wind meets our faces as we peer out at the gym teacher in the driveway. Ma is with him, she's got him by the arm and he's limping.

"Have her home by midnight," Dad yells, "or she'll turn into a pumpkin."

c h a p t e r
28

It's Saturday night and I am a hostage to this place, the time, these people.

It's his doing, Dad's, and he isn't even here to endure the color and flash of RollerDome Duplex, a skating joint that the senior class at Pinelawn has rented out for their Christmas party.

They got it all at the RollerDome: a rotating strobe overlooking a rink that includes an incline lap on the outside. The incline is definitely the Boss. It's got a slope that damn near free-falls, about twice as mean as the angle skateboarders do, guaranteed. Only the hotshot skaters are trying it, the ones who ignore the knee and elbow pads. Them guys, the daredevils, they'll maintain the needed speed to stay on top of the curve and wouldn't brake even for a brick wall. You're supposed to wear a helmet when you're on the incline, but Yogi's been whipping around it completely out of control, challenging anybody who thinks they can keep up.

She's got that look in her eyes that says she could go for a bash right about now, a fight with any willing body, preferably a guy. She's gotten punched out by guys plenty of times 'cause she'll keep after them till they got no choice.

Twice last summer she got into scraps at the Coed Hard Court Tournament in Sayville. First she takes a swing at a Jewish guy in the handball semis. This Jewish guy, he's just a spectator, he was on the sidelines cheering for his brother and Yogi takes offense. She took two swings at him, the first being your tactful excuse-me-while-I-stretch sucker punch; then she took a second punch when she saw she'd hit him square the first time. It's addictive, I guess.

Only reason she wasn't disqualified is 'cause a buncha white people were running the competition and they were paranoid about appearing prejudiced against anybody black, especially a female. But when Yogi took a poke at the referee during the final, they gave her the boot. Who's gonna blame 'em for not inviting her back. I've tried telling her a million different times, but as far as she's concerned, adrenaline's got no use except for fighting.

Tonight though, I envy her. Her frustration is mine as well. Just watching her tearing around the rink eases me. She won't lose her edge; Yogi won't fall, not my sister. She can come as close as she wants to the nastiest spill, and still she keeps her feet, pirouettes in the air, and lands in perfect position to do that gliding swizzel-stick you can only manage on single blades.

Terrell's got on the regular four-wheeled skates 'cause she can't play in a league with Yolanda tonight, not when Yogi's this reckless. Terrell's down for trouble only when it's somebody else taking the risks; she'd never gamble on injuring her own body, and that makes perfect sense, don't it?

Here Yogi comes flyin by. You can just about hear her motor rev. Without a ceiling on this place she'd be airborne.

As it is she's doing the laps twice as fast as anybody else, going backward when she feels like it. Or sometimes when she's coming off the peak turn, the highest one at the far end, she'll do her crossovers, then swoop down on an un-suspecting classmate to cut them off. They think it's fun and games, but she's serious. If she busts somebody's ass to-night, she won't be apologizing.

I've always known Terrell's mom was a bitch, I just didn't know she was ignorant too. Cruelty that comes out of ig-norance is ugly 'cause it's pathetic. Everybody gets mud-died by it, including the person being cruel.

I'm sitting in the lounge that's partitioned by a glass wall so that the chaperons can see the kids skating but not hear the noise. The lounge is lit in blue light with a cigarette machine in the corner and a row of video games. Along the opposite wall is a bar for the adults, and somehow, after all these years, it's become evident that Ms. Daniels couldn't pass a GED if her life depended on it.

There's a cheap, aluminum brightness in her expression that has humbled my mother. It's not shame I see in Ma's posture, but she's close to it. Shame is something she'll have to learn, what with the whole neighborhood in on *it* by now, that Dad came back from the hospital nowhere near the same guy he was when he went in.

After the monthly block association meeting last week, I saw a group of neighbors standing out on the sidewalk across from our house, looking up at the oval window of our library. They know he's up there and won't come down to see anyone. Next they're expecting the guys in white suits to come to cart him off kicking and screaming, harnessed in a straitjacket and muzzle.

Tonight Ms. Daniels has the appearance of a vulture bid-ing its time, anxiously preparing herself to pick over the remains of my parents' marriage. Is this a natural fact un-derstood only by adults: that marriage is a war of tolerance, a test of will, a matter of stamina? In the past, Ma has never missed an opportunity to remind Ms. Daniels that she's a three-time loser at the game, so I suppose she's got it coming.

Ms. Daniels sips her bottled mineral water through a straw, tilts her head and makes a face, as if something has occurred to her (doubtful), then starts to say something but tactfully decides against it. Uncle Benji's at the table with the two women. He's drinking a Fresca with crushed ice. Ma's not having anything. She hasn't even taken off her coat, her mouth a straight line.

Once more something's occurred to Ms. Daniels, or maybe she's got the hiccups. You wouldn't say she's an ugly woman though her head is oversize in comparison to her body, and I think her hair is rebelling against the dye job she's laid on it: a sort of metallic black that glints with the suggestion of halloween blue. From the neck down she's constantly on display. Her attire for this outing is a tight V neck and spandex cycling pants.

"Have you considered sending Frank away to one of those mountain resorts in Vermont?" she asks, tugging at her bra strap. "I saw it on 'Days of Our Lives' once when Dr. Hammerstein had these impotency problems after breaking his collarbone while rescuing his neighbor's cat from a tree limb. It was all in his head, not being able to get it up."

It's a dumb enough remark to ignore, but she's made the same suggestion three times in the last half hour, the same little story about the hammerless doctor. She's so desperate to make insults, she's repeating herself.

"Filona," Uncle Benji says, exasperated, and a little ticked off that he's gotta share Ma's company with a gaudy dingbat. "Your suggestion was, and still is, totally inappropriate."

By the way, Filona is Ms. Daniels's first name, of which I've been trying not to mention that 'cause it has that sound to it, like I gotta give some sorta explanation. Anyhow, Uncle Benji's been intervening on Ma's behalf, trying to keep sweet Filona off her ass. He goes, "I should think that any suggestion you might dream up has already been considered and rejected."

"It's only that the mind and the body are so closely related," Ms. Daniels chirps, batting her eyelashes. "And although I don't recall that Frank was ever a terribly vigorous man—"

Without a word Ma stops Ms. Daniels in midsentence. From my angle I can't catch the look in my mother's eyes but it immediately brings the bullshit to a halt.

I meander across the lounge to see what's happening over there. The age group is a bit younger, though the crimes are similar. As far as I'm concerned, they all deserve to be pardoned, even Filona Daniels. They're unaware of being hostages, but they are, and you can't blame a hostage for crimes committed while in the midst of a crisis.

There are sixteen shopping days left before Christmas and Sonny is in a tizzy about her marriage. Mind you, she's been witness to what's been going on in our house so we won't waste any pity on her.

All night she's been bending Stacy Rodriguez's ear about her own little screwed-up marriage. Seems Gil's been more concerned with getting ahead on his job than spending time with Son. Stacy's trying to explain to Sonny that men are more concerned with what they want than with what they have. Sonny doesn't follow though. I guess she was expecting Gil to continue to passionately court her even after they were married.

Stacy isn't condescending with her explanation. She's drinking rum and Coke and is close to getting shit-faced. Quite naturally she looks stunning. I keep trying to get her to talk to me, but she only winks. We had a brief conversation about fabric in the car on our way over to the rink. Enlightening, yet not quite as satisfying as seeing her naked.

There are a few others with Stacy and Son, mostly people I don't know. The only ones I recognize are Burt Hopkins, who teaches biology, and the guy named Stan Lapari, who I don't know what he teaches. All the other faculty present tonight are strangers to me and more than likely they will remain strangers. Being hired at Pinelawn High is the same as being placed in the endangered species category.

Ma's got a reputation for firing teachers. She even compiled a list of their names, a reminder to watch her back. It wouldn't surprise me if handing somebody a pink slip actually gets her off. She keeps the list of names, and the reasons for dismissal, in a document on our family computer in the library. Supposedly the document is safeguarded by a password to keep prying eyes from minding her business. You'd think she'd know better than to try to keep secrets. But to be honest, I wouldn't have paid the document any mind if she hadn't safeguarded the stupid thing. It's sorta funny and it's sorta perverted too, the way she formats this document the same as the obituary page in *Newsday*. Talk about a God complex. I got two-thirds of the Trinity as parents and believe me when I say, it ain't such a nice thing.

This year's crew of teachers is young, but E. Hazzard is the only one worth noticing. He's here too, or did I mention that he's been standing up along the bar for the last half hour, equally spaced between Ma's table and Stacy's. He's turned in Ma's direction though. Has been all night, yet it's taken me till now to trace her eyes back to him. She could be staring just beyond him—that's if it were really up to her. Then again, if it was up to her she wouldn't even be here. Neither of us would.

c h a p t e r
29

It's not a bad thing to have only a one-voice conscience, if only I could be sure Dad knows what he's doing. Shouldn't there be two voices though, one weighted against the other? What if my one voice is schizo? That might work.

My father is selfish. Before we left for the rink, he had me bring Ma up to the library for another visit.

"You fuck him yet?"

"Fuck him who?" Ma was expressionless. She glanced at me. I'd heard her use the word a few times in phone conversations.

Dad said, "It was a Monday, the first time, me and you."

"I remember."

"You've always been at your best on Mondays."

"No, Frank. You were always at your best on Mondays. I let you lead. I didn't want to embarrass you."

Dad laughed. "Well, at least we both got something out

of it." He looks at me. So does Ma. She smooths her hand over my eyebrow.

"I love you," I tell her.

"I know."

"And you love me, and I love Dad. Can't we make it a complete circle and leave this other business?"

Ma paused, then decided to ignore the question. She couldn't bring herself to say it was out of her hands, but it was. She was like me, doing what he wanted 'cause she loved him. That was what I preferred to think.

"Then it's Monday," she told Dad. "And my choices are . . ."

I looked from one to the other. These were serious negotiations. "Wait a second," I said, "you aren't really talking about what I think you're talking about."

Ma said, "No, of course not, Randall. We aren't talking about anything you would understand."

"I don't get it, Dad. You said you wouldn't keep secrets from me. You said we were one."

"And I said your mother was the person who joined us."

"Yeah, but that don't mean you can keep secrets with her and not let me in on it."

"Shut up," Ma said simply, and turned to Dad. "My choices, Frank. Give me my choices and we can get this over with as quickly as possible."

"Mitchell or the other fellow. The tall one."

"I know lots of tall men."

"Are there any you'd like to—"

"Fuck? No. But I'm flexible to my husband's preference."

"Details, baby, details. I can't be expected to fill in all the blanks. You choose, and when it's done, you'll tell me all about it, right?"

"So be it. Come along, Randall."

———

My old man. You should see him. I should draw you a picture of him, slumped over in his wheelchair in the study, tediously cleaning the dirt from his nails.

One afternoon I asked him, "Why don't you cut them?" He just grunted.

I see him every day, watch him intently, but he won't see me when I'm trying to make sense of his fury, the anger that fires up in him from time to time when he shouts at me to go to my room where I huddle behind my door to listen to the yelping cries coming from the library. He was yelling so loud one morning that the mailman called the cops; thought we were torturing somebody.

When the cops showed I don't think Ma said a single word to them. She let them in and let Yogi explain. That seemed to tell the whole story, told the coppers all they needed to know and then some. "His wife don't want nothing to do with this guy," I heard one whisper when I followed them back out to the squad car.

"Can you blame her?" the other one chuckled.

Sure, why not? Let somebody else handle that problem; it was out of their universe. At least they knew to leave well enough alone. They won't be learning any lessons from this house. They've got other responsibilities. They aren't hostages, stuck in a place called the RollerDome.

Ma has made the slightest signal to E. Hazzard standing in front of the bar in the lounge of the RollerDame skating facility. She didn't even tell him what kind of soda she wanted. It doesn't matter. She just wants to bring him closer to her and Eric doesn't waste any time approaching.

He hands her the soda then notices that Ma's taken her coat off and put it in the fourth chair at the table. There's no place for him to sit. I can sense the expression of embarrassment on the gym teacher's face just from the look of

satisfaction Uncle Benji is wearing. What a jackass. He probably figures it's his job to fetch things for Ma.

Yogi comes rolling into the lounge and sits at the table in
the corner. I bring her over a Snickers. She's been alternating
between coffee, chocolate, and Coca-Cola. She's wired to the
gills.

"Have you and Terrell tailed this guy Hazzard lately?"

Yogi undoes her skates and starts massaging the arch of
her left foot. "Who says we ever did?"

"He did."

"How do you know?"

"I mistakenly overheard him talking about it."

Yogi shrugs. "Tailing him wasn't my idea anyway. Terrell's the one interested."

"So am I. You should be too."

She takes a bite of the candy. "Go on."

"Monday. Follow him Monday."

"I don't like the mothafucka, so why should I bother following him?"

I wait a second, peer into her eyes. If her choice of words
means she's figured it out, that's cool too. But she's not giving that away. Everybody's got their little secrets, but it's
no secret E. Hazzard digs Ma. All the male teachers do,
especially the young ones.

"You gonna do it or not?"

"Yeah. And when I do, how does it end up?"

"Can you take him?"

"How do you mean?"

"Hurt him. Cut him maybe. Do him the same as you're
supposed to do that kitten."

"If I got reason, I can take anybody."

"You'll have to be quick. And strong. He's no wimp. He's
huge."

"I got eyes, I can see. But if he don't give me reason, I'm
not touching him."

"Don't worry. Come Monday he'll give you plenty reason."

"Says who?"

"Does it matter?"

"Says Dad? Is this coming from him, 'cause if it is, the least he could do is speak to me about it."

"Naw. This is for us to take care of. This is between me, you, and the mothafucka."

c h a p t e r
30

Sonny stops by late Sunday night. The house is still and quiet and I haven't seen anyone all day. Dad's in the library agonizing over one of his speeches titled "Misplaced Aggression: The Fuel to DeEvolution." He can't quite get it right and it's put him in a royal blue funk. Yogi is home too with her door shut.

I'm reading my Bible when Son shows up. She's here to see Ma.

"I don't know where she is," I tell her. "Probably over at the school, but you can visit with me instead." I pull her by the arm toward the stairs. "Or do you gotta rush home to that guy?"

"Gil's out of town on business again."

"He a brownnose."

"No," she laughs. "He's just getting ahead."

"So then how come you can't stay if he ain't home anyhow." I've got her about halfway up the stairs.

"Looks like I don't have a choice in the matter," she smiles. She's acting as though things are the same, and I don't want to shake her loose from the notion until I get her to my room.

I dive onto my bed and open up my Bible to where I was reading. Even when she isn't interested in what I'm doing, Sonny always pretends to be.

"Lookit," I show her my new King James version. The cover is made of old leather with gold lettering. In the New Testament, every time Jesus says something it's written in red.

"That's Dad's, isn't it?"

"He gave it to me."

"And you're reading it for a project in school?"

"No. Dad said I should. He said there were some pretty good stories in it and I was probably old enough to understand 'em."

Sonny moves closer. "How far have you gotten?"

"To the time when God sent down the angel of death on the Egyptians to kill the firstborn. You know that one?"

She nods. "But you're going to tell it to me anyway." She gives me a tired smile and slumps into the chair next to the bed.

"What happened was the Israelites were slaves to the Egyptians and God didn't like that. So he did all these miracles to make the Egyptians let the Israelites go. The Egyptians didn't want to let 'em go, so God planned to have the firstborn of every family murdered. Only thing was, he had to make a way for the angel of death to know whose kid to murder. So he goes to the Israelites and tells 'em to wipe lamb's blood on the doorpost so the angel wouldn't kill their oldest kid, just the Egyptians'. That's pretty wild, ain't it?"

"Yeah, it is."

"If our family lived back then, you woulda got killed by

the angel of death, Son. Our family woulda been Egyptian 'cause they're black. The Israelites were Jewish.''

She moves onto the edge of the bed and I position myself to watch her, moving only when she does. I feel composed. Controlling Son isn't anything new. Everyone controls her.

"When did Dad tell you to start reading the Bible?"

"The other day."

"You talked to Dad the other day?"

"Sure."

I zone my eyes into her mouth to anticipate her words as they come to her lips, calculating what I might say next to pull her even farther. "I talk to him every day," I say, watching her mouth.

"Does he eat his meals with the family?" She already knows. I've heard her and Ma discussing Dad.

"Nobody eats together," I answer her slowly. "I never see Ma eat at all. She just cooks, and she don't even do that lately." I put a bookmark in the Bible and close it. I'm staring into her eyes. There is no reason for her to be frightened, but she has grown careful of me. It's taken only five minutes to get her to this point. I had expected it to take longer.

I've always been careful of everyone, at first because I was shy, and then because I found that when you leave gaps in a conversation, it makes people uncomfortable. That's when they usually speak out of turn and mention things they hadn't planned on. It's passive aggression, a rough con. Like right now, I've taken Sonny's tongue with my silence. She's looking at me instead of where I'm taking her.

She glances at the Bible, then at my hand next to it. I let her picture it good, and smile, then open up to tell her something.

"Wanna hear about this dream I had the other night?"

"OK. But not a long one." She kicks off her shoes and puts her feet up on the bed. We're side by side, our backs resting against the headboard.

"Well, it was one of them dreams that seems real 'cause

it takes place in a place you been before." I pull a poster from behind the dresser and handed it to her, the sketch of a mountainside under fog.

I had learned to draw by watching Son when I was real small. She would draw mindless patterns or race cars in motion or physiques. She'd done this to occupy me when I was bored, or when Yogi had beat me up and I'd be crying and stuff. She could draw anything I wanted with a sweeping wide motion of her hand and quick, deep-penciled curls to fill out a detail. When she drew, I saw her face mirror the touch of the pencil on the paper.

"Most of my new drawings are in pencil but sometimes I use the charcoal you got me. I ain't too good with it yet."

"It'll come." She looks at the drawing of the mountainside. She's never come out and said it when I draw something really lousy, but I can always tell if she likes it by how much time she takes to look it over.

She points to where the mountain flattens out to a landing. "Good definition. Everything's relative."

"I used a number 3 pencil on just about everything else except right there," I explain. "That's how I got it to look like that. Plus, I turned the pencil sideways." I move her hand across the poster, lightly skimming it to show her the stroke. "Then I smudged it a little right here."

"I see. The rock has texture. Good. Did someone teach you that?"

"Probably. You recognize the mountain?"

"Should I?"

"It's the mountain we drove up a long time ago. We were way up in the air and it was cold and misty and our ears kept popping."

"Mount Washington. But how do you remember? You were a baby."

"I wasn't never a baby."

"Yeah, you were. You couldn't even walk or talk yet."

"But I could see." I take the poster and put it behind my

desk with several others. "Anyway, that's where this dream happened, except this time I was by myself. It was real windy and I saw myself getting carried by the wind, lifted off the ground by a gust of air, and I flew through the air about twenty feet to the edge of a cliff."

I wait to see if she wants to hear more. "You felt yourself fly or you saw it?" she asks, as if it actually matters to her.

I think about it for a second. I hadn't considered the difference between seeing a dream and being in it. "I'm pretty sure I saw myself. You think that would make it a vision instead of a dream?" I move my face forward, closer to her. She shrugs.

"Maybe I'll ask Dad. He'd know. Anyway, I saw myself getting blown in a wind toward this cliff. Just over the side there was a long drop to a bunch of rocks, but out in the distance was green land. It looked warm and beautiful, like spring. It was so beautiful that I wanted to move closer to the edge of the cliff to see it better. Only thing, I didn't want to fall off and kill myself on the rocks. It was like—"

"A dilemma?"

"Yeah. That's it. A dilemna. I got on my knees so the wind couldn't carry me and I thought for a while. I was thinking, should I try to see or should I get down off this mountain. I was thinking, 'Man, if I don't see it now, I'll blow it and I won't be able to draw it or tell anybody about it.' I felt like everyone was depending on me to risk falling off the side of the mountain to see. So I crept closer on my knees and looked out over the edge. That's when a rainbow appeared and it reached out over everything I saw."

"Is that the end?"

"Kinda. But I have to describe it. See, the colors in the rainbow were mostly true. There were solid blues and reds. Then, where the colors joined, they blended into each other to make crazy colors. Like colors you get when you swirl paints. That's when I woke up. I was happy too, you know.

'Cause I seen it up close before the dream ended. That's how come I can tell you about it."

I wait for a reaction. Sonny hides a smile in her hands. She nods soberly.

"You think it's a boring dream?" I ask.

"No."

"Yeah, you do. It is unless you saw it. I can't tell it like I saw it, not exactly. I got better ones though, ones that happen indoors with everything close. In those my hands are different, you know? It's like I can make stuff bigger or smaller by touching it with my hand. Or sometimes I can make myself fly, except I can only fly in slow motion and my body tumbles and flips through the air, except it's like the air is real thick and it keeps me from falling."

She forces a smile. "Are these dreams supposed to mean something, honey?"

"Maybe so, maybe not. But the colors are nice. And sometimes I can make my own colors and scents and textures. Once I made a ball of soft, fluffy cotton out of a plank of wood. Just with the tip of my finger."

"It's like you can create?" she asks. She wants to simplify my dreams so we can drop the subject.

"Kinda. And sometimes I get a head start on the next day. Say suppose if it's not raining before I go to bed, then it starts while I'm sleeping, there'll be wetness in the dream."

"Is the bed wet when you wake up?"

I laugh. "Naw, I'm too old to wet the bed."

Sonny laughs too and reaches over to touch my face. I let her. "Is Yogi home?" she asks, getting out of bed.

"Yeah. She's in her room."

"Then we'll see what she's been up to, huh?"

On the way down the hall, Son stops in front of the library. I try to pull her along, but she just stands there, standing at the door.

"He's probably sleeping," I lie. Dad rarely sleeps at night.

He rarely slept at all anymore, choosing instead to get strung out on the buzz of a million uppers. He's got a legal supply stashed in his doctor's bag.

"He's probably asleep," I say again, trying to pull her down the hall. There wasn't anything in the library she wants to see. Not really.

"He isn't asleep," Son says with such certainty that it startles me. It's not like her to be alert to things that aren't proven by fact. "I can feel him," she says.

She cracks the door open just enough to poke her head in. I move in close to her side as we both edge into the room.

Dad's at the far end, sitting perfectly still in front of the oval window. Sonny puts her fingers to her lips so I won't say anything. We're hand in hand, approaching the wheelchair like Dorothy and her friends in *The Wizard of Oz*. A floorboard creaks causing Dad to stir. He tilts his head to one side to hear better. The closer we get, the smaller our footsteps get. I want to speak up since I'm not a stranger to his presence, but I don't. There is a thrill in the room that is built on the unstableness of Dad's disposition.

"Stop right there." The voice coming from the chair is deep and loud. He doesn't turn around though. Us seeing him and him not seeing us seems to give him a magnificent authority.

"What do you want, Sonny?"

She looks at me and mouths, "How did he know?"

I shrugged. "You'd better answer him."

"Just wanted to say hello," Sonny says to the wheelchair, "to see how you were doing."

"Is that so?" Slowly Dad begins to turn his head until we can see his profile. His head is turning with small clicking sounds, like it's happening mechanically. It keeps turning until his chin is tucked just behind his left shoulder at an extreme angle.

"Oh, my God," Sonny whispers.

"Mine too," I whisper back. "I think we'd better go."

c h a p t e r
31

Yolanda is sprawled across her bed with a paperback novel, her hair braided in circles round her head.

"What the hell is going on here?" Sonny asks as we enter the room. I trail close behind her so Yogi won't see me right away. She's made it plain often enough that I'm not welcome in her room.

Yolanda continues reading without looking up. The room is a mess: four jelly donuts on the dresser and a pile of clothes in the middle of the floor.

"Hey, Yogi!" Son tries to grab the book but Yogi pulls away.

"Yo, you can't be comin in here yankin shit outta my hands."

"Why does Dad have Randall reading the Bible?" Sonny asks. I guess the answer I'd given doesn't count.

Yolanda looks up at the mention of Dad. Her eyes are glazed. "Randall's lying. He always lies, the little retard. Or maybe it's another one of his secrets that don't make sense." She points me over to a chair in the corner. "The first time he opens his mouth, he's outta here."

"That's exactly what we don't need," Sonny said. "We *need* to come together."

"Don't be gettin adult with me. I ain't the one actin crazy, everybody else is."

"Well if you keep calling your brother stupid, he'll start believing it."

"I didn't say he was stupid. I said he's a retard, and he is."

"Are you puffy?"

"No. Haven't been in a month."

"You say that like it's an accomplishment."

"Don't you got a husband to take care of instead of pestering the fuck outta me?"

"How can you talk to your only sister like that?"

"Easy. Now shut the fuck up."

"If you use that word one more time—"

"Fuck," Yolanda yells defiantly. "Fuck fuck fuck fuck fuck—" Sonny turns out the light on the dresser and grabs Yogi by the shoulders. I can barely see them on the bed by the moonlight coming through the window.

"All this has to stop. You understand? It has to."

"All what?"

"This whole thing with everybody going in different directions."

"I didn't start it, so how the fuck am I supposed to stop it?"

Sonny's voice is panicked in the dark. "We have to do something."

"What? It ain't like we can fake anything. He won't go for it. What you think? You think me and Ma haven't tried to make things get back to normal? We can't. He won't let us. He's guarded himself in that library and won't let anybody in except doofus over there. And that little mongoloid loves every second of it. I'm through dealin wit it. If he wants to cut off his daughters, then that can work both ways."

"Yogi, why do you keep calling Dad 'he'? That's our father in there whether you want to own up to it or not."

"It's not me who doesn't want to own up, it's him. He always liked Randall better anyway."

"No—"

"Yeah, Son, it's true so just get used to it. That's the way guys are, even the ones related to you. They like each other more 'cause they think they're better."

"That's insane."

"No, they're insane. Both of 'em."

Sonny turns on the light. "You think Dad's going crazy?"

"Going crazy? I'm sayin the shit done already happened. Did Ma tell you about the mirrors? And what would you call Thanksgiving dinner?"

"He was drunk that night."

"Bullshit. The man is losin it. He stays in that library twenty-four hours a day. Randall goes in with a basin and towels to wash him in the morning and at night. He brings him his meals in there too. It's pretty sick, but what are we gonna do about it, send him to a nuthouse?"

"It's the stroke, that's all. We have to help him adjust."

"This ain't medical, Son. It's more. Can't you feel it? I turned the thermostat up to eighty-five and I'm still freezing."

"Randall says Ma's at the school. Why would she be there this late?"

Yogi looks over at me. She's thinking about mentioning E. Hazzard. I can just about see the name flash across her mind. She shakes her head. "I dunno what Ma's doing," she says, still looking at me. "I guess she's got her own little secrets to attend to."

"What does that mean?"

"It means there's shit already in motion and you got no choice but to accept it."

c h a p t e r
32

What do I make of this deal my father has cut for himself
—for us all?

Is this what Ma's always wanted, for him to take charge,
to tell her what is to be done? Or is it that she's given in to
the notion that our family serves no further purpose? He
isn't going to force her to sleep with anybody, and at the
same time, she doesn't really want to. At least she didn't
appear overly enthusiastic. Yet it will happen, shortly, and
only my parents know why.

Unreal, that they would strike such a bargain. Could be
that it's a trade-off. But who's getting what? Payment, perhaps? Maybe something happened in the past, something
he can hang over her head, threaten her with. Something
legal. There is a coolness between them now, a comfort level
that takes into consideration all their faults. She can't ask
any more of him. It's his turn to ask of her. He doesn't have
to make demands, just as he can't make demands of me. He

knows that neither of us will deny him. What charm this man has, what balls.

His leverage over us must be respected. He tells me I'm the only one to profit. What does Ma think of that? Does she know? How can he tell her to do something so wild if she doesn't know everything I know? But she can't. For all her strength, she doesn't have the stomach for the bloodshed that is to come.

Monday has arrived. I didn't sleep last night because I've been anticipating today. Rainy Monday and all is right with the world. For all the suspense my sleepless night has brought to me, nothing has happened yet. It is evening and the rain is drumming heavily on the roof and splattering against the windows. We're protected though, safe and dry inside our happy haunted house.

Ma and Yogi are out in the weather, taking care of their nasty little deeds, while Dad and I sit here in the library. Mrs. Harewood fixed Dad a huge meal but he doesn't want it. He's satisfied to nibble on a piece of burnt toast and mumble incoherently to himself. He might be talking to me, the way he looks at me expectantly from time to time, but I haven't any idea what he's talking about.

I tear a piece of soft boiled chicken from the bone and look it over.

"We started practicing for the Christmas play." I lay the chicken to the side of the plate to save for last.

"What's it about?" Dad asks, rolling his eyes toward me. He's been slowly moving toward being fully awake for the last half hour.

"The same Nativity bit," I tell him.

"What are you playing?"

"One of them singing angels."

"Weren't you a wise man last year?"

"Yeah. I was supposed to do it again, but Mr. Simpson, he got mad at me and let Jamaal Phillips take my place."

"Why'd Mr. Simpson get mad?"

" 'Cause I told him I wanted to be Herod, and he said there wasn't any Herod in the play. Then I said that there wasn't any baby Jesus either, just a manger and a wooden baby with marbles for eyes. I said it was a dumb play 'cause the two most important people weren't even in it. I tried to tell him to look in the Bible if he didn't believe me. He said he had his own script and I was gonna be one of the singing angels."

"He punish you for talking back?"

"No. All the other kids laughed at me. That was my punishment. I didn't mind though 'cause the other kids laugh at me all the time."

"Why?"

"They don't like me, same as Yogi don't."

"Why's that?"

"Somethin different every year." I shrug and start in on the spinach.

"What did you do this year?"

"Like a few weeks ago when Donnie Masterson and a coupla other guys burned the legs off this daddy longlegs spider for fun. I tol 'em to stop, but Donnie wouldn't so I snatched the matches outta his hand and threw them in a puddle. Then everybody got mad and Donnie cuffed me in the head and I kicked him in the stomach. That's how come they got mad, 'cause they like Donnie more than they like me. He's an eighth grader and his brother's some kinda CIA operative. I used to like Donnie all right, but now he don't like me. None of 'em do."

"They ever try to bother you?"

"No. I wouldn't be afraid to fight any of them. Well, maybe Kathy Mason. She's a good soccer goalie." I pause to picture me and Kathy Mason in a fight. She is tall with long arms. "I could take her though" I decide, "as long as I get her from behind."

"That bother you? The others not liking you?"

"No."

Dad tosses the toast aside, missing the trash can by several feet. "Good."

"Sometimes I wish I was part of everything though. Not 'cause what they do is fun. I mean burning the legs off a spider ain't much fun, you think?"

"No."

"Maybe I shoulda just let 'em do it and minded my own business. By the time I snatched the matches, the spider had only three legs left. It was gonna die anyway. I shoulda let 'em kill it quicker with the matches."

"Maybe. But it doesn't matter if they don't include you in their games. You need to be alone to watch the things that happen. Watching leads to understanding—understanding is peace."

"Yeah, sure Dad."

He starts fidgeting through the pockets of his robe for a cigar. "You don't believe me?"

"Yeah, I do." I light him and watch him puff and wheeze on the stogie. "I'm just a kid though."

"But you're different."

"They say I'm spooky 'cause I stare."

"They don't understand."

"And they don't have peace." I stifle a yawn. "Dad, I don't think they really care about the peace of understanding. Don't get mad, but I'm not sure I even care much."

I reorganize everything on my plate, sliding the glob of spinach aside and shoveling the mashed potatoes to where the spinach was. "I mean it's OK," I tell him through a white cloud of potatoes, "but what happened at the hospital to make you start actin like a nut?"

He gives me a look of warning.

"I ain't gettin smart or nothin, but before you always wanted me to get along with the kids at school."

"That's before I understood you."

"Uh-huh. Then let me in on it."

"Keep it up and I'm gonna smack you."

"If you can catch me," I laugh. Dad smiles. "Be quiet and listen," he says. "You're sanctified."

I stare blankly at him to let him know he's gotta do better.

"That means 'set apart.' You're like a special kite, way up in the sky, looking down on everything. Watching everyone."

"Are you drunk again?"

"No."

"Maybe you should be."

"Your mom threw everything out."

"I figured she would so I stole some more. I like it when you're drunk."

I run to my room to get a bottle of Yugo vodka and the checkerboard set. Dad likes checkers with his vodka and Scrabble with his gin. Down in the kitchen I fill a Tupperware bowl with ice. I can feel things coming to a head. Not the stuff with Ma and Yogi and E. Hazzard, but the stuff between me and Dad. I don't want to seem too anxious though.

I balance the table game on my head and walk very slowly back into the library. "Hey," I grin, "lookit."

"That means you have a flat head."

"If I do, you do too." I open up the folding card table and put it between us. "I'm just like you."

"Keep it up, smart-mouth."

I put three ice cubes in the empty glass on the desk. "You want mixer?"

He shakes his head and motions for me to fill it to the top. "You stole this?" he asks.

"Yep. And I got another in my room." I broke the seal. "If Ma finds out, she won't talk about smacking me, she'll do it."

"Then it'll be our little secret. So who taught you to steal?"

"No one. I learned by watching. That watching sure does come in handy. You get understanding, peace, and booze."

"It's no joke," he says coldly. "Who taught you?"

"Yogi." I pour the clear liquor. "Her and Terrell steal something every time we go to the mall. And they don't never get caught. They're pros, just ask 'em."

Dad tries to smile but can't. "I had no idea Yogi liked to steal." He looks at his hands and mumbles something about his hands being his kids' hands.

"What's that?"

"Have I missed that much?"

I shrug. "You're here with me right now."

"What about Yogi?"

"What about her?"

"How is she?"

"She's OK. She's gonna outlive you. Sonny too." I open a bottle of uppers and give him a dose of three. "Let's play checkers."

c h a p t e r

33

"What was it you and Ma were arguing about the other day?"

"When?"

"The time she decked you."

Dad runs his finger over the Band-Aid above his eye. It was the backhand that did the damage. She must've caught him with her ring.

"Oh yeah," he recalls it with a wince. "That argument."

"That was the best one so far. She told you off pretty good." I position myself for a double jump. "I'll bet that's the last one. She's fed up."

Dad blocks me. "Think so?"

"I know so. Why was she ticked?"

"Who knows, who cares." He surveys the board. "She was tearing herself up inside for no good reason. I think she knows it's over. Crown my king."

"You still love her?"

"Sure." The pills shake him with a convulsive shiver. "But I love me more now."

I lift my face to him, a little surprised that he's admitting to how selfish he's become. Not like it ain't obvious, but still it makes me more open to anything he says if he can judge himself so honestly.

"When I realized I was about to die, I figured it was time to stop trying to share so much. I've been doing that for too long. No more sharing—except with you."

I slide one of my men to a safe position, out of range of the hostile king. The game is almost over. He's got three kings and I'm hopelessly trying to elude them, moving one square at a time along the outside boundaries. Finally I give up and we start a fresh game.

"If you don't share, you won't be going to heaven."

"Doesn't matter. I'm contented now. I've got what I always wanted. I finally stopped hoping for it and got it. All I had to do was stop fighting against what comes naturally, even if it's messed up."

These words catch me square but I caution myself not to rush. If I rush, I might get scared, and we're too far down the road for me to chicken out.

"Even if what's messed up?" I ask, trying to pay attention to the checkers.

"Our nature. The thing I've been getting paid to change, the nature of human beings."

"You found out you didn't like being a doctor. That's simple enough."

"It isn't that simple though. I wasn't appreciating wickedness. I thought I was supposed to change people, but I was wrong. Life isn't my creation to tamper with."

I let his words ride.

"That sounds wrong?" he asks.

"A lotta things you been saying sound wrong."

"If something occurs to you, speak up."

"OK. It sounds like you're a quitter."

"Then maybe I am a quitter. I did my best and it wasn't good enough. So what? If I can't change our heritage, then let it be."

"What's our heritage?"

"We're born in sin and shaped in iniquity."

"That's nothing new," I come back at him. "You always knew that. It's in the Bible."

"I didn't know it, I only read it. After I spent all that time dealing with people, I learned. I understood after I watched."

I stretch my legs beneath the card table and touch his. He smiles. He's gonna give me all I want, all I can handle. He's gonna put it right between my eyes. I can feel the transfer beginning, I can feel myself being filled with his spirit.

"After you understood, you quit? The stroke taught you to quit?"

"It taught me to understand what I am."

"Why should I wanna understand if it's gonna make me quit?"

"You won't have to quit because you won't ever start. You won't ever think it's your duty to help others. Your duty is to reflect what you see, that's why you have to watch."

"If I don't try to help like you did, will that make me stronger than you?"

"That's for you to find out."

A question comes to me, but I stop to feel how peaceful the house is, as though it's listening in on our conversation. It has been waiting for this night. I take a look around the room, scanning it quickly at first, then looking it over a second time more slowly. I feel keen, my eyes inching closer together and focusing in on his mouth, the place where I will lay the business end of the rifle. That will be his payment for the gift he is now giving me.

For a moment I lose my question, but then it returns to me. It seems odd to be so aware of everything, yet nothing

takes on a singular importance, or rather, all things are coming together in the fullness of truth. Dad is smiling. For the
remainder of his life, and perhaps my life as well, I will be
his, solely and completely.

"Let's say I decide not to ever be helpful to others, won't
that mean I'll be doing the opposite of what God wants?"

"Perhaps you misunderstand what God wants, just like I
did. For prestige and monetary rewards, I willfully diso-
beyed God and pretended I was doing His will. I was in-
terfering with His handiwork; that's why I got chopped
down."

"Foul!" I yell at him. "That's wrong, that thing you just
said. God wants you to help."

"It's not wrong, just backward. There's a difference."

"What does He want then?"

"For us to appreciate our wickedness, which is our nature, and celebrate in it."

"But why does your appreciating our beauty have to
mess up everything around here so much?"

"You mean I've done a total about-face?"

"Come on, Dad, don't kid me. You don't have to ask that.
You know what you've done. If you tell me you're going
crazy after all those years working with disturbed people, I
could buy that easier than what you're feeding me now. Or
say suppose you tell me things can't be the same with you
and Ma 'cause you're a cripple, yeah, I could follow that.
But right now you're not giving me anything. There's only
one thing I know for sure and you haven't even come out
and told me. I figured that out on my own."

"And what's that?"

"That you're gonna kill yourself," I say flatly. The words
are not shocking to either of us. "You're gonna do it," I tell
him as a command. "You're gonna off yourself."

Neither of us has touched the checkers for several minutes, looking directly into each other's eyes, a give-and-take

stare. He moves his gaze up to the rifle on the rack over the window. My eyes slowly follow.

"No," he wheezes and says slowly, "I'm not going to kill myself."

I flinch. Not enough for him to notice. Or maybe he does. "Nothing worth anything is easy," he says, as if proving he's still the father, the one who's controlling everything. It makes me breathe easier. I don't want to push him around, though if that was the way he wanted it, I could manage. He's no punk. He could probably take it as rough as I wanted to dish it out. Torture, even. Pain that could last so that we both got a bellyful of it. But he's going to go easy on me.

"You've got the toughest job to do," he says. "Tougher than my job and your mother's put together."

Suddenly I feel restless. I walk over to the African artifacts locked in the glass display case in the corner. He's on top of my every move, dictating what to do. I look at myself in the glass atop the display. On the lower half I can see a flattened-out reflection of him in the chair. I move my fingers lightly along the edge of the glass. In the distance I hear the lazy bass drum banging heavily for the first time. The drum is deep, making a hollow sound. I see the sound as a wave rolling toward us. This was in a dream I had once, the beat of the drum. A simple, rolling beat.

"Please don't run from me, Randall."

"I ain't runnin." I move a small step away from him.

He motions at the chair with a pleading smile. His hair and beard are matted and his eyes are backed up in their sockets. It seems he's watching me from the depths of his skull. Except for the tight skin spread over his features, he is a skeleton.

"Sit down, son. We have more to talk about."

I obey, slowly, with foreboding. It's as close to true fear as I've ever been, the danger looming all around me, the evil closing in on me, remaking me. The peaceful quiet of the house isn't calming anymore. It's making me feel uncomfortable.

"I don't think I like what's happening, Dad," I say truthfully. "You're rushing me and I'm missing it. Let's just back up a minute. You got sick, and it taught you?"

"Even before, I was putting it together. How long have people been searching for peace of mind? Listen at the phrase. We clump it together into one word, like that'll make it simpler to grasp. Peace-of-mind. Men hopelessly searching. But they don't want what they're searching for. They crave discord. Pretending to search just adds to the discord."

"That's wrong," I fire back at him.

"It's backward—"

I hold up my hands to silence him. I'm frustrated and he seems pleased.

"OK then, if you don't pretend to search, neither will I. But that isn't all you want from me, is it?"

"Now you're rushing. Just relax and it'll happen. You're the only person I can share my peace with."

"But sharing isn't all you're gonna ask me to do."

"Just let it happen."

"What about Ma? Why can't she share this with you?"

"Don't go soft on me, Randall."

"I ain't goin nowhere. You know, I think you're past goin nuts. I should just finish you now. End it. That's what you want anyway."

chapter 34

He throws his head back to let his rasping laughter fill the room.

"Hey, I'm just a kid and I gotta sit here while you act like a kook. I'll tell you the truth, if you weren't my dad, and I just walked in here and you were sayin this stuff and lookin like a fruitcake the way you do, I'd think you were danger-ous."

"And you'd be right."

"Yeah, it's funny to you, but how'd you like it if I flipped out, or if I just all a sudden got stroked and started droolin all over myself?"

He looks out the window, the seriousness coming back to him. He relights his cigar and I pour him up another drink.

"Peace of mind and men searching. Yes, that was it." His robe and pajamas are rumpled and stale. He closes his eyes and begins to shake, an aftershock from the laughing. "That was it, my peace." He fishes an ice cube out of the glass.

"What a loon," I mumble, then louder: "Hey, Dad, get to the point."

"Exactly. I wanted to be a hero and came off looking like a fool. Funny thing is, I thought I was chasing peace and it was chasing me. I had to fall down for it to finally catch me. It's simple, once you realize that it's backward to what would seem proper."

"Why's that?"

"It's backward for the simple purpose of creating friction that leads to sparks, and then a flame, and finally a conflagration of massive proportions. Organized confusion. Armageddon."

"You were confused because it was backward," I say, and nod.

"The whole world is confused, Randall. It's organized though, that's why most people don't realize it. But I do, and you will too."

"Show me an example."

"Martin Luther King. He was gunned down for offering unity and equality. The majority didn't want it. They said they did, but when he brought it, they killed him. And not just one man either. It was popular opinion, a collective choice. They crucified Jesus for the same reason, and he knew as much would happen from the beginning. So did King. If you move against the current of humanity, you get chopped down."

"King and Jesus were offering the same thing you've found?"

"No. This is the exact opposite." He holds out his hands. They are trembling. The wrists are like toothpicks. He brings them to his chest and I can hear his labored breathing, a slow lazy beat.

Thinking is better than talking. You can think anything you want, whereas with talking there's always someone else to worry about, what they think of what you say. Thinking is safer, it is whole and pure. But during this talk with my father I could speak as if I were thinking, and Dad, his eyes spinning wildly from the pills, would attach answers to my questions that were so bold that I imagined they were conclusions I would have come to anyway as I matured.

"We are as one," he smiles. "The words I speak to you are the basis of what you will draw, and this will be our link to forever. It is God's will."

"Yeah, well, let's skip the drawing. I wanna know about King and Jesus. Were they stronger than you?"

"For the time being. They are of the Holy Ghost. They were used by God as proof to the world that the nature of mankind is wickedness. Still, people don't want to give in. Yet, if you held up a picture of Louis Pasteur and a picture of Charles Manson, who would people recognize? When a choice was offered between freeing a sinless Jesus and a murderer and bandit named Barabbas, again the natural choice was made by the masses. Yes, in this world there is love and peace and joy. Then too, there are drugs and crime and violence. It is a matter of potential. It is a matter of realizing potential without being ashamed of it.

"Yes," he continued, "King and Jesus are stronger than I am for now. But that's where you come in. When my blood is shed I will be, like them, a method used by the Holy Ghost. Soon the Holy Ghost will be in you also."

"If you say this, that your blood will be shed for use by the Holy Spirit, it might be true. But it ain't so nice."

"You think Isaac might've said that to Abraham on their way up the mountain in the land of Moriah?"

"I know that story. It ain't very nice either."

"But it's pure, and you will follow. The Lord will provide a way."

The telephone on the desk rings, causing me to jump. I watch it ring seven times and stop. I look again at my father, into the depth of his skull. "I don't scare easy," I say for no apparent reason.

"No one is trying to scare you, Randall. The word 'fear'

comes from your mouth, not mine. Either way, don't forget that there is a greater force controlling the collective choice of humanity, as well as the choices you will make. Never forget who the strongest is."

"You keep talking about God, but you aren't really talking about good." I look around the room. "You hear it too, don't you?"

"No, but I feel His presence."

"Whose?"

"Would the presence of Satan frighten you?"

"He's here, isn't he? You keep talking about God, but there's evil here. I already know, so just say it."

"It's God."

"No, it isn't."

"How would you know the difference?"

"How would you?" I shout back, a little unnerved.

"I love you."

"How do you know the difference?" I ask again, forcefully.

"There isn't one. My peace is the understanding that they are the same. One is an outgrowth of the other and they've lived together for longer than we can imagine. They're more like each other than we are like either of them. We are the product of that union."

"Stupid!" I yell, my voice cracking.

"It frightens you?"

"Nothing frightens me. It just don't add up."

"Sure it does. Open your mind and listen. Few people understand their origin because it's frightening to them. So they make it easy and put God over here and call him righteous, and put Satan over here and call him evil. And when they struggle between the evil passions of the flesh and their moral conscience, they don't understand it. They don't understand that there is one God capable of two faces, and it is in His image we are made."

"One God, two faces."

"Exactly. Satan is the alter ego of God."

"Like Dr. Jekyll and Mr. Hyde?"

"Sort of. But He has control of both faces."

"You still haven't said how you figured it."

The phone rings again. He nods and I pick it up. "It's Ma," I say, covering the mouthpiece.

"Tell her I'm asleep."

I relay the lie and hang up. "She said she'd be home late." We both know why but I don't bother trying to imagine what her world is like tonight.

He drags on the smoldering cigar and looks away from me a moment. He's considering Ma, I'm sure of it.

"Hey, you were saying something."

He turns to me, a little distracted. "Yes, that was it. I was saying that from the perspective of men, evil doesn't exist without righteousness, nor righteousness without evil."

"They cancel each other out, like in math?"

"No, son. Evil can't be explained without mentioning righteousness. Knowledge of one is dependent on knowledge of the other. It's like explaining darkness as the absence of light. You have to know what light is to start with. You follow?"

"Sure, I got it. Like with Adam and Eve and the tree of good and evil. There wasn't one tree for good and another for evil, there was just the one."

I get the King James version from the bookshelf and turn to Genesis.

"They gained the knowledge of good and evil and just like that they were ashamed 'cause they was buck naked. They musta figured it was dirty and got scared."

"It was at that moment that mankind was created," Dad explains. "It was the birth of a new set of instincts. The beginning of our need for discord. Their imaginations exploded and they found they were capable of creating destructive vices. They became not just the created, but the creator. And that was the way it was meant to be. It's a God-given talent."

A photograph jumps in my head. "To create destruction?"

"There's something backward about it all," he says, trying to help me grasp the correct picture, "yet it's something to appreciate."

"Why?"

"No other creature in the universe has it. We are victorious, yet tragic. Blessed, yet cursed. We reflect the diversity of God."

"Hey, don't preach, man. Say it simple."

"Listen, I wanted to be a doctor because of the mystery of our iniquity. I didn't know it at the time, but I was amazed at how deviance can make itself appear in the most decent of people whose only flaw is being mortal, and that simple fact controls their behavior. If I told you you were going to die in the next five minutes, it'd make you act differently, wouldn't it?"

"I suppose."

"Death is the reason for whatever we create. Without death hanging over our lives, we couldn't express life with such disparate completeness. That's why God told Adam and Eve they'd surely die if they ate the fruit. Death has always been the fuel to life, the driving force."

He waits a second to see if I disagree, but I cannot anymore. His words are truth. "Keep going," I urge him.

"Supposedly, there's a great controversy going on between good and evil and we decide our fate depending on which side we choose. But why has it taken so long for this controversy to be solved?"

"For the sake of organized confusion?"

"Not just for the sake of it, but for the beauty of people struggling with a dilemma that doesn't exist. That's what

caused the Apostle Paul to write, 'I die daily.' In First Co-
rinthians he says, 'For that which I do I allow not: for what
I would, that do I not; but what I hate, that I do. For the
good that I would I do not: but the evil which I would not,
that I do.' He was talking about his need to create and destroy, his need to do evil and good, his appreciation of life
and death. It was the dilemma inherited from Adam and
Eve's eating from the tree."

"That's confusion, all right."

"It's poetry."

"It's kinda stupid. You think he was hittin the bottle
when he wrote it?"

"He was in exile."

"You think he went nuts."

"He was looking over his life with utter clarity."

"Yeah, right."

"Don't scoff."

"I ain't scoffin. If the guy is a kook, he's a kook."

"But he wasn't a kook, don't you see? Paul was a man of
conviction. When he did wrong, he did it with great deter-
mination. And when he did right, he approached his duty
with the same conviction."

"He was the guy who persecuted Christians, right?"

"Yes. And then one day he was shown the light. In a way
you've got something in common with Paul. He experienced the guilt of reflected sin, which means he killed a part
of himself when he persecuted and murdered the Christians. But after his conversion to Christianity, he expressed
the beauty of this mistake through art. Likewise, you will
express this beauty."

"How's that?"

"Paul and the Christians, you and your dad. You see?"

"Yeah. Murder." I nod and try to see it the way it will
happen between us.

"What are you thinking?"

"I'm wondering what it'll be like after you die."

"Look at it this way, I'm the one choosing when I leave, so I won't leave till I have nothing more to give you. The same as I did with your mom."

"I'll miss you."

"Sure you will, but we don't have time for sentiment. How far have you gotten with your Bible?"

"Almost to the New Testament."

"Good. When you read the first four books of the New Testament, you'll see that right before His death, Jesus told His disciples to watch and pray, just like I'm telling you."

"And they fell asleep, right?"

"That's because they were scared to watch. They were afraid to understand what was to come to pass. They didn't realize the peace they would have if they would only watch, and understand who Jesus' murderer would be."

"God?"

"Though He slay me, yet will I trust Him," Dad recites. "You won't be afraid, will you?"

"No."

"You'll keep your eyes open when you pull the trigger?"

"Yes, I'll watch."

"And you're not afraid to understand that the destruction of mankind cometh from the Father, who has created to destroy."

"What father you mean, you or God?"

"Both. You see it?"

"Yeah. But it ain't beautiful that you're destroying my mom and sisters."

"It's an unavoidable truth though. And truth is always beautiful if you aren't afraid to recognize it by sight, and use it."

"Use it?"

"There are ownership powers in sight." He takes hold of

my hand and kisses it. "When the time comes, you will inherit the view to an act of violent truth. Let it be at the center of everything you draw. My death will give you an enlightened view of life; just as Jesus Christ's death offers salvation, my death will offer you an evolution."

c h a p t e r
35

At a little past midnight I'm on the stairs, about halfway between the top and the bottom. The living room is dark and Yolanda is sitting on the couch. She is aware of my presence but we have not spoken. I can hear her crying. I can smell the reefer. She's torched a joint right in the fucking living room. Incredible. She's been sitting there for the last half hour, too wasted to know how wasted she is. When Ma's car finally swings into the driveway, the momentary flash of headlights startles us both. I creep back up the stairs and find a spot where I can see but not be seen.

I have no idea what is about to happen. For the last month, her and Ma haven't been able to stay in the same room without there being an argument. But tonight I don't know that there will be arguing. Yogi hasn't bothered turning on the lights. Whatever she's got planned, it will not be rational.

"Where the hell you been?" she says as the door opens.

Ma hasn't adjusted to the darkness yet. She takes an uncertain step backward until she makes out Yolanda, standing in front of the couch.

"Yolanda? What happened? Did your father—"

"My father isn't who I'm asking about. I already know that joke. It's my mother. Where the hell you been?"

Ma closes the door and moves to the center of the room to flick on a lamp. "What's that godawful," she frowns. "Girl, if you've bee—"

Before she can finish, Yogi's on top of her, grabbing her by the lapels of her trench coat and flinging her onto the couch. As Ma gets up, Yolanda throws a hail of punches but only the first one lands, a glancing blow that grazes the top of Ma's head.

"How could you!" Yogi screams. She rushes again but Ma's ready this time and ducks, allowing Yogi's momentum to carry her into the piano, sounding a few discordant notes. Ma assumes control now, calmly tossing Yolanda onto the couch and putting a knee in her stomach. Yogi tries to get up but Ma's got her shoulders pinned, restraining her.

"Now wait a minute here."

With a frenzy of movement, Yogi wriggles free and sinks her teeth into Ma's wrist. Ma responds by cuffing her twice and putting another clamp hold on her, this time with her forearm across Yogi's neck. She's grabbed a handful of Yogi's hair too to keep her from taking another bite.

"Hi," I greet them cheerfully and come down the steps. "What's going on." The lamp has been knocked over in the short melee and the light casts a shadow on the wall behind me. I've got a straight razor in my hand with blood on it.

"What'd Yogi do?"

They both look at me in disbelief, then look at the bloody razor. Ma lets Yogi up. "Why aren't you asleep?"

I shrug and grin. "I wasn't sleepy, then Dad wanted a shave. Then I heard you guys playing the piano. Want me to leave?"

"Is he hurt?"

"Who, Dad? Naw, I just nicked him. Hey Ma, know what? This seems like a weekend."

"Well, it isn't. Now go to bed."

"No, Randall," Yolanda speaks up anxiously.

"Go ahead," Ma orders.

I wipe my nose with the back of my hand, flashing the blood-stained razor in front of my face. I have a picture in my mind of how I must look to them, my head bowed slightly. I feel my eyes move closer together, almost crossing. I've never shown the crossed eyes to Ma.

She tilts her head at me. "I said go to bed," she says again, cautiously.

"Why should he listen to you?" Yogi says with contempt. "You aren't our mother. You're nothin but a slut."

Ma turns on her wildly, her hand flying to her mouth to stifle the gasp. When she steps toward Yogi, I step forward and flash the razor. Ma backs off and almost trips. Neither Yogi nor I move to assist her. We watch her back away, careful not to take her eyes off either of us.

"Your briefcase." I hand it to her. "Dad's waiting for you in the library. He wants the details."

The room is frozen for a second. Ma's dazed, and this time the tears begin to roll down her face without hesitation.

"Go on," I tell her softly. Her head is bowed as she leaves the room.

"Details," Yogi says blankly.

"Don't worry." I wipe the blood from the razor with my finger. "Ain't nobody done nobody wrong. Everything happened just right. Go on to bed and I'll look in on you in a while."

In the kitchen I put on a pot of water for tea and stare out the window. I have seen through all the windows in the house and am convinced it was ready to fall. Like a house built on sand, it is just about ready to go. Everyone is prepared for it now. After Dad's fall, everything else has come down with him. Soon it will be time for me to finish it.

"What was it?" Dad asks when I return to the library. He sits in his wheelchair by the oval window with a towel around his neck.

"Ma and Yogi."

"Fighting?"

"Yeah."

"Was there blood?"

"Just yours. I put Yogi to bed with a cup of tea. You want any?"

"No."

He tilts his head back to stretch the skin under his chin. He has a cigar in his mouth and a steady stream of smoke rises to the ceiling as I clean the shaving cream from his face in neat, even strokes.

"I'll be up all night," he says. "Wanna stay up with me?"

I wipe the blade on the towel. "Maybe for a while. Do I get to stay home tomorrow?"

"Your mother might not like it."

"She won't mind. I told her I had to be about my father's business."

"Then so be it." He takes the cigar out of his mouth and blows a ring. "How'd she look when she got back tonight?"

"Tired."

"Tired like fatigued, or tired like depressed."

"Both. Why?"

"You know where she was coming from?"

"From betraying you, like you said."

"You know what that means?"

"Yogi called her a slut."

"That make you mad?"

"No. You?"

Dad shrugs but I know he has to feel something. "Don't worry," I say, "I'll make sure everybody gets what's coming to them."

I dip the towel in the basin and wipe his face, holding his chin to see how good a job I've done. Except for the scrape on his neck, it's perfect. I hand him the mirror.

"You're a butcher." He laughs and kisses me on the cheek.

"What you wanna do now?"

He shrugs. "I'm so tired, baby."

I open the bottle of pills and shake a few out on the table. He downs them with a swig of vodka. "Been a coupla days awake since I been asleep." His words are slurring, his eyes heavy. We wait a moment for the pills to drop, raising his lids.

"You'll make it all right," I yawn. "I'll take care of everything."

"I'm not scared when I'm this tired," he says. "When the times comes, I'll be tired enough to want sleep."

"You don't want the cup to pass?"

"Not unless you do."

I shake my head.

"Good. Just remember, 'The Comforter, which is the Holy Ghost, whom the Father will send in my name, He shall teach you all things, and bring all things to your remembrance, whatsoever I have said to you.'"

c h a p t e r
36

December 12

One last dose. He makes it seven pills, for the sake of completeness, and off he goes a-whizzing through a wind tunnel, back into the past.

They're driving down the highway, the five of them, his wife in front and the three kids in back. They're playing the alphabet game, taking letters off license plates and billboard ads. The first to Z wins. The boy isn't playing though. He's started up on one of his solitary games, the one where he counts the cars they pass and subtracts one from the total each time a car passes theirs.

"Ten points for a police car," the boy says from the backseat. The father finds him in the rearview. The girls are looking out the other window. He's six years old, baby-faced, that timid smile, the eyes twinkling with mischief.

Rules never existed for this boy-child. As a father, he had tried to make him understand that rules weren't made to be broken, they were made to keep order. The kid's response was to retreat into his own little world where he ruled.

What's that? The victim whirls his chair in a complete circle to catch a thought.

Yes. When he was maybe five, the younger of his two sisters had pushed him down the steps—a busted lip, a bloody nose. The baby-sitter had witnessed the whole thing, yet when they had gone to punish the girl, her brother threw a fit. Said he had tripped. None of it made any sense but they hadn't worried much about it until three months later when his mother found the bloody T-shirt under his mattress. When she insisted on washing it, he didn't speak for two weeks.

For his seventh birthday, they gave a surprise party for him. That's when it became obvious: the boy was weird. He took himself hostage, locked himself in the bathroom and demanded all the strangers (friends of the family) had to leave. He took refuge in the bathroom facing the front to make sure his demands were met. He never left anything to chance, never trusted anybody. His mother spanked him twice for that stunt. She always spanked him twice and it never seemed to matter.

"You don't run things around here, little boy," she yelled while whaling away at his bottom. She'd made the victim watch to show him how it was done. Of course it was his fault, never mind her own ego-driven obstinacy.

But the boy won. He got his way. He cried some after the spanking and that was the last time they threw a party for him.

While time closes in on his execution, the victim sits out on the cold icy driveway in front of his home, his mind aflutter with pills and memories. He is wearing only his pajamas and a robe, and though the temperature has dipped into the teens, the chill cannot touch him. He has exempted himself from all consequences.

The sound of laughter cautions him. Two figures come walking up the street in the uncertain light of dusk. The victim shrinks low in his wheelchair to camouflage himself in the falling darkness as he watches them mistrustfully through narrowed eyes.

A bouncing ball—the Nelson boys—stopping at the edge of the driveway—saying something in drawn-out words that come from farther away than where they stand, their mouths finishing the sentences but the words arriving to his hearing seconds later. Useless words. Drawn out like from a tape recorder with drained batteries. Their eyes are wide, their expressions hesitant, fearful.

He shoos them once, then again more deliberately with a curse. Finally they walk away several steps and disappear into thin air, leaving him alone. The street is deserted like a ghost town.

He looks down and sees the broken-down body that has carried him through life, finally collapsed in this metal chair by illness. But his soul, it has arisen to escape on a cloud bound for immortality. It will not take three days for him to burst forth triumphant from the clutches of death. Like Enoch, he will be translated.

He inhales, drawing his lungs full, exhaling loudly, hawking up a wad of crimson phlegm and spitting it as far as he can. He has let go of the old. His failures no longer exist. It doesn't matter that he was born in sin and shaped in iniquity. The stench isn't so bad anymore. He can live with it. He can die with it too, the smell clinging and rotting his flesh as his soulless body lies beneath the ground.

The house occurs to him from the recesses of his muddled mind and he spins the wheels of his chair around quickly to see it. His house, owned by sight and financial investment, built comfortably upon a generous lawn, set back a distance from the sidewalk to be seen impressively by those driving by. It is a perfect house, though now diminished in importance as his body has diminished, even as his eyes have matured.

He rubs a hand across the hair on his chin and runs his tongue over the filmy roof of his mouth. He can't remember the last time he brushed his teeth. He tries to remember the last time he looked at himself in the mirror. Some things aren't worth looking at or owning, not anymore.

He maneuvers himself across the broken ice in the driveway, around the side of the house to the backyard. There is the small sound of falling water in the distance, pulsing at his temples, comforting him with a pleasurable light-headedness. He smiles and considers an appropriate farewell to his home and family.

In back, he stops on the patio, allowing his sight to adjust to the dark. Out in the middle of the frozen lawn, his eyes are closed to picture and hear the past in his mind.

During the autumns of their youth, he had tossed around a football on bright Sunday mornings until the neighborhood kids came by. His oldest, she had the best arm on the block. That's why they started calling her Sonny. He'd taught her to throw with a true overhand motion, gripping the seams with her finger-tips so as to release the ball with touch and velocity. She'd even knocked out another kid's tooth once. The second girl was the more athletic of his two daughters, but she'd always shied away from playing quarterback. She didn't want to compete with her older sister. That was probably his fault. Of the three, Yogi had needed him the most and he'd given her the least.

It was true. Damn right it was. She'd said it several times; not straight out, but in so many words. She figured he was smart enough to get the message. He did, then at the same time, he didn't. Or he put it off. Rearing Sonny had been a privilege, not a chore. Not that anything was wrong with Yolanda, she just wasn't Sonny.

Was her waywardness due to his neglect: the shoplifting, the drugs and alcohol?

No. That was too easy, too smug. Every mistake a kid made wasn't a cry for help. Maybe getting stoned was her personal signature, what made her different from Son. That's why he couldn't take it from her, even if he had really tried, the way he should've. Maybe he didn't have the right to. He'd never say that to a parent in therapy, but now, with all the facts on the table, he understands what made families so complex. In the end, they were all just individuals.

He reaches down to stick his hand in the snow, trying to feel the brittle cold, trying to inflict some pain for his sins. He feels nothing. Some failures you could never quite reconcile. They were too close to home.

Sonny. He had no regrets about how he raised her. All she needed was a roof over her head and three square meals a day. At school, it was nothing but A's from kindergarten through college, and on top of that, she doubled as a son. Funny thing how she was never a tomboy the way Yolanda was. She could just do things that guys could do, same as her mother.

At sixteen Sonny could whiz a tight spiral up to thirty yards, or maybe a little less, but always a perfect spiral. Then some guy named Hazzard came along to take her away. He had just the name for that kind of thing, Hazzard. A name like Hazzard and you automatically ended up with something that didn't belong to you. Hazzard. Icy roads. Slippery when wet. Georgia was gone.

No, that was Turner. Gil Turner. The outsider. The toehead. The id. He was the one who had taken Son away. The Hazzard guy just got lucky, or so he probably thought. He'd met Hazzard once. Yogi called him E. Hazzard and said he was a giant, though Georgia wasn't too impressed. Her act of betrayal wasn't even two hours old and already her memory of it was sketchy, or maybe she'd lied when she calmly listed the facts: the gym teacher was watching the fights on ESPN when she showed up at his door— he'd offered her warm beer and cold chicken—she'd told him not to say another word, just strip—he did, somewhat anxiously, al- most tripping while he struggled to get his jeans off—there was no foreplay, Eric hadn't needed any—she didn't let him kiss her —his condom was ribbed and pre-lubed, and it took him three minutes to get on—they did it on the floor in front of the TV— he came quickly and he swore that had never happened to him before—they'd done it with her on top. She hadn't wanted to admit the last part, but the victim had gotten it out of her. His wife had always liked it better that way. Forever the fucker, never the fuckee.

"Aw, hell," he sighs.

Hazzard. Turner. For all it matters now, they are interchange-

able. No point wasting his last moments thinking about them.
  His wife. His kids.

There were four years between Son and Yogi, then five between
Yogi and Randall. They had planned the spacing very carefully.
Georgia insisted on having the final say. She'd had the final say
on everything except the falling apart.

He turns to look at the back of the house. On the second floor
is Randall's bedroom, a bathroom, and the girls' room. The front
is taken up by the library and a guest room. He remembers chang-
ing the blueprints to put the library in front, removed from where
the noise of the children could be heard. In the basement is the
game room and another room for entertaining on informal occa-
sions. All of these will survive him. They would have anyway,
but when the house was a dream to reach for, he had never thought
of it still standing after he was beneath the ground.

From one of the darkened windows he senses the boy watching
impassively. For the last few weeks he has felt Randall's furtive
care almost constantly. There will be no cold feet at the end, no
whimpering. This is not his child any longer. He might have even
known the ending first. He is a bright boy. A curious boy. Bright
enough to know that his curiosity has a steep price that will be
paid over the course of a lifetime.

c h a p t e r
37

Tuesday morning Terrell Daniels pulls up in front of the house and blows her horn for Yogi. She knows what happened with the gym teacher. I beckon her from the front door, "Come on in," but then stand in her way when she approaches.

"Don't gimme no hassle, Randall. And stop staring like a moron. I know you aren't as dumb as you act. No one could be that stupid."

I let her in the house.

"Where's your sister?"

"Upstairs. Were you with her last night?"

She looks me up and down. "Who wants to know?"

"I already know." I shrug.

"Then why'd you ask?"

"I like to hear you lie. I'll go get her."

I go up the steps, but stop in the upstairs hallway to peek back down at Terrell. She's looking around the room, her eyes wide, a surprised smile on her face. The lamp is still on the floor. The cushions from the couch are strewn to the far corner of the room and the piano bench is knocked over.

She goes over to one of the end tables to straighten up our family portrait, which is facedown. I ease back down the steps and tap her on the shoulder.

"Jesus Christ. What are you doing snoopin around?"

"I live here. What are you doing?"

"I'm waiting for Yogi, if that's OK with you?"

"We'll be ready in a few minutes."

"We?"

"Yeah. I'm going too."

"For what?"

"Don't worry about it," Yogi says. She comes down the stairs wearing a baseball cap over her uncombed hair and the same clothes she had on the day before, which isn't unusual, except she looks like she got only five minutes of sleep last night.

Out in the car, Yolanda starts scrounging through the ashtray. Terrell hands her a freshly rolled joint.

"I figured you'd want one," she says, "even though I think it's best you chill considering all the shit that done gone down. You need to keep your head on straight."

"Just drive the fucking car." Yogi lights the joint. I roll down my window and slump down in the seat.

I never like it when Yogi smokes 'cause it makes her mean. But today, she will need it. She needs to be a little off center so that what she has to do won't occur to her straight on. I don't pity her though. I've still got my own business to take care of.

Yogi takes a long drag. "There's too many people in this here world," she exhales. "People who hurt you by mistake and people who do it on purpose. And more often than not it's the ones you trust that hurt you the worst."

"Hey," Terrell motions with her head at me in the back-seat.

"So what? Think he don't know?"

I move to the other side of the seat so I can look crossways at my sister. "That's enough," I warn her. "You don't wanna lose your reflexes."

"Lookit, everybody done set things up to where I gotta do this whether I want to or not. And that's cool. But don't try 'n tell me how to do what I gotta do. Let me take care of it my own way."

"Whatever."

"What you guys talking about."

"Don't worry about it, Terrell. You just stay outta harm's way."

The night before, Yogi and I slept together.

She was lying perfectly still when I came in, but I knew she was awake, waiting for me. I had climbed into the bed and she turned over so that we were face-to-face.

"Why you all the way over there." She grabbed my T-shirt to try to pull me closer, but I stayed on the far edge. She said, "You're probably gonna be the type to touch your-self and not let anyone else do it."

"How you mean?"

"You know what I mean."

"What about you? You ever let Terrell touch you?"

"Maybe. But you, nobody's ever going to touch you, are they? Nobody's ever gonna touch your body or your emo-tions."

"Is that wrong?"

"No. Nothing you're ever gonna do will be wrong." She said it again, "Come closer," and I gave her my hand to hold. Her voice went flat. "What's gonna happen to him, Randall?"

"Nothin he don't want."

"Don't talk circles."

"Just leave it to me, all right? 'Cause all I'm doin is leavin it to him. He's our father and what he says is how it'll happen."

"You think he might hurt himself?"

"He won't."

"What else?"

"What else like what?"

"Like what do you guys talk about when you go in there?"

"Sometimes he asks about you, Ma, and Son."

She perked up. "What does he say?"

"He keeps saying, 'You think they're used to it yet?' and I tell him, 'No.' "

"Is he gonna talk to us before—before whatever's gonna happen?"

"No."

"But why?" she whined. "Doesn't he love us anymore."

"Kinda."

"You're not being any help, stupid." She kicked me under the covers. "What the fuck does 'kinda' mean?"

"It means that's what this whole thing is about, 'love.' He says love is a dollar bill and we already spent it."

"Then what did we buy?"

"Each other."

"How's that when he's locked himself away from me?"

"You still got me, and he's inside of me. You got me and I got you, for always."

"Promise."

"Yeah," I said, "I swear it."

"So what woulda happened if he didn't get sick? That's what changed him."

"I said the same thing. He says every day changes everybody, and the stroke was like the coming of another day."

"You musta didn't hear him right. Take me in to see him and I'll ask him myself."

"OK. Tomorrow, after school, if you still wanna see him I'll take you in there. But by then, I don't think you'll want to anymore. All he wants from you is to make up with Ma. He wants you to know that last night wasn't her fault. He wants you to know that he's the one who sent her."

"Did he say why?"

" 'Cause it finishes the love between them. He says he was the first and only man ever to touch her, and since he got sick and she ain't so old that she won't want another man to touch her, he wanted to be the one to give her permission. He didn't want her to do it behind his back or to wait for him to die and then do it. It's like a divorce, I guess."

Yogi started to cry. I didn't try to comfort her. I just let her go ahead so she could finish quicker.

"What happens now?" she asked when she was done.

"Tomorrow, you'll do what you have to do. And don't ask me what that is 'cause you already know, right?"

"Yeah, I know. I'll take care of him."

"There's a way to get him without him knowing you did it."

"No. Whatever I do, I'll be looking him right in his face."

c h a p t e r
38

We're nearing the high school. Terrell's driving extra slow to give herself a chance to find out what Yogi has planned.

"Hey, look, you can't let it bother you, Yogi. It happens to a lot of people."

"I'm not a lot of people." Yogi looks out the window. She keeps flexing her hands, getting herself psyched.

"If I told you it happened to me would it make a difference? My moms sleeps around. My father does, too. And they both know. It's called an honest marriage. It's maturity, reality. People get tired of the same thing every night. One day you'll see it the same way."

"My parents and your parents are different."

"What are you trying to say?"

"Nothin. Come on, step on it."

"This shit is gettin outta hand, Yogi. Just 'cause of what happened, you can't be talking like your family's better than mine."

"I didn't say it, you did."

"But you think it, don't you? You've always thought your mom was better than mine, but now you know that's bullshit. Get that straight once and for all. Your mom ain't no better than mine, and you're no better than me."

"If you gotta make a statement like that, then that tells us both all we need to know."

"Cute. Real cute."

"Terrell, drop it, OK? I've had enough of your bullshit. You think you know everything 'cause you got a car and you sleep with guys. But you can't tell me how to react. I'll choose my own way to react."

My sister might as well be wearing war paint. She's already got a puffy welt under her eye from her scuffle with Ma. In bed last night, I told her that any violence we did was all aboveboard. No one else could see that the way me and her could, not even Sonny. When the whole mess got started, Sonny was already moved out. It wouldn't be long before we were all moved out.

The three of us go in through the front lobby of the school and stop at the registrar's desk. They need late passes and I need a visitor's pass. First-period classes have already started and the three of us head upstairs to the girls' lockers. The lockers are tucked away in a secluded alcove just off the main hallway on the third floor.

"This is where you get lost," Yogi says to Terrell.

"No. I'm down for whatever."

"Is that a fact?" Yogi pulls out the knife, the one she was supposed to use on the kitten.

"Nice knife," I grin at Terrell. Her eyes are as wide as saucers.

"Stick it down in your sock," Yogi hands me the knife, "and go keep a lookout."

I do as she says, but don't go so far that I can't hear Terrell whispering, "Get a grip, girl. You start talking about cuttin somebody, you're talking serious shit."

"It's not your family, Terrell."

"Maybe, but this isn't just wrong, this is the twilight zone. I'm scared. You know what's next, the cops and everything. I can't let you do it."

"Do you love me? If you do, you'll let it all happen."

"It ain't about all that."

"Yeah, that's exactly what it's about, love. Now I'm telling you for the last time, back off."

"No. You're gonna have to make me." Terrell's expression is uncertain, but she's doing something with her hands, stroking tenderly at Yogi's face and saying things that don't make sense. Evidently, this is supposed to have a calming effect. I know better than to interfere. Besides, Yogi is geeked out of her skull. All night she was tossing and turning, getting herself "up" for it. Once she gets to a certain point, it's no holds barred; she's capable of anything.

Terrell puts her mouth on Yolanda's and I take a few steps toward them, not to stop them, but to get a better look. I'd seen them kiss once before, but just a peck. This here is the slobbery kind though, with open mouths, the way they do it on the soap operas. Terrell's eyes are open and its obvious she knows she's in over her head. I can't see what's in Yogi's eyes, but I can imagine. I've felt the pain of her anger before, the surge of energy that erupts like a volcano and then the damage that results. We've yet to discuss the consequences of what we've agreed to do. They are coincidental. Terrell has positioned her right leg between Yogi's legs. Yogi pulls her face away for a second and Terrell starts something like, "We can go somewhere, back to my house if that's what you want. I'll rub you down, do it right. I know just how to make you feel better," but my sister is shaking her head no.

She reaches her right hand up so slowly that maybe Terrell thinks it's a caress, but then Yogi grabs the other girl's throat, and with a very neat and simple movement she trips Terrell backward as though she were dipping her for baptism. Terrell doesn't struggle, she doesn't seem afraid anymore. She just lays flat on her back with Yogi straddling her. Terrell's eyes are closed. She knows it's all over.

"I love you, Terrell," she says, and bounces her friend's head three times off the floor. By the time I rush to stop her, Terrell's eyes are rolling back up in her head.

"You didn't have to do that," I push my sister away. The look on Yogi's face is blank. She's numbed herself to everything, and I start to worry that putting revenge in her mind was a stupid thing to do. Not that she can't handle it; she might go too far.

I feel the back of Terrell's head. There is a lump but no blood. "What the hell, Yogi."

She shrugs. "You think that's bad, well, things are about to get a lot worse. Now gimme the knife and let's go do this."

I hand her the weapon and wonder whether she'll remember all of this a few years from now. At least she'll have something to regret, something to point to and say, 'I did that.' The way the nightmare has happened so far, she's been standing idly by while our family burns.

Down in the gym the tenth-grade girls are in the middle of class when Yolanda walks in. They're playing basketball, I think. With tenth-grade girls it's hard to tell. I go down to the second set of double doors that is closest to Hazzard's office. I wait to hear Yogi's voice before I step in. I want to be sure everyone's attention is on her.

"Son-of-a-bitch," the words ring out and echo. Everything is frozen as I step in the gym and slip into the office. I peek around the corner and spot E. Hazzard with a whistle in his mouth. He looks stunned as Yogi walks up on him. She's approaching him as if she is gonna do him right here in front of a bunch of tenth-grade girls. The whistle falls out of his mouth. He looks guilty as sin.

"You know why I'm here," she says.

There's a pause. It's so quiet you could hear a pin drop.

"Yolanda, this is neither the time nor the place."

She jabs a finger in his chest. "Like hell it isn't! Now move!" The girls begin to gather around the confrontation, just as we figured they would. When we planned it the night before, we imagined that there wouldn't be any trouble getting him alone in his office because he wouldn't want the whole class to hear his business. He's the one on the defensive. He's the one caught with his pants down.

"OK, let's do laps," Hazzard instructs the class. He's trying to maintain control of the situation. "Three laps, then hit the showers."

He begins back to his office with Yolanda close behind. I take a seat at his desk and wait for them.

"Hi, big brother," I beam cheerfully.

He shuts the door. "I think I've had my fill of you people."

"Feel?" Yogi sneers. "Rumor has it that that's all you could manage. Rumor has it you don't know how to do nothin else."

"Let's skip the jokes," he says. "You don't amuse me and neither does your family."

"I thought you kinda liked my mom." I wipe my arm across his desk, knocking his books onto the floor. "Or at least she said you liked her a lot more than she liked you."

He gives me a look of disgust, then pity. He turns to Yolanda. "I don't know what sick games you people are playing, but letting a kid this age in on it—"

Yogi cuts him off. "OK, that's quite enough, Mr. Motherfucker. I don't think you're in any position to get self-righteous with us." While she says this, she doesn't look him in the eye. I'm not sure whether she's trying to spook him, or maybe she's looking him over to see how she was gonna take him.

She moves a little to his left as though she's measuring distances. He turns his body so that they're still face-to-face. He seems tense, alert.

"Are you stoned, Yolanda?"

She ignores the question. She's looking at his arms, the position of his body.

"Would you like me to call the guidance counselor?" His voice sounds insincere, like he's just saying it to get her to stop looking at him the way she is.

Yogi's getting turned on, that little smile at the corners of her mouth. I read it once that people bleed more freely after a struggle. E. Hazzard is big-game prey. He will bleed like the woman in Dad's journal.

"Last night isn't my problem," Yogi says, still sizing him up.

"If you calm down, I can explain everything. Here," he offers her another chair and she sits, which strikes me as odd. I shift in my chair. Hazzard turns to eye me, suddenly considering me as though he'd forgotten I was there.

With his back turned, I glance at Yogi and she shakes her head. Hazzard's wearing shorts and his muscles flex impressively each time he moves. He's sweating heavily now and I close my eyes to get an image of him and my mom.

"Does she still call you Harold?" I ask him.

He doesn't answer. He's starting with more bullshit, trying to talk Yogi out of what she has planned. But he's got it all backward, that's the funny part. He's worrying about his job, not his health.

"First of all, you shouldn't be driving up to people's houses spying, should you?"

"Ain't this a bitch," she laughs.

"I think maybe you've stumbled onto something."

Yogi stops him abruptly. "Check you out. All a sudden you come off just like all the rest of the teachers. Well I ain't goin for it. I—am—so—sick—and—tired of adults thinkin they got immunity from anything 'cause there's nobody to punish them. You're bullshit, E. Hazzard, and you can tell your daddy I said so."

The phone rings. Hazzard answers. "Terrell," he says, a

little puzzled, "where are you? You sound hurt," and immediately we both know Yogi has to do him right here and now. But as she moves toward him the knife drops out from under her jersey with a clank.

Their eyes meet, and for what seems like eternity, all three of us are seduced by the moment. We can't move. There is pure excitement in Yogi's eyes, but in Hazzard I see a mix of disbelief and maybe even amusement. In years to come, when we discussed that moment, Yogi and I would both agree that he could've gotten to the knife first. It almost seemed like he knew he deserved something, like a stroke of bad luck had caught up to him and there wasn't anything he could do about it. Yogi took the moment of indecision to go for the knife.

Hazzard falls to his knees to cover her with his body, grabbing hold of her arms, moving one hand down to her wrist to try to take the knife. I sit motionless in the chair, watching them struggle, wondering how Yogi is going to pull it off, though I know she will. It's her kinda fight.

Hazzard almost has the knife free when she brings the back of her head up and butts him in the face.

There is a sickening crunch, cartilage and bone being reshaped by impact, his nose turning to the side of his face with a whimper. Yogi turns to see him tumbling over the desk, falling spread-eagled on the floor. I walk over to where he has fallen and look down into his face. His lip is busted too, and when I look up at Yogi, I swear she's about to hurt him in the worst way, so he will never forget.

He moans softly and begins to struggle to his feet, using the chair to pull himself upright. His right hand is over his nose, the blood gushing red between his fingers. I think he's saying something but I can't tell whether it's a threat or a plea. Yogi doesn't seem to care either way. For her, the gym teacher is meat waiting to be butchered.

She kicks the chair away to make him get up by holding on to the desk, then waits, patiently, as he puts his left hand on the desk for balance. As he gets to his knees there is a stark, expectant terror in his eyes. Yolanda focuses in on his middle finger, her own eyes wide with anticipation. Just as he exerts pressure on the hand to push himself to his feet, my sister raises the knife up over her head with both hands and brings it down with all the force she can muster, separating the finger from the hand at the knuckle in one clean chopping motion.

c h a p t e r

39

Time can blur details, like the name of that kid in third grade who could turn his eyelids inside out and make all the other kids scream. Other details, the ones worth pictures, time can't touch.

The rest of what happened in the home where we lived and loved each other, it's all mine, to be used by me. The crime is mine too, though there is no victim. My actions are only the completion of a simple truth I have learned at my father's feet.

The sun has gone down and I'm sitting across from him up in the library with the rifle cradled across my lap. I'm completely naked. Dad says there's gonna be blood, and blood washes off of skin better than it washes off of clothes. We've got everything pretty much all planned. Now that my time has come though, I want to back out. But he isn't going to let me. He's anxious, I can feel it. He looks ready to go. I'm sure he could probably die all on his own, but that isn't the way he wants it.

We haven't talked the whole day. I wanted to, but he said no. So I left him alone to drink and do his pills, and to sit off in the driveway to watch the sun go down. When it was dark, I had gone around to the windows facing the back-yard and watched him mumbling to himself and laughing. He's relieved and it makes me feel good to make him so happy, but still I'm a little frightened, constipated.

As I approach him slowly, he rolls his head one way, then the other, as if he can't see me too well. There are evening shadows on the wall and the rifle is heavy in my arms. I'm holding it the way I've seen guys in a parade do it, the way you hold a baby.

"Do you know how?" he asks.

I nod.

"And the cane?"

"It's right here." I touch it with my foot. "I'll lay it next to you with the tip by the trigger, just like you said. Don't worry, no one'll think I'm guilty, 'cause I'm not."

"The fingerprints?"

"I'll say I picked up the rifle after I came in the room."

He sighs. "It is finished," he says and beckons me close. He puts his good hand behind my neck and kisses my mouth. "Into thy hands I commend my spirit."

After I did it, I freaked. The walls seemed to close in on me and I ran to every room in the house to make sure no one was there. Back in the study, I checked the body one last time before calling the cops. I was looking to see if he had moved, and then I'd laugh and shake him and he'd tell me it was all a joke. He'd led me, after all, down this dark hallway, and now he was gone.

I grabbed my coonskin and called the cops, then waited out in front of the house till they came. I pointed them up to the oval window. The street was empty and dark but people were peeping out their front doors.

The ambulance took only a few minutes. The driver was a lady. She took my hand and led me into the living room like it was her house. We sat on the couch while two plain-clothes guys went upstairs to check the corpse. They each had a pistol stacked on their side in a holster. I wanted to go upstairs too, but the lady made me sit on the couch with her. She tried to say a few comforting things that didn't come out right, then she sat still, probably waiting for the drama of the moment to hit her. I got the family portrait off the piano and pointed Dad out. She appreciated that and told me I was very strong.

One of the cops, the one named Dolan, he had hard blue eyes and creases in his face. He seemed like the only one who wasn't afraid to think the worst. With cops you never know, they can act like you're guilty just to see what you do.

"Where were you when you heard the shots?"

"It was just one," I said. "I was in my room."

"And then?"

"Then I went in, and, and—" I put my hands to my face and the lady came to my side still holding the picture.

"Can't this wait?"

Dolan wouldn't even consider it. Whatever he was gonna find out, he seemed convinced it was gonna be right then. He moved across the room to stand in front of me. "Go on," he said. There wasn't any budge in his voice and I imagined he'd maybe shot somebody himself once.

I paused, giving him a chance to take a long hard look at me, to see if he would react to the evil, but he wasn't giving nothing away.

"Then I saw he was dead," I said, "and I called you guys."

"Had you seen him today?"

"Yeah, out back."

"Did you talk to him?"

I shook my head and looked up as Ma came in the door. She moved directly to the couch and grabbed my shoulders. "What did it come to?" She was looking desperately into my mouth and I could see the repulsion in her eyes. I could barely look her in the face.

She asked it again, "What did it come to?" but she didn't really want the details. What for?

Dolan eyed us steadily. Once there's blood on the ground, wasn't nothin private no more. But regardless of anything —the facts, the body, the rifle, my guilt—this was beyond him. Him and me both.

He had questions. They weren't difficult. He already knew what he could never prove. Finally they decided to take the body and be done with it. The corpse. It wasn't really Dad anymore, just flesh weighted by bone, the stuff that remains after the spirit is set free. And I could feel him within me, though not as strong as it would become later.

The body was wrapped in linen on a stretcher. Me and Ma stood at the door while they carted it out. It was pretty solemn, like I was supposed to salute or something. I felt a small laugh come up in my throat while Dolan watched me hide the smile.

"You'll be hearing from us." He put on his fedora and paused at the door to light a cigarette. He could've been waiting for a tip.

After they left, the house was quiet like a mausoleum. Ma went upstairs, and I went up to find her in the library sitting motionless in the wheelchair. The lights were out. I crept up behind her and at first I didn't think she knew I was there.

"And what happens now, Randall?"

There was something in her voice, a farewell, and it frightened me. If I came from within her, then anything I could do, maybe she could do it too. And probably she could do it better. We were all playing by different rules now. I stood very still, waiting for whatever.

"And what happens now, Randall," she asked again, her voice so flat that I knew things couldn't get much worse for her.

"I was gonna ask you the same thing, Ma."

"You were, were you?" She wouldn't look at me, she just kept staring out the window. "Remember the day your father had the stroke, at the hospital, down in the cafeteria?"

"Yes, Ma," I said, and she turned on me suddenly and I could see there was still the potential for violence in the room. She was stronger than Dad. I was certain of this and fell away from her against the wall. I wanted to hurt myself so she could come to me and tell me I was still her baby, but all she had was hate.

She rolled toward me in his chair and leaned her face at me. "Don't ever call me that again, boy. Do you hear me? Not ever."

"OK," I said, wanting to be helpless for her. "Georgia," the name caught in my throat, my back sliding down the wall. Anything more that happened would be all my fault. Anything that happened till the day she died, she could pin it on me.

"I'll do whatever you tell me to do." I was on my knees, crawling toward her, reaching for her. "I'll do whatever you want," I begged.

"Since when did you start doing what I asked, Randall?"

"Why you talking to me this way. You're making me scared."

"Scared of what?"

"Scared of what you think of me."

"Maybe you were scared when you shot him. When you murdered my husband, you were scared then too. And you liked it, didn't you?"

I climbed up the side of the chair and buried my face in

her chest, but she was stiff as a board, her face turned away from me. There wasn't any use trying to make her love me anymore. We stayed there in the room for a long while, me holding her as if she were the corpse. Her punishment, I guess.

Later in the evening, we picked up Yogi at the detention center and paid a bail fee. I waited in the car while Ma did the paperwork. But when they came outside, Yogi didn't want to get in the car. Ma was pulling her, but Yogi kept looking at me and saying no. Finally I got out of the car and she took a wild swing that brushed my chin. There was a struggle and a cop came outside so Yogi cooled out and we got in the car. I sat in the backseat next to her and she grew very weak and dim. After that we went to a lobster house and had dinner.

The funeral came two days after the shooting. It was pretty disorganized. That morning when I awoke, Ma was already gone, so me and Yogi got dressed and waited in the living room. Yogi was watching me carefully, and I wished she would say something, but she just kept her eyes on me and finally I asked if I could make her a cup of tea. She said she'd like that, and smiled.

Finally Ma came back and the three of us drove over to the funeral home. It was a private ceremony. Dad was an only child and his parents were dead, so it was just us. When we got there Sonny and Gil were leaving. I caught Son's eye to see if she knew. She did, and then she tossed a pretty wild crying scene. Gil just stood there like a dumbbell. Then Son started getting real hysterical, saying something about 'How could you? He was my father too,' but nobody was there to hear her but our family and a baldheaded priest who had a giant mole on the tip of his nose.

Yogi ended up going with Gil and Son, so she never saw the body. Nobody did. It was a closed casket affair and I told myself that the casket was empty, that Dad had been translated to wherever it was that Enoch and that other guy who got translated hang out. The thought of it made me happy as we stood silently and listened to the priest making his prayer. Ma didn't close her eyes; she was looking at me, and then we were looking at each other for a long time until the prayer was finally over.